THE
ACCIDENTAL
PATRIOT

An ordinary man. An extraordinary dog. A nation needs them.

JOSEPH BAUER

Archway Publishing books may be ordered through booksellers or by contacting:

Archway Publishing
1663 Liberty Drive
Bloomington, IN 47403
www.archwaypublishing.com
844-669-3957

Author Photo Credit: Eugene W. Davis

ISBN: 978-1-4808-9619-2 (sc)
ISBN: 978-1-4808-9617-8 (hc)
ISBN: 978-1-4808-9618-5 (e)

Library of Congress Control Number: 2020918053

Print information available on the last page.

Archway Publishing rev. date: 11/04/2020

For my daughters, Leah, Lauren, and Halle.
Who could need other inspiration?

The only title in our democracy superior to
that of President is the title of Citizen.

—Louis D. Brandeis, Associate Justice of the Supreme
Court of the United States, 1916–1939

CONTENTS

PART I

PART II

PART III

PART IV

PART IV

PART I

PART I

1

THE DELIVERY

★ ★ ★ As the elevator door opened, Leo Kinz looked again at the delivery slip taped to the top of the pizza carton. "Apartment 1216," it read. He stepped into the hallway and turned to the left without hesitation, without apprehension, clueless that he was walking to his death.

Leo knew the building well, as he did most of the apartment complexes around Dupont Circle. To his eye, they were pretty much the same. Entrance lobbies brightly lit; floor hallways, just moderately. Tightly woven commercial carpeting with vague, almost indiscernible patterns. Inexpensive artwork, usually boring florals or abstract pastels, hanging in the hallways in cheap oversized frames, as predictable and original as the pizzas he couriered in thirty minutes after order, guaranteed.

He was sure he had been to apartment 1216 before, but the name on the customer slip was unfamiliar: Ruth Morgenthal. Probably a new tenant, he reasoned. They were always coming and going in this part of Washington. Most were government workers or professionals from the law firms or trade associations that lined the neighborhood. And there were many foreigners too, working in the embassies, interesting people who did interesting, maybe even important, things. Deliveries to new customers were the best, Leo thought. You never knew what you would find, what you would learn.

He was not supposed to make small talk or ask questions of the customers. It was a turnoff, his manager said.

"Like when the guy who brings your bags to the hotel room," his boss advised. "Or a cab driver. He asks, 'How long you staying? What are you doing in town?' Makes you nervous. People don't like it. Just give them the pie and leave 'em alone. Don't ask them things."

But Leo did anyway. It was the thing he liked best about the job, meeting interesting people. And you didn't learn anything just handing somebody a hot box. As he walked down the hall to apartment 1216, he planned what he would ask Ms. Ruth Morgenthal and how he might warm her up. *Nice to have you as a customer, Ms. Morgenthal,* he might say. *Hope you enjoy it here. Anything I can tell you about the neighborhood?*

But as it turned out, Leo Kinz did not ask Ruth Morgenthal any of his questions. He didn't get the chance. It wasn't clear that he ever even saw her face. Because just as he rang the doorbell at apartment 1216, two men stepped rapidly, soundlessly behind him in single file. They had been lying in wait for him to pass the small janitorial closet halfway down the hall. When the doorknob moved and Ruth Morgenthal had begun to open the door only a fraction, the two men crossed their arms in unison and bowled Kinz forward violently, pressing high on his back and shoulders so that the deliveryman would stay upright as the weight of all three men forced the door open into the apartment. The force of the flying door knocked Ruth Morgenthal back and made her stumble to her left, behind the door, but she did not fall. She gripped her face, too startled to scream immediately. The first intruder stepped deftly around the door and was next to her in an instant, covering her mouth with a gloved hand, and spinning her so that her back was to his chest. In timed precision, the second intruder leapt to Leo Kinz, who was still holding the pizza carton, instantly silencing him with a firm hand over his mouth.

"Where is your daughter?" the first intruder asked Ruth Morgenthal. His tone was low and controlled—eerily calm, as if it were a perfectly normal question to ask. He used his foot to close the entry door. "Motion with your head. Where is she?"

Ruth Morgenthal wriggled and tried to bite his hand. She was forty-four years old and fit. She was a bicyclist and still jogged regularly, including that very morning in her first week in the city. She thought her attacker was about the same age, and not too much taller. Perhaps she could bite him and spring free at least enough to scream. The woman next door might be home, or coming home, from her job at the French Embassy. Maybe she would hear her. But it was useless. He was a professional, and strong, and he clenched her mouth too tightly for her even to bare her teeth.

"Where is your daughter?" he asked again. His tone was unchanged, but now he twisted her neck firmly. Not nearly as harshly, however, as his accomplice twisted Leo Kinz's neck. His partner threw the deliveryman to the floor, facedown, with cold efficiency. Ruth Morgenthal could see everything as it happened, not eight feet in front of her. She saw the attacker withdraw a stiletto, place it under Leo's neck, and pull it fiercely, deeply, and upward across his throat from ear to ear. Leo Kinz, the amiable man who liked to meet interesting people, who used to drive a taxi until he worried—brutally ironic in the moment—that it was too dangerous, lay on the floor next to a spilled pizza carton, blood belching from his neck as from a tipped jug.

The killer looked to his partner, who signaled silently to the hallway leading from the living room. Taking his cue, his knife still in hand, he started gently down it. As he approached the bathroom, Melinda Morgenthal emerged. She was eighteen years old, intelligent, naïve and pretty. Not worldly, but adept at appearing to be. She was wearing what she seemed always to wear: faded jeans torn open at the knee and a V-neck T-shirt, her barefooted toenails polished in sky-blue. It was impossible for her to digest the scene she found before her. She took no step, made no sound. The attacker took her arms in an instant, the way a dancer takes his partner's, and twirled them to her back. She let out the beginning of a scream, but merely the beginning, before the man's gloved hand clamped her jaw and marched her forward to the living room.

The intruder holding Ruth pulled a small roll of duct tape from his overcoat, reached around her waist, and handed it up to her.

"Strip off a piece. About two feet."

Ruth Morgenthal did as she was told.

"Hand it to him."

He forced her closer to her daughter's captor so that she could reach him. Ruth could see that he was hurting Melinda as he pulled the girl's grasped mouth close to his chest while reaching with his free hand for the tape. He snapped it quickly and in a single motion wrapped it twice—tightly—around the girl's face. Melinda's nostrils flared and her skin flushed. Terror filled her young eyes. How wretched and crazy it all was, she thought. How could this possibly be happening? She saw the deliveryman and the sea of blood spreading from his body on the floor. A wave of nausea came over her, fueled by hot fear, stayed by adrenalin. Her skin was burning. All she had done was come to Washington to spend a month with her mother and help her settle in to her new job. It was a city for young people, her mother had said. "Maybe you will make some contacts for your future," she had said. "A good experience for you before you go off to college after the visit." My God, how crazy this was, she thought.

For the first time, Majir Asheed looked into Ruth's eyes, turning her head and leaning down over her shoulder. At first she looked away, glancing down and then up. But the taller, dark man kept his face, expressionless and still, close before hers, until finally she looked into his too. When at last she did, he nodded, ever so slightly, in acknowledgement.

"Now perhaps we can communicate, Ms. Morgenthal," he said calmly. "Take the daughter to the couch," he instructed the other attacker. "Do not be rough with her." The mother watched him as he gave the order. He sounded sincere. She felt a rush of self-deluding comfort.

"I am going to remove my hand from your mouth," Asheed said. His tone was oddly matter-of-fact, almost languid. "But I must know there will be no screaming. Do you understand me? There must be no screaming. If there is screaming, your daughter will die immediately. Do you understand me?"

Ruth nodded. But only once. It did not satisfy Asheed.

"Do you understand me?" he repeated, again in the flat quiet tone.

This time Ruth nodded aggressively in the affirmative. He responded in turn.

"All right then, Ms. Morgenthal." He took his hand from her face and stood before her. "Let us communicate."

"Do you know why we are here, Ms. Morgenthal?" he asked her.

"No," she said. "Or why you killed that poor man." Leo Kinz lay lifeless. The gurgling had stopped.

"We take no pleasure in it," he said. "No pleasure. It was necessary, as such things are."

Asheed was Syrian, but his spoken English was near perfect, even elegant. Deep cover work in England and the United States for twenty years will do that for an agent, especially when he knows his life may depend upon it. But what he had said was true. His actions had *not* been driven by personal derangement or perversion. He truly did not take pleasure in Leo Kinz's killing, nor would he in the killing of these two women—mother and daughter no less. No pleasure, truly.

"Why did you come to Washington?" he asked Ruth.

"To work on a project for the government," she said quietly.

"What part of the government?"

"The Pentagon."

"You are a soldier? We do not think you are a soldier."

"I am not a soldier. I am not in the military. But I have come to help them. As a civilian."

"To do what?"

"To work on a project at the Pentagon. I am an engineer."

"A nuclear engineer?"

"No. Civil."

"For what project?"

"I don't know yet. No one has told me yet."

"But you have been here a week," he said. "You have gone to the Pentagon four days. This is known. This is known by us. And you say you know nothing about what they want from you?"

"No, nothing. Nothing! They have been questioning me about my life. And giving me tests. They say it's about my security clearance. They will not tell me anything about the project until that is done. Please, leave us! Just leave us! There is nothing I can tell you."

It was the saddest kind of situation, Asheed feared. *He* was telling the truth, and *she* might be telling the truth too. And if she was, there was nothing either of them could do to make it less than true. It could only become truer, and more terrible.

He led her to the front of the couch and released his hands from her. He motioned, almost courteously, that she should sit. She did. Only a small space separated her from her daughter. Melinda was crying, and her eyes above the crude tape gagging her were red, raw, and filled with terror.

Majir Asheed stood in front of the couch. He looked from side to side and shifted his weight, as if pondering a difficult thought or considering possibilities.

"Do you think we are going to kill you?" he asked Ruth Morgenthal finally. He bent slightly and looked directly in her eyes.

It was his first utterance that carried any expression, but it wasn't in his voice, which remained even and flat. It was in his dark eyes. His brows lifted slightly, and the faintest warmth was reflected in his eyes.

"I am very afraid," she said. "I am afraid for my daughter. I am afraid for myself."

"But do you think we are going to kill you?"

"Yes," Ruth Morgenthal said. "I think you are."

The Syrian assassin had not expected a different answer, but still he sighed, as if somehow disappointed. He stepped back from the couch and paced for a few moments.

"I believe there is nothing you would not tell me if it meant you would not have to see your daughter die." He knew that this was the truth. He knew she would disclose all that she knew. He paused. He stood staring down at her. She saw no malice in his eyes. Nearly a minute passed. His eyes never left hers.

"Tell me what you are working on at the Pentagon," he said. "If you tell me everything that you know, you will not see your daughter die. And she will not see you die either. That is my word," he said.

Ruth Morgenthal broke down in tears, tears of frustration, fear, and—worse—understanding. Asheed waited patiently, watching her eyes. She gathered herself and spoke to him.

"I don't know anything! I don't know anything that I *can* tell you. They are supposed to tell me soon, but they have not told me anything yet!"

"Not even where the project is? In Syria? In Israel?"

"Nothing! They've told me nothing yet! Don't make me watch her die! I have told you everything. I don't know *anything*, so that *is* everything."

Asheed turned silently and considered the utter sadness, the utter truth, of the moment. All truth. All terrible truth. Two people speaking the truth, and nothing but loss to come from it.

And then he kept his word.

2
INSUFFICIENT PRECAUTION

⋆ ⋆ ⋆ Jack Renfro had been to a thousand murder scenes, but never one like this. Normally, the first glimpse produced an immediate intuition. And, often for a detective as observant as Renfro, that intuition turned out in the end to be pretty nearly correct. The scenes of drug-related murders, legion despite unprecedented national efforts to address addiction, and the demand for substances that it produced, always seemed to carry identifying markers. Location. Paraphernalia. The victims themselves, who usually could be tied to prior criminal records within minutes.

If it wasn't a drug killing, and the victim was female, it was usually domestic violence. Those scenes were more variable. Signs of rage and fury. But domestic killers tended to alter the scene, often to make it look like a robbery or a sexual assault, with drawers pulled out and their contents strewn in the other rooms, and with torn and removed clothing and lingerie. Experienced detectives like Jack Renfro could sense such connivances in an instant. *It's domestic; find the husband or boyfriend,* they surmised. And it was almost always the right place to at least start.

But this scene at apartment 1216 of the Dupont Lofts was perplexing, outside the norm. A triple homicide in a tidy two-bedroom in a pricey enough neighborhood. Almost certainly there were at least two perpetrators, since two of the victims, the women, were bound with duct tape and found in separate rooms. No apparent forced entry. No ransacking. Jewelry untouched on the bedroom dressers. No indication of sexual assault or mutilation. It was too early to have a dusting report, but Renfro doubted that any prints would be found other than the women's. These were neat, clean, quick killings silently performed and, curiously to Renfro, very possibly with a single weapon, minutes apart.

Jack was no medical examiner, but he may have been the next letter over from one. He bent close to the slashed necks of each body, studying the incisions. The blade had entered each more deeply on the left side facing down, severing the carotid, before being drawn up and slightly to the right, leaving a shallower exit wound that did not quite reach the right carotid. It didn't need to.

"Same guy killed all three," he said to Susan McShane, the CIA official who stood, per Renfro's instruction, in the doorway next to the uniformed patrolman from the Metropolitan Police Department.

Jack Renfro rarely seemed to speak in complete sentences. "Three-Word Jack" other detectives called him, which was only a small exaggeration. But in truth, his concision was a strength, appreciated in the department and especially by the prosecuting attorneys who knew that nothing impinged credibility like extra words. In Jack Renfro's reports and testimony there was never anything extra, never anything superfluous, and never anything wrong.

"Pizza man first," he said. "Then the women. Not sure which first."

"The mother first, don't you think?" McShane said. "She's here near the couch. You said the girl's back in a bedroom."

"Maybe," said Renfro. "But I think the girl was out here before she was killed. The blood smear on the carpet." He pointed to the smudge in front of the couch. "Out here, barefoot. On this couch.

There's blood on her foot back there." He gestured towa~~rd the~~ bedroom. "She was taken back there and killed. Instead of ki~~lling~~ her here."

"Why?" asked McShane.

"I don't know. But there's a reason for everything," Renfro said. "And we'll know, for what it's worth, who died first, if I'm right about the weapon."

"What do you mean?" asked McShane.

"The same knife was used to kill them all. Pretty sure. Whoever was killed first—probably Kinz—will have only his own blood in his wound. The second, her own and Kinz's. The third, all three."

It was grim deduction, but if Jack Renfro was right about the weapon, irrefutable.

"What brings you here, Ms. McShane?" he asked.

"You called me," she said.

In fact he had, because the Pentagon contractor's badge he'd found on a lanyard in Ruth Morgenthal's purse listed her on the back as the host contact.

"But I didn't ask you to come to the scene," he said. "I was just following protocol. We always notify if there's military or defense identification. Usually nobody comes. Were you worried about her?"

"Not like I should have been," McShane answered.

"She worked for you?"

"Yes. I recruited her. She was just starting."

"To do what?" Renfro asked.

"I can't say."

Renfro's expression showed surprise, but he nodded as if he understood. McShane took one step into the room, extending her credentials to him. Renfro held up a hand, as a stop sign, and moved over to examine them. Susan McShane, Deputy Director, Clandestine Operations, Central Intelligence Agency.

"Spy stuff?" he asked.

"I can't say," she said.

"You don't have to," Renfro said. "But maybe that helps explain *this*."

He reached into a pocket and withdrew a plastic evidence pouch. He handed it to McShane.

"Found two of these stuck to the ceiling, on either side of the light fixture. The others in the kitchen and the hall. All on the ceiling."

McShane turned the pouch over and looked closely at the small, oval, cream-colored discs in the baggie.

"Don't open it," Renfro said.

She held up the pouch to the light. There were six of the tiny devices, each the size of the nail of her ring finger.

"Listening devices," she said.

"That small?" Renfro asked. "If they were as white as the paint, I would have missed them. I only looked up to see if there was blood spatter up there."

"They are military grade," she said. "Highly sensitive."

"They were listening to her," Renfro said. "That's how they knew this poor guy was coming." He looked down at the pizza man's body. "He was their ticket in. This was planned. Professional."

"There must be video surveillance at the entrance," McShane said.

"Oh, there will be video, all right. And it will show two or three guys entering and leaving in dark clothes and sunglasses."

McShane asked if she could take the evidence pouch with her. CIA specialists might be able to identify the source of the devices.

"You'll have to sign for them, but sure," Renfro said.

"There's something else, Detective," she said. "Can I speak to you alone?"

Renfro stepped out into the hallway, and motioned for the uniformed officer to go inside. He closed the door.

"Thank you," McShane said. "It would be very helpful if what I've told you about Ruth Morgenthal did not reach the media. I think you can see that she was involved in a covert operation. If that comes out, there will be questions and implications. Nothing good could come of that."

"I see," said Renfro. "I can manage that."

McShane reached into her pocket for her car keys.

"You leaving?" asked Renfro. "Don't you want to see the other body? The daughter?"

She turned and, for the first time, seemed physically shaken.

"No, Detective. I really don't."

3

SIX WEEKS LATER

★ ★ ★ Stanley Bigelow could not have known that lumbering into the small sedan awaiting him that April morning at Reagan National Airport would change his life forever. Later, he would ask why he had not been more inquisitive from the beginning. How, at his age and station in life, does one slide so casually, without forethought, into a world he does not know and is unsuited for?

It was not as if there were no signs. It was not every day that he received an email without a subject line from a civilian he had never heard of working at Wright-Patterson Air Force Base. And why would an air force civilian in Dayton be asking if C. Stanley Bigelow, the old founder and chief executive officer of CSB Engineering Group, could kindly come to Washington the following Tuesday morning to meet with "some personnel" about a matter of interest to the government that might involve CSB Engineering? Meet where in Washington? With whom, precisely? Could more information be provided in advance? Why did the email, in the last of merely three sentences, ask that he not discuss the request or his trip with anyone?

He had asked none of these questions before pecking out his unconsidered, thick fingered, one-word reply: "Sure."

To which came the immediate response from the civilian he didn't know: "A blue Toyota sedan with Maryland plate CIV 819

15

waiting at door five of the arrivals area at National Airport
United Flight 1361 arrives from Pittsburgh. You will not
require lodging and will be returned in time to board Delta Flight
667 back to Pittsburgh, departing at 3:12 p.m. Boarding passes will
be emailed to you Monday next. Thank you."

And so it all began for Stanley Bigelow, the second life he'd
never intended, the one that began, unbeknown to him, because
Ruth Morgenthal's had ended.

He carried only his scarred, square-framed leather briefcase to
the gate counter at the Pittsburgh airport. Still, the ticket agent
surveyed it with sweeping eyes as if there could be some question as
to its eligibility for carry on. *My word,* he wondered, *how little are
they making these planes nowadays? If they get any smaller, you will
have to check any large ideas on the loading bridge.* His ticketed seat
was in row nine. He hoped to move to an exit aisle for less cramping.

To Stanley, the older he grew, the larger he seemed to be. He
knew it wasn't true. Every fall, as he pulled his tuxedo from the
closet to dress for the annual Pittsburgh Engineering Society black-
tie, he worried it would no longer fit comfortably, but it always
did. Still, he felt bigger and a little clumsier each year. Now at age
seventy, he carried his six-foot-three frame above a forty-inch waist
and very large feet. On first impression, he was not a fat man per
se, just oversized all over. His well-proportioned facial features, full
head of wavy salt-and-pepper hair, and thick brows that turned
upward at the bridge of his nose, lending the impression of an ever-
present smile in his blue eyes, earned him, he would be amused
to know, the rating of handsome enough by most. But even if he
knew it, he would not have much cared. In matters of appearance,
though always well-groomed and never poorly garbed, he was not
self-conscious. He was long on loneliness and short on vanity.

He leaned over the gate counter to make his request. "Is there an
exit row seat available? I am pleased to pay extra for it," he said to the

middle-aged agent. Her smile was broad and stretched, seemingly near permanent.

"Not your day, sir," she said. "They're all taken. I'm sorry. But it's a very short flight."

It was true, but it was little consolation to Stanley. The short flights were sometimes the worst. The seat belt sign might never come off; you could not get up from takeoff to touchdown. But you might as well argue with city hall as argue with an airline. He wrenched himself into row nine, folding his legs in, accordion-like. Thank heaven for small mercies; he had an aisle seat.

He rumbled through the automatic door below the big number 5 in the baggage area of Reagan National and saw the blue Toyota neatly placed to the right of doorway. Its rear license plate was easily observed. Stanley approached the passenger's-side window, which was lowered. The driver turned his head toward him. He wore a windbreaker over a pale blue shirt and a thin dark tie. His hands were not on the steering wheel. Stanley thought it slightly odd that he made no gesture at all when Stanley announced himself.

"I am Stanley Bigelow."

"Yes."

"May I sit up front?"

"The back, please." If the driver spoke with any expression, it was imperceptible to Stanley.

"May I ask where we are going?"

"Arlington."

"But Andrews is in Maryland," Stanley said, referring to the joint military base.

"We're going to the Pentagon." The driver extended his hand to the back seat as Stanley muddled in behind the passenger seat, but it was not to shake Stanley's. "I need your cell phone," he said flatly.

Halfway across the world, in the small Afghan city of Turj, another man, much younger, embarked on a new assignment too that morning. But, unlike Stanley Bigelow, this man knew exactly what he was doing and why. And he was not asked to surrender his cell phone and its camera. He drove his Nissan pickup truck to a side road near the small hospital compound operated by Doctors without Borders. He wore a laborer's clothes and a tool belt. He retrieved a screwdriver and a rag from the glove box. Without reluctance, he took the tool in his right hand and drove it angularly into the fleshy underside of his left forearm. He wiped his blood imperfectly from the shaft and placed it beneath the blanket on the passenger's-side floor that lay covering an automatic long gun. He wrapped the wound loosely and walked to the hospital. The Afghan security guards at the front doors looked quickly at his wound and handed him a paper pass granting entrance.

A pleasant Finnish doctor, reasonably proficient in Farsi, treated him without delay. A nasty puncture wound, the doctor said. A careless coworker and his electric tool, the injured man said. It was the one holding up the plywood sheathing that always seemed to get hurt, he said.

Treatment for his alleged workplace accident required eight stitches and antibacterial salve, and took nearly forty minutes. In between calls from the nurses, there was ample time for an unsupervised walk-around of the hospital and a few dozen photos including, in particular, one of the basement, to which the patient descended unnoticed, before leaving as he had come.

The two men, continents apart, would never meet. Neither would know the other existed. Only their pursuits would intersect.

4

THE PRESIDENT'S DIARY

★ ★ ★ Del Winters had been the president for just fifteen months, but the next meeting on the Oval Office diary had been in the making for more than twenty years. Other presidents had prepared the footings and advanced the program in tight—the tightest—secrecy. Violent Islamic extremism had exploded on US soil on September 11, 2001, and had roiled incessantly, mostly in faraway places, ever since. The nation had committed its resources on multiple fronts, from broad-scale military invasion in full global view, to thousands of covert missions to find and destroy extremist killers.

Each president was compelled to consider all options. For one thing, the political life of each of them demanded it. In the White House, in the congressional leadership, and certainly in the highest ranks of the military, it was clear as gin, as Winters's father would say, that the American homeland itself would never be territorially vulnerable to the small fraction of Islamic believers bent on bringing death to those who would not succumb to them. And it would not be vulnerable even if the splintered and scattered extremists grew in numbers. Yes, there would be—and had been—sporadic attacks within the United States borders. Radicalized individuals would move from websites to public gathering places and wreak killing havoc. Eventually, undetected cells germinated in urban centers and succeeded—once, twice, three times—in staging deadly attacks. To those innocents who fell to the hands of the irrational hatred, the loss was inexorable. But in a nation of 320 million, an individual citizen was exponentially more likely to be killed by an Uber driver while crossing Pennsylvania Avenue than at the hands of a foreign terrorist.

But Del Winters and the other presidents understood that a different calculus applied. The overwhelming power of the armed forces could defend the land and nearly every one of its citizens. But the spread of terror in other parts of the world was still deeply harmful to the United States and its people. Both moral principle and self-interest—Winters believed in equal measure—required continued US participation in the eradication of the terrorist impulse. Citizen shoppers in the malls and diners in the country's restaurants would be safe, but American soldiers and aid workers would be butchered. And other nations, even if smaller and distant, were cogs in the global economy that American businesses large and small needed now, and would need increasingly in the future to distribute products, services, and technology. There was no looking away, no taking a back seat.

Still, Winters could not help but feel that the earlier presidents had had it a little better. The drumbeat of extremist activity had marked their terms, to be sure. Since 9/11, those presidents had been mostly successful in protecting the homeland but had not been able to stanch the spread of extremism elsewhere. They had done what they believed they could do, directing explorations into all manner of antiterror strategies, including the preparation of the extraordinary program to be discussed in the next meeting on the president's diary, obliquely calendared "Assets Review." Planning was the easy part. Implementation was difficult. And the decision to implement had not come to the earlier presidents. It was coming now.

The door opened without a knock, something that only occurred when the opener was one of the young armed marines in dress blues who stood on shifts at the door of the Oval Office.

"They're all here, Madam President."

5

A CIRCUITOUS ROUTE

✦ ✦ ✦ As the little blue Toyota pulled under the canopied entrance of the JW Marriott a mile from the Pentagon, large Stanley Bigelow bent restlessly in the back seat and watched as his quiet driver stopped to speak, needlessly he would soon learn, to the bellman who stepped out to greet the car.

"The garage entrance?" the driver asked, all for appearance's sake. He knew very well where the entrance was. He had performed this routine many times before.

The bellman gestured to the street. "Next drive."

"Where are we going?" Stanley asked with measured alarm.

"I am handing you off here. Another driver will take you on to the Pentagon."

"That seems odd."

"It will all be explained to you. There is nothing to be worried about. Just precautions in case we've been observed."

Once inside the garage, the driver took an immediate down ramp to the left, passed the basement hotel elevator, and drove to the opposite side of the level, where a black Ford Focus waited. Instead of occupying a parking place, it rested laterally, engine running, across two spaces. Stanley's taciturn driver pulled into the next open space next to the trunk of the waiting car. He seemed to spring out of the sedan even before the Toyota engine drained to silence. He walked to Stanley's door and opened it.

"This man will take you now. Please sit in the front seat this time."

"Well, that's a relief," Stanley said. He climbed out stiffly, adjusting his pants and rumpled suit coat. "May I have my phone?" he asked.

But then he saw that his driver had already walked briskly to the other car and was handing the phone to his replacement.

"I think I should be told what's going on," he said.

"That's understandable," said the second driver, who had never left the Ford. He looked up to Stanley and directly into his eyes, which was somehow comforting. His tone was businesslike, not unfriendly. Stanley noticed his sturdy build and open-collared white shirt.

"This car was used yesterday by two vendors from Omaha. It's a rental that they picked up at this hotel and drove to the Pentagon on routine business. We can't know when our vehicles coming and going are being monitored, and usually it's of no interest to us if they are. But somebody upstairs must care about you. We were instructed to avoid observation. We do this when it's necessary to prevent anyone from knowing that a person came from the airport and went to the Pentagon. One car brings you to a hotel. Another leaves later and goes to the Pentagon. No one can observe the exchange. The cameras down here are ours. If this rental car was observed yesterday, it will probably be observed again today. But whoever observes it will conclude that the same vendors from Omaha are going to the Pentagon again the next day."

"But I'm not from Omaha."

"Exactly."

"So I go through this drill again when I go back to the airport after this meeting?"

"That depends on whether somebody still cares about you."

6

SUDDEN EMERGENCE

★ ★ ★ Del Winters's path into public life was unconventional. Nine Eleven, two words that had been lodged indelibly in the world's vernacular after that course-changing day in 2001, marked the end of many conventions in US military life and structure. And a good bit of it was not seen by the general public, including the rise of Delores Winters. The broad strokes of George W. Bush's restructuring of the nation's security and intelligence apparatus after 9/11 were well publicized. His consolidation of numerous law enforcement agencies, intelligence functions, and formerly mundane departments, including some within even the Commerce Department, under the umbrella of the new Department of Homeland Security, was well-known, was generally understood, and came to be actions that earned him growing historical credit as his legacy took shape in the decades that followed their provocation. But there were important realignments that became known only later.

Among the most significant of the changes was a marked reshaping of the military's special forces under the Special Operations Command, known as SOCOM. It was decided that the uniquely trained, but theretofore mainly independent units of the various branches should be answerable to a unified command reporting directly as a new battle function to the secretary of defense, and then to the president. The new command was to have its own dedicated resources in areas that previously had been positioned in the traditional branches. Formerly, when Special Forces activities required logistical, engineering, or other support functions, these were supplied by the other branches because appropriate personnel resided there. With the new SOCOM force, these support functions and capabilities were moved inside SOCOM under its direct control. Especially important was the establishment of dedicated technology, weapons development, and procurement expertise so that the unique needs of Special Forces teams could be met promptly—and covertly. The new resources developed or procured everything from special night vision devices, to specialized detection tools, to unique mission aircraft.

All of this created a need for dedicated legal support to guide technology contracts for devices and weapons the development of which was nearly always classified and not even known to the other branches beneath the level of the Joint Chiefs. For this need, Colonel Delores Winters, the army lawyer from Joint Base Andrews, was deemed the ideal resource. Her father was then second-in-command of the air force, dividing his time between MacDill Air Force Base in Florida, where his branch's top command resided, and Joint Base Andrews in Maryland. His principal assignment was the coordination of air support for special operations missions against terrorist targets. Technically, he was not in the SOCOM chain of command, only the liaison between it and the air force. So it was concluded that no direct familial conflict of interest existed between father and daughter. Neither would receive orders from nor give orders to the other. But General Winters's extensive experience in covert missions and intelligence, it was observed, would make him a valuable advisor to his daughter.

What was not observed when she was tabbed for the role was how her new assignment would entail so much exposure to the highest levels of government, even to the president. She reported directly to the SOCOM commander, who was then navy admiral Carl Banks. Admiral Banks, almost singularly revered as a good judge of talent, was deeply impressed by the army lawyer. Her assessments were razor-sharp. Her style was direct but unassuming. She was confident but careful. As the admiral confided to a listening President Obama, "She has a big-picture mentality and still pays attention to detail." By the end of Obama's second term, Winters, though not yet forty years of age, had been promoted to lieutenant general and nearly always accompanied the SOCOM commander to meetings at the Pentagon and in the Oval Office.

In the private meetings that always take place between new presidents and living predecessors, Obama spoke about her to one of his successors, leaving him a handwritten note bearing the names of three persons he knew still to be in government, essentially unknown to the public, whom he believed capable of any position—any—in government. Her name was listed first.

Regardless of political affinity, the confidential words of one president to another are weighty. The new president made a point of instructing his defense secretary to ensure that Delores Winters remained in her leadership post within SOCOM though she had already served there for years and would normally be due for reassignment. West Point wanted her for the legal training of cadets in human and electronic intelligence. But she stayed instead in SOCOM, assuming additional duties and stature. She began to conduct the secret briefings to the congressional leadership that were necessary to secure SOCOM funding requests. These were frequent affairs. Her clarity and lack of evasiveness struck them all. She was trusted and liked. Eventually, she became known, albeit marginally, to the media. She never appeared on television newscasts or cable news panels, but she didn't have to. Senators and congresspeople kept referring to her when *they* did. When there was a terrorist event anywhere in the world—and there were many—the networks clamored for interviews with committee members thought to have some inside knowledge of the United States response. The elected officials were eager to indulge them with airtime. "We were briefed by General Winters, and we can assure you that our military and intelligence community is doing all that can be done," one was quoted. "I can tell you that if you had spoken, as I have, with General Del Winters, you would feel confident that in spite of this attack over there, our forces are well positioned to continue to protect us," said another. And on and on. Still, she steadfastly declined interviews. But an article in the *Atlantic*, exploring the inner workings of the country's intelligence and Special Forces capabilities, called her "the nation's secret guardian angel."

And then it happened. No one could have predicted it. With less than a year remaining in his first term, the popular sitting vice president suffered a debilitating hemorrhagic stroke while traveling in Oklahoma. The country was gripped with concern. As surgeons labored, initial reports were discouraging. The president addressed the nation and reported that while the best care had been given, the stroke was severe and the vice president, while alive, was "medically unresponsive." It was not likely, he reported, that the vice president's faculties would be restored. The vice president died the next day.

The president huddled with his cabinet in the White House immediately after announcing the vice president's death. Most had no suggestions; it had all happened so quickly. All were sensible enough to refrain from suggesting themselves. One raised the name of an aging senator who had announced he would not run again in the election just nine months off.

The president excused them all and sat alone for thirty minutes. He opened a desk drawer and withdrew the note Obama had given him. He reached for a pen and crossed off the second and third names.

7

THE POWER OF NOW

★ ★ ★ Much was unclear when the SOCOM lawyer Del Winters received the call from the White House asking her to come to see the president right away. The vice president's funeral was barely completed. The world press was swirling in speculation with a curious mixture of grief, sympathy, and anticipation. It was all so unexpected, so abrupt. With the presidential election approaching, the campaign was so far a one-sided affair. The incumbent president enjoyed a high favorability rating and was unopposed in his own party for renomination to a second term. His first-term vice president, Walter Such, was handsome, youthful, very popular, and well positioned to carry the party's presidential mantle after the next term. For the party, it had seemed to be a period of exceptional stability. And now Such was dead. Who would the president choose to replace him? It was not a decision that could wait, obviously, but it was a decision heavy with political ramifications. A choice that seemed imprudent could change the upcoming election dynamics dramatically.

The pundits were weighing in by the hour. Most assumed the president would select one of several state governors who were known to have presidential aspirations and had been wise enough to resist challenging the incumbent seeking his second term. Their advocates were working the back channels in earnest, urging their selection. But the president was uncomfortable with each of them for one reason or another. He did not know any of them closely. None had been deeply vetted, as would normally be the case, and there was no time to do that vetting now.

The White House released a statement the day after the funeral. It said only that the president expected to nominate a new vice president for consideration by the Senate within a few days. In the meantime, Secret Service protection was dispatched to guard the Speaker of the House of Representatives. He had already announced that he would not accept the vice presidential appointment, but, want the job or not, he was next in line to the presidency until a vice president was confirmed.

Del telephoned her father at Joint Base Andrews immediately after she received the call summoning her to the White House. Henry Winters was meeting with his own senior staff when she called. She told him it couldn't wait. After asking them to leave the room, he took the call. She told him about the White House summons.

"You should prepare yourself for a big thing," he said to her.

"What are you saying?" she asked.

"Look at the timing of this," he said. His tone was measured. He seemed neither enthused nor negative.

"He probably wants to know if anything is afoot in the terror cells," she said. "Everyone is distracted. There could be an attack, trying to take advantage."

"Delores," he said. She knew that he reserved that usage for moments when he was certain of himself. "At a time like this, he wants to talk about one thing. You need to think about that one thing and what you will say."

"It seems out of bounds. I am not a political person."

"In any other situation, it would be impossible," her father said. "The party people would not accept it. A person does not come out of nowhere and become the vice president. But this is unique. He knows you. He knows you understand the most critical problem in foreign affairs. And he knows the public does *not* know you."

"How does that make me attractive?"

"Because it means you are not *unattractive*. To anybody. At least for now, you're a safe pick." He paused. "The real question is, are you just a placeholder for the rest of the term? Will he want to run with someone else in the fall? And will you be willing to run at all? You said it yourself, you're not politically ambitious."

"What do you think, Dad?"

"About what?"

"Please." There was some exasperation, borne of nervousness, in her voice.

"I think he wants you to be the vice president but probably will not want to commit to you about running with him for a second term."

"And what do you think I should say?"

"I think you should tell him you're not looking for short-term employment. If you are capable now, you are capable for a second term."

"I don't even know if I *am* capable," she said.

"You don't know now, but you will in time. And if it turns out that you do want the job, you need to have the opportunity."

"But it's his prerogative entirely."

"You don't believe it, but you have more leverage than you think, Del."

"How so?"

"He's decided he needs you *now*. Now is more important than November. When you have *now* on your side, you always have leverage."

Henry Winters knew a thing or two. He continued, "Reverse the issue on commitment. Try to make it so the choice is yours, not his. Tell him that you'll do it now and that the choice is yours about the future."

"But we both know I don't have aspirations like this."

"No, we both know you haven't *had* aspirations like this. Yet. You've never had this kind of thing within your grasp. How do you know you won't love it?"

She knew this was why she had called him. His words rang true to her.

"If you do this right, you'll have the chance to find out whether you want this," her father continued. "The line between ambition and a desire to serve is sometimes pretty fine. The line between being ambitious and being competitive is blurry. And God knows you're competitive. But going longer or not going longer should be your choice. The presumption should not be that you have the job only until January. The door has to be open for more. Otherwise, you're just a footnote to history. I don't think of my daughter as a footnote."

"It's a lot to think about," she said.

"Call me after?"

"No, I'll come over to Andrews. We can either celebrate or drown our sorrows."

There was a quiet moment.

"There will be no sorrows for me, Delores," he said. "I just hope there are none for you."

8

AT THE OFFICERS' CLUB

★ ★ ★ The officers' club at Joint Base Andrews was one of the best appointed in the world, and one of the most frequented by senior military brass. The large officer corps associated with Bethesda Naval Hospital was welcomed on the premises, and used the courtesy generously. The different uniforms of the joint base personnel, particularly with the addition of the navy officers, gave the place an almost cosmopolitan feel. The lounge and dining areas were twice the size of those of a typical base club.

Del walked in and spotted her father at one of the small tables positioned in front of a long buttoned-leather bench. Three officers were sitting across from him in comfortable round-backed matching chairs. As soon as he saw her, he stood up, gesturing to her with one hand and, less demonstratively, to the three officers with the other. The officers retrieved their drinks and moved away immediately. He must have cued them that she would be coming. She navigated the room toward him, avoiding eye contact with anyone except him. She felt calm, a sense of quiet within herself, almost an emotional numbness after her meeting with the president, a meeting unlike any she had ever had before or would ever have after. She was smiling, but only slightly. Her father, on the other hand, was smiling broadly.

"What are you so pleased about?" she asked him as he embraced her.

"You," he said. He looked into her eyes intently. She thanked him with hers.

"I won't make you drag it out of me," she said, still standing. "But have you ordered for me? I am ready for one."

He had. A double Gentleman Jack waited in a glass, neat. Ice cubes sat in a sidecar. She dribbled two cubes into the bourbon glass and took a chair that one of the young officers had vacated. Her father folded his hands on the tabletop, a showing of patience. She leaned forward over the table and spoke quietly.

"I said yes. We reached an accommodation about the term. Now keep your voice down."

In truth, Henry Winters did not need to be cautioned. His reaction was equal parts pride, happiness, and concern. That mixture did not produce outburst. In fact, his smile lessened, which Del noted immediately. She put it down to the power of the moment.

She told him everything about the meeting in the Oval Office. The president was alone when she walked in, sitting on the sofa near the fireplace. He rose to greet her but did not extend his hand. She asked if he wanted a briefing on terrorist movements since the death of Vice President Such. Yes, he said, but he had something else first. They were both still standing, and he motioned her to sit. Then he sat.

Henry listened earnestly as his daughter described the conversation, asking only one question at the beginning: "How long were you in there?"

"Seventy-five minutes."

Go on, her father gestured.

She told him how the president had said he thought she must know why he had her called. She answered that she presumed nothing, but wondered if it related to the vacancy. He sounded a lot like her father in their telephone call just hours earlier, saying that in normal circumstances she would not even be on a short list. But the loss of the vice president could not have come at a worse time. His relationship with the dead man had been excellent. It had been comforting to have a number two whom he thought actually best for the job and whom the party felt best for its future too. He liked Such personally, and his family. He appreciated his loyalty. He was truly in grief himself. Obviously, no advance thought had been given to a vice presidential selection for the second term.

"What about others considered for the first term?" she'd asked. She thought it was probably the only poor moment of the meeting. He seemed surprised by the question, surprised she would feel entitled to ask it. "Not offended, exactly," she told her father, "but not pleased."

"I'm not surprised he didn't like the question," said her father. "Another general asked me once why I'd passed over a certain colonel for promotion. I could have punched him in the nose. Evaluations of others are personal subjects. When it's entirely up to you, and you make your judgment, your reasons are private unless you say otherwise."

"Well, he didn't answer me."

"I like him better that he didn't," said Henry. Her father had always had mixed feelings about the president.

She went on to describe the president's view of her own qualifications. They liked her at State and they liked her at Defense, including in the civilian leadership. To the public she was an unknown quantity, but to him she was known well. Interestingly, he asked her if she agreed with him that he knew her well.

"No one has ever asked me that in my life," Del said to her father.

"Get used to it. You're going to get a lot of new questions," he replied. She saw empathy, and a little worry, in his eyes.

Del said that, yes, she thought the president knew her well. They together guessed how many times they had met in the White House, or the Pentagon, or somewhere else. A hundred times, they surmised. But only three times alone, before this day. She did not have to bring up the issue of the upcoming election and the nomination of a vice president for a second term. He did. He said he would not ask anyone to be vice president unless he thought that person was qualified to be the president. He believed she was. And there was no reason to anticipate he would feel differently in a few months. He did not consider her absence from the public eye or elected office a political liability. Maybe it was even an advantage. The public had long ago begun to embrace the "outsider" to establishment politics. Anyway, he calculated that the unforeseen death of the vice president would cause the country to focus even more on him as the nation's face. He should assert himself as the reliable leader to whom the people could look, and look pretty much exclusively, in a period of leadership change. The entry of a well-known political figure, certain to have his or her own political coalition of support, could bring unpredictable consequences, and perhaps rivalry and tension. A new face—oddly—might be less disruptive. He told her about the handwritten note from Barack Obama but did not show it to her.

Her father returned to a full smile. "I never felt that guy got the credit he deserved!" he proclaimed. He ordered more drinks.

Del continued with her relation of events at the White House. When the president finally came around to actually asking her to take the job, she answered quickly and firmly that she would. She said she appreciated his statements about the next term but that she wanted the option to determine if political life and authority was "not for me," allowing her to withdraw before the party convention in July and return to her military career. The president said he understood. He asked only that if she was unhappy in the job that she tell him as soon as possible. Then he went to his desk and retrieved a formal statement that had already been drafted for the announcement. He would make it that evening at eight o'clock Eastern time. The networks had been advised that the president would make a brief statement and did not intend to take questions. She would not be present. He was satisfied with it, but he wanted her view. It read as follows:

I will send to Congress tomorrow morning the
nomination of Lieutenant General Delores Winters,
a career military officer in the United States Special
Operations Command, for the office of vice
president of the United States.

General Winters has been a senior leader in our
country's military intelligence community and
an integral part of the nation's counterterrorism
activities. While not yet well-known to the general
public, General Winters is very well-known to
the leaders of Congress and many agencies of our
government. She is respected by all. I have been
advised by Congressional leaders on all sides that
her confirmation will be effectuated very quickly.
I am confident that the American people will
conclude that she is not only a suitable choice but
also an excellent one.

Because the next presidential election occurs within
the year, I want to be clear that this appointment
is not intended to be an interim or temporary
appointment.

When Del had read it, she told her father, she looked at the
president and said that it appeared to commit her unequivocally to
running with him for reelection. She repeated that she needed to
assess her interest in that before committing. The president took
the paper back from her, she said, moved to his desk, and penned in
a small addition to the last sentence. As revised, it read as follows:

Because the next presidential election occurs within
the year, I want to be clear that this appointment,

as far as I am concerned, is not intended to be an interim or temporary appointment.

It satisfied her. The option was hers.

"Did he get personal?" her father asked.

"What do you mean?"

"Did he talk about the fact that you're single?"

"No. Why would he?"

"Because other people will. This is politics, if you haven't noticed."

"Well, he didn't. It didn't occur to me that he might. My personal life is my business."

"It will be the public's business soon. Or they will think it is. Like in a half hour."

"Things have changed," she said. "Not everybody marries, like they used to. Look around. There are a lot of unmarried women. And men."

"I suppose," Henry said. He waved his empty rocks glass to a waiter standing near the bar.

It was seven forty. A large television hung at one end of the bar.

"Will you stay for this?" her father asked.

"No, I think I'd like to relish my last moment of obscurity. Thank you for all you did. Your advice helped."

She rose to embrace him and walked to the entrance. Officers were lining up for refills and gathering near the television. A navy lieutenant opened the door for her and saluted. Immediately outside, a civilian in a dark suit stepped up to her abruptly. She was startled.

"Agent Burns, ma'am," he said. "Secret Service. I didn't mean to scare you. You won't need your car. If Agent Wilcox here can have your car keys, he will take it to your residence." He pointed to a black SUV just a few steps away, its rear passenger door open. "That one is for you, General."

9

PROJECT EAGLETS' NEST

★ ★ ★ As President Winters rose from her desk, the entering men stopped and stood straight, awaiting her acknowledgment, which came instantly with a slight smile. They moved to the sofa and armchairs positioned in front of her desk, but the guest in uniform remained standing, as did she, behind the desk.

"General," she said, and the two of them saluted in well-practiced unison. General Ben Williamson, chief in command of SOCOM, then lowered his fit frame into the chair near the right front corner of her desk, as she sat down behind it.

The other two men seemed gently restive. The saluting thing was always a little unnerving, distancing. There was no taking it out of her, though, and they knew better than to show overt discomfort lest it be interpreted as disapproval, or worse, envy. They say Kissinger had mastered the skill of concealing the inevitable insecurity of civilian advisors in the presence of a president and uniformed military. Complete acceptance and palpable reverence to both was the trick, and it always helped to ask, as the meeting concluded, for a moment alone with the president. They might have uniforms, but he had access. And it was useful to make the point.

President Winters, as they all well knew, was deeply military in every way. The daughter of the retired air force general now living upstairs in the White House residence, she had lived in nine cities and five countries before she graduated high school. Her mother had died when Del was eleven years old and her father never remarried. Henry Winters was inclined to career service anyway, and had for years resisted overtures to move to private industry. His wife's death from cancer closed the discussion, at least in his mind. Offers continued to come from the defense contractors, but the then major Henry Winters knew that the military life and the community it offered was a better place to raise his only child than a foreign new outside world he knew little of. Inside the military culture, he understood the expectations and the privileges. Out there, who knew?

Del was not pressured to seek a military life in her father's footsteps. If anything, Henry resisted the notion, for example, urging against application to any of the academies, though acceptance at Annapolis, West Point, or the Air Force Academy could have been easily arranged, and on the merits. The general's daughter was a student scholar of the first order: well-rounded, athletic, comfortable with science and languages. But her father was pleased when she chose to attend Georgetown and more so when she stayed on there for law school. His air force assignments took him all over the world, but he was able to see to it that Joint Base Andrews near the capitol was his residential posting. He and Del saw each other often as she moved into adulthood and, as it turned out, her own military career.

Having spent her youth on military bases left an indelible mark on Del. In truth, it left an indelible mark *in* her. She was moved by the commitment and affection she saw between the servicemen and the officers, and the mutual respect that marked their interactions. At the officers' clubs, where her father was inclined to be, seemingly all the time, usually with her along, she observed a world unto itself, with all that a world needed. It had structure. It had roles. It had pride and pressed uniforms with beautiful ribbons and pins. Everyone had a purpose, and to each it was something important.

You didn't know when you would be called, but you would be important when you were.

At first there were hardly any women wearing uniforms in the officers' clubs, but then there were more, and then more yet.

By the end of her first year of law school, the daughter of the then air force colonel Henry Winters knew she would enlist in the Judge Advocate General's Corps when she earned her law degree. Her father expressed measured neutrality to her announced intention. She was a top student at Georgetown, excelling in a highly competitive environment. She was attractive and likable. A national law firm enticed her with a summer internship. For two and half months' attendance she was paid what her decorated father earned in six. He beamed at her success and promise.

"We can afford better gin if this keeps going," he'd told her.

But he knew his daughter.

"I will only say, it would be better if you go to the army or the navy," he told her over dinner in Washington a month before her law school graduation. She had told him her mind was made up. She was joining the military; the question was, which branch. "In the air force, everyone at high levels will know me," he said. "When you're promoted or awarded, some will think it's because you're my daughter. I can live with that, but you might think it too, and *that* I can't live with. The navy has the best food, by the way. Since Lincoln, they've cooked for the presidents when they travel. Still do at the White House mess."

Instead, she applied to the US Army JAG Corps, but never forgot his comment about navy cooking. The rest was history, as sudden as it was unlikely. Events had swept her without notice from hardworking obscurity to the very center of public life, with only five years as the vice president to prepare her for being—or for that matter to prepare the nation to accept her as—commander in chief.

But accept her it did, and when she was elected, she insisted that her father move into the White House with her. He agreed without argument. It was not that he was infirm in any way, or that he was in need of the accommodation, or even that he had signaled any desire to live there. It seemed it was more that she needed him. There was no First Gentleman, and no First Partner, as Del had never married. There was no other in whom she trusted so completely as retired general Henry Winters. And the media and most of the nation thought it at worst unobjectionable, and at best somehow comforting, to have a First Father at 1600 Pennsylvania Avenue.

Against this background, the Assets Review meeting began.

"So who called this meeting?" the president asked.

"Technically, I did," said Secretary of Defense Vernon Lazar. "As usual."

"Because you asked for a classified briefing on the Special Forces new assets deployment program, Eaglets' Nest." She could see he was surprised by her comment, and a little defensive.

"Don't be so sensitive, Vern. I know I asked for the meeting. And it's good to see you. And thanks for bringing General Williamson too. It's helpful to hear information unfiltered, especially when it's too classified to write about."

"How is your father?" asked Williamson. His tone was warm, sincere.

"He's well, thank you. I think he likes it here."

"If he didn't, he wouldn't be living here. Believe me."

"He still enjoys the prerogatives of a general, after a fashion."

"As he should," said Williamson.

"Agreed," said the defense secretary, Lazar. "General, why don't you go first? Set the framework."

"Sure." The general lifted one broad leg over the other and adjusted his chair slightly to better face the president. "You know that we have always looked at this program in four pieces: the aircraft, the munitions, and the deployment base construction."

"That's three," said the president.

"The fourth is security," said the general. "It applies to all of the other three, but especially to the deployment base. That is that is least developed. And that's because we need so much involvement. A clandestine construction job like this has not been undertaken since the Greenbrier complex." He was referring to the secret installation of a compound beneath the West Virginia hotel, constructed in the 1950s to house the entire Congress in the event of a national attack. Now a tourist attraction for history buffs, its existence was kept secret until a *New York Times* reporter disclosed it four decades later.

"We have to select a contractor with the capability to do this, and to do it so that no one knows what is being constructed," General Williamson continued. "We have to trust this outfit with information known only to us and a very few others under our direct control. It takes enormous covert planning and spy craft. That's why Jack is here." He nodded toward the slim civilian on the sofa, Jack Hastings, the director of Central Intelligence. "Jack has assigned a deputy, Susan McShane, to work with SOCOM on that piece, and with NSA."

Lazar interjected, anticipating the president's question. He knew she would have expected the chief of the National Security Agency, a close confidant of hers, to be there.

"Jack is covering today for Meryl Jennings," Lazar said. "There was inordinate chatter overnight and she wanted to run it to ground with her team over there."

"I think you mean *Admiral* Jennings," the president said, referring to the absent head of the NSA.

"Of course."

"Because I noticed you called Ben here 'General,' but you didn't call her 'Admiral.'"

And I *am sensitive,* thought Lazar. In the past there had not been these gender trip wires.

"But let's not stand on ceremony," the president said. "Anyway, she called this morning to explain why she wouldn't be here. She's fine with going ahead without her, but I don't want to get into her end of this without her present. We've got enough to talk about with the aircraft and the munitions. We'll defer the deployment base until next week when she can be here."

Lazar did not seem pleased. "But there are a couple of early decisions that are not controversial. Jack could catch her up."

"We will wait," Winters said, neither strongly nor mildly. "So, General, you were saying?"

"Yes, right," he said. The president noticed that he rustled in his chair before continuing. "So we have these four parts to the program. We started with the aircraft, the smaller drones, because that's where this idea began. On that piece, we can say we are almost ready. The new drones are through prototype and first assembly. A dozen have been made and flown. They meet all of the requirements we established. We can direct them remotely from any air force installation in the world on minimal or no notice. We've conducted thirty-six test firings of mock munitions. All the new drones hit their coordinates within forty-eight inches, most within eighteen inches. We're talking altitude of fifteen thousand feet and higher. That's at least as accurate as the Predators at lower altitudes."

The Predator drone was first deployed in the 1990s, initially as a reconnaissance craft. Later it became the principal unmanned aircraft delivering Hellfire missiles and laser-guided bombs to destroy terrorist camps and high-value targets. It still was. But it was awkwardly large, one hundred feet nose to tail, with an eighty-foot wingspan. And it was relatively slow. Its maximum air speed was two hundred thirty-five miles per hour. For this reason, it typically had to be deployed hours in advance to a general area where credible intelligence suggested a target would, or more often *might*, become exposed. It hovered and circled at high altitude, necessary because of its noise, awaiting opportunity. Worse, the Predator and its improved models required five thousand feet of return landing surface and nearly half that for takeoff. This meant that the fleets needed access to established military airstrips, which were not always nearby, necessitating long mission times.

A key driver to the development of Eaglets' Nest, as the program was secretly called, was the need to more rapidly deploy a weaponized unmanned aircraft, the small Eaglet drone, and to base it nearer its usual operating zones. This meant the Eaglet needed more airspeed, and the ability to put down on either a very short runway or none at all, such as the Harrier fleet. It needed to fly in complete stealth. And, most challenging of all, its principal deployment base must be covert, for the troubling reason each planner knew from the first concept meeting in the Pentagon five presidents ago.

"You say the drones meet our performance requirements. Even the runway and lift parameters?" asked the president.

"Very nearly," continued Williamson. "The vertical landing and takeoff has been difficult in blowing sand conditions. The engineers believe they can solve it. The basing pad may have to be larger than we thought to allow for that. And in bad weather we could always divert the Eaglets to a landing strip if we needed to—keep them there temporarily."

"I don't think that's really an option. Not with its ordnance," said Lazar.

"We can't call it a good option, that's for sure," the president agreed.

"Remember, it's because of that payload that the Eaglet will rarely fly anyway," said Williamson. "Hell, it may never fly. The implications of deployment are enormous. Even the core viability of the program is premised on damn few deployments, at least with the new munitions. And what are the chances of coming home to a sandstorm? We would be crazy to send it in the first place if there was any chance of that."

"Especially since the mission time would be so brief," said the president. She looked to Lazar. "I assume we have not changed those parameters?" she asked him.

"We have not. Mission times would vary by targets, with distance from base being the main variable. But with the speed of these things, maximum deployment time should never exceed three hours from departure to return, no matter which of the three candidate base sites is selected."

The president seemed satisfied on the point. "You would think if we can figure out how to make and hide this equipment, we ought to be able to figure out whether a sandstorm is coming in the next three hours. What about the munitions?" she asked.

"You or me?" Williamson deferred to the secretary of defense.

"Ready and as certain as we can be," said Lazar. "Until one is actually deployed, of course. We tested a miniaturized version of the warhead underground and it behaved as expected. With a placebo charge, of course."

"A miniature of a miniature," said the president.

"Yes, but with every functional component of the actual ordnance. The engineers all agree there will be no issues in scale-up."

"That's the great thing about engineers. They usually agree with each other," she said. "That's why there are so few of them in Congress."

"Or maybe it's the worst thing about them," said Williamson. Small smiles appeared, except on the general's face. "They make me nervous always saying things will work."

Which was why every feature of Eaglets' Nest, mechanized or human, was designed with three, even four, backup redundancies. Only nuclear submarines were so imbedded with alternative systems and parts. The drones had three secure satellite communication channels, each with its own detection software to move between channels in the event of suspected intervention. And as a last resort, if the unthinkable happened and all three failed, a fourth channel, though open and insecure, could be used to get the craft out of the sky, if need be with a self-destruct order.

The new weapons were unlike anything in the arsenal. They

were much smaller than the conventional Hellfire missiles fired from the Predator drone, which measured over one hundred inches long and weighed, depending on ordnance charge, as much as one hundred thirty pounds. The Talons, as the small missiles in the new program were named, were just sixty-six inches from tail to nose tip. Each weighed only fifty-eight pounds, allowing a single drone to carry up to four of the warheads, permitting multiple sites within the drone's range to be targeted in a single flight.

"Whatever their certainty, we *will* test the actual missile, won't we?" asked the president.

"We have to, yes. But you know better than anyone the problems with that," answered Lazar. "The treaties make it a challenge. And the legal red tape isn't the half of it. We have no assurance that even an underground or undersea detonation in the remotest place will be completely undetectable. To use a poor term, the political fallout could be extreme—abroad and at home."

President Winters leaned forward and rested her head on her hands. "Oh, I understand that. But I don't want the detonation to be undetected. I want it to *be* detected. We're going to make sure terrorist commanders know we have this, and its power. Then we might never need to use it. The important thing is that no one detect *where* we keep it."

She closed a folder on her desk, an unambiguous signal that the meeting was concluding. "Ben," she said to the general as she rose, "are you going up to see my father before you leave?"

"He's meeting me by the door to the old building in a few minutes. We're playing golf this afternoon at Burning Tree."

"I know," she said. "His security detail told me." Immediately, she regretted saying it. "But it would be nice of you not to mention it," she said.

"Trust me, he knows."

"Why do you say that?"

"Because he told me to say that since you've found out that we're playing, I should see if you want to come along." She curled her lips, an expression of minor regret. She knew her father did not like her monitoring his comings and goings.

"Well, in fact I would," she said. "But I'll have to meet you at the tenth tee. You two can play the front nine and warm up for a new bet. As I remember our match last time, you'll need it, General." Williamson smiled, saluted, and trailed the others out of the Oval Office.

10

AN UNSOLICITED INTERVIEW

★ ★ ★ The conference room in the Pentagon was not what Stanley had conjured in the fifty minutes his mind had to envision it. For one thing, it was down, and not up, on the third subterranean level of the complex. Escorted down a long corridor resembling a hospital hallway without the artwork, he noticed the high ceiling. He estimated twelve and half feet, unusual below ground in his experience. He presumed the meeting room would be plain and bright with an austere table and uncomfortable chairs. But the table was massive, walnut, assuming. The chairs were fulsome, inviting. The walls were paneled; the lighting, ample and tasteful.

His young uniformed escort introduced him as soon as they entered the room, as the awaiting contingent rose. "Sirs and ma'am, this is Mr. Bigelow."

"Thank you, Lieutenant," said the gentleman at the far end of the long table. The door closed behind the departing escort, and everyone except Stanley sat down. There was no handshaking. Stanley sensed his own perspiration. The corridor walk had been long, his collar just a bit tight.

"Mr. Bigelow, please take a seat. We thank you for coming. We know you must have a lot of questions, especially what this is all about. You may know very soon. First, let me introduce us to you.

ld you like coffee?" he asked, with the first smile Stanley had
since the one permanently taped to the face of the ticket agent
in Pittsburgh. This one seemed more relaxed.

"If there is nothing stronger," Stanley replied flatly.

The host smiled again. Stanley lurched his large frame to the
center of the table to reach the chrome coffee carafe. He noticed that
the cup and saucer, placed next to a leather place mat, were high-end.

"My name is George Steeden," said the host. "I am undersecretary
of defense for Special Forces operations. My boss is Vernon Lazar,
the secretary. Have you ever met Mr. Lazar?"

"No."

"Across from you is Susan McShane. Susan is deputy director of
the Central Intelligence Agency for clandestine planning." McShane
nodded, with a curled expression that could be said to be either a
smile or a frown.

"I've never met her either," said Stanley, producing a warm laugh
from most of them around the table.

"At the other end of the table is Wilson Bryce. Wilson is director
of technical operations for NSA, the National Security Agency. Are
you familiar with the work of that agency?" asked Steeden.

"Only what I learned on the way over here." Another laugh.

"And sitting next to Susan is Captain Tyler Brew." He gestured
to the wiry black uniformed man who had kept, Stanley noticed,
a serious eye on him from his moment of entry and who, he also
noticed, had not laughed.

"Captain Brew is a Navy SEAL," Steeden said. "The SEALs, the
Army Rangers, Delta Force, and a few other units are—together—
the specially trained forces that form the mission units of SOCOM.
That means Special Operations Command. While these forces come
from different service branches, all of their activities are centralized
under a single commander, presently General Ben Williamson. Last
fall, Captain Brew turned forty. At that age, SEALs are normally
required to leave field operations. Many leave the military at that

time, but their special skills and background with intelligence in the field make them valuable in managing special asset programs. Especially covert programs." No movement from Captain Brew, just the serious stare. *Has he even blinked?* Stanley wondered.

"So, Captain Brew was asked by SOCOM to take on responsibility for the daily management of the program we are speaking with you about," Steeden continued. "Given the nature of something like this, it is important that as few people as possible know everything about it. Participants know their role, their part. But they don't know the roles and activities of others. You can understand why this fragmentation is needed. There is always the risk of a security compromise. We can deal with that; we plan for it. So long as the compromise of one component of the project cannot cause the compromise of others or of the whole program."

"Yes, I can see that," said Stanley. "People can't disclose what they don't know."

"Correct. Only Captain Brew knows the details of each part of the overall program, including where the personnel are and what they are doing, each and every one of them."

Tyler Brew was born and raised in the Deep South, the descendant of slaves on Alabama cotton plantations. Though born a generation after the tensions of the civil rights movement of the fifties and sixties, and raised in a family that urged optimism and hope for his place in society, he encountered, as all blacks had, constant reminders of his race and implicit hurdles to advancement. "You can try to ignore it and be resentful," his father had instructed as he reached middle school age. "The longer you resent it, the more it gets to you. Or you can be aware of it and deal with it. I don't mean you accept it. *Never* accept it. It's wrong, and you never accept wrong. You can use your feelings to want right, and your mind to do right. And when you do right, you'll please yourself and your family. That's more important than anything." Tyler excelled in school and athletics, despite a quietness often mistaken for shyness. He enlisted in the navy after high school, when his leadership capacity was observed quickly. His mother, a highly intelligent woman who shared her husband's pragmatic attitude about racial division, questioned her son's decision to enlist in the military. She'd wanted college for Tyler, as had his high school teachers. An athletic scholarship, at least to a smaller school, was possible. But Tyler wanted to join a larger team. He assured her he would go to college after service, and said that the financial burden would not be so great, as the government had refortified educational benefits, needed because fewer talented young persons enlisted for service. And his choices might be wider for admission, he'd told her, as the veterans' benefits would allow him to select a school that the family might not otherwise consider affordable. His mother could see the strength of his desire and knew that the military was by then a place where a young black man could truly advance. The uniform had a way of diminishing the importance of the color of the hands and face that extended from it. Besides, her husband was supportive. "He will lead," he'd told her. "Let him lead."

Undersecretary Steeden still held forth in the Pentagon conference room. "I am glad you appreciate the need for limited knowledge," he said.

"Just how much *will* I know?" Stanley asked.

"Nothing, unless we decide you are suitable," said Steeden. "That's what this meeting today is really about."

"And also whether I am willing to do whatever it is you are talking about, right?" asked Stanley.

"Well, first things first, Mr. Bigelow."

11

LADY AT THE TEE

★ ★ ★ As far as anyone knew, no woman had ever played golf at Burning Tree Golf Club before the passenger in the third of four Cadillac Escalades cruising up the asphalt drive at a rude but safe speed. Four Secret Service agents flooded out of the second vehicle like synchronized swimmers to surround the third, while two from the front car and two from the rear emerged to take stations fore and aft of the caravan. The president waited for the required approval, which came ten seconds later, and then opened her own door and stepped out. She looked toward the tenth tee box and saw her father and General Williamson, waving.

Burning Tree, or simply "the Tree," as it was known to its legendary membership of dignitaries and Washington elites, had been, until the problem of Delores Winters, firmly—seemingly inexorably—committed to its exclusively male tradition. In recent decades, many marveled at, and many others despised, its intransigent refusal to admit women, even as social visitors. There were no women's restrooms anywhere on the premises and no female employees. Membership was strictly by invitation only, and Burning Tree boasted that every president since Calvin Coolidge had walked its hallowed grounds, and many had been members. The club had offered honorary membership and privileges to every justice of the

United States Supreme Court until Sandra Day O'Connor, a good athlete who enjoyed golf, was confirmed to become the first woman to sit on the court. Membership was not offered to her, and the practice of offering membership to future justices was discontinued, though Justice Scalia, who'd been invited before his elevation to the highest court, continued to be a member.

It was even known that when a female Secret Service agent was sent in advance of an earlier president's visit to inspect the premises for security, she was turned away and made to wait in the parking lot while male agents surveyed the facilities. Augusta National, home of the fabled Masters Championship, perhaps succumbing to national television revenues, or maybe because the club's secretary noted that the twenty-first century had arrived, had thrust aside its pride and invited Condoleezza Rice into its membership many years earlier. But not the Tree.

Consternation ran high in the fall of 2016 when many believed Hillary Clinton would be elected as the first woman president. Members feared it would be impossible to deny a president an invitation. But her polarizing reputation, whether earned or not, provided enough cover for the stalwarts opposed to change. The board let it be known that a president Hillary Clinton would not be invited. The reasoning was that she was not a golfer anyway, so the insult would not be so overt. Donald Trump's startling election made the point moot anyway.

But the election of Delores Jane Winters seriously challenged the Tree's prior excuses. She was respected and personally liked by prominent leaders across the spectrum. And she was a notoriously avid and able golfer. Between Election Day and the inauguration, talk within the club buzzed. At first, the entrenched senior members, opposing her admission, appeared to be prevailing. But more than a few souls, including board member General Ben Williamson, good friend to the president-elect's father, knew it was time. He excused himself from the board's deliberations, but probably preordained their outcome with a procedural suggestion. He urged that a short letter be mailed to the home of each member, with a return card marked only "Yes" or "No," on which members could cast a purely advisory vote to the board. It would not be binding, the general noted, but it would serve the purpose of informing the board of overall membership sentiment. What harm could come from simply polling the members?

The president's father had not urged his fellow general to do anything of the sort, but his friend had told him of the letter and voting card.

"I want the wives to know about this," Williamson told Henry. "Wives always see the mail."

"But they can't vote anyway."

"They can in the bedroom," the general said.

By early January, older members could be seen downing scotch silently well into the evening in the Burning Tree lounge in moods dimmer than usual. Glum acceptance was setting in, as thirds and fourths were poured by waiters betraying, on close examination, slight approving smiles.

Of course, concessions were necessary lest the speed of change be overwhelming. Only one restroom would be afforded, a converted walk-in closet off the main room, wearing an embossed sign that read not "Women" or "Ladies," but simply "The President." No locker-room accommodation would be undertaken until it could be determined if additional women might be invited in the future, which was not at all certain. And the club's staff would remain all male until the board, at its discretion, chose to revisit that question.

On Inauguration Day, a club member with a senior post in the State Department discreetly delivered a formal and confidential invitation to a Secret Service agent he knew on the White House detail, for forwarding to the new president's father. Late that evening the envelope lay beside a rocks glass filled with two fingers of bourbon in the library of the White House residence, as father awaited daughter. Reports among staff suggested that an extended discussion ensued, marked by long pauses. Apparently, the new president was underwhelmed by the invitation and, mindful of the snub to earlier women, prepared to decline it. Henry Winters urged temperance.

"You shattered the most important glass ceiling in November," he said to her. "But there are many more, Del. Maybe this is the first of the rest."

The next day a handwritten presidential note card was dispatched by courier to the club secretary.

"Invitation received and accepted. Prefer the men's tees. — DJW" was all it said.

12

STANLEY EXAMINED

★ ★ ★ The mood in the Pentagon conference room was stiff, cool. To Stanley it felt like an interview that he had not solicited, a mixture of curiosity, pressure, and slight resentment. But he could not say that he had been brought against his will. He was asked, would he come to Washington to meet with "some personnel"? And he had answered yes, he would. There was no room to argue that he had been duped. The security measures used to bring him from the airport were unnerving, and certainly unexpected by him. But it was hard to call them unreasonable or physically too imposing. And the email had put him on notice—had it not?— that his trip was of a secretive quality.

Anyway, he was here now. He had committed to nothing and would be home in Pittsburgh that evening. The best course was to be friendly and calm and hear them out. Besides, so far it was all sort of interesting, and even a bit exciting.

"We know all of this must have you feeling off guard," said Undersecretary Steeden. "You probably have questions that we should address up front."

"Up front before what?" asked Stanley.

"Before we start asking *you* questions. We have a lot of them.

About your company. About yourself. So that we can make a judgment as to your suitability."

"You make it sound like I am trying to be hired for something."

"When we can explain more fully why we asked you here, you may conclude that this is an opportunity."

"For my company or for me?"

"For both. But for you personally, it is an opportunity to serve your country."

Stanley finished his coffee, and allowed that to sink in for a moment. *So, this is more than just business,* he thought. He felt a small stirring inside himself. It was not unpleasant, more like a slight heightening of his senses. At his age, that was always interesting.

"I do have an obvious question," Stanley said. "How did you find me for whatever this is about? You could all be my children. I should have retired years ago."

"We identified you because you have the skills and the background that align with the unusual profile for a critical need we have for a program under development," said Susan McShane, her first words in the meeting. "And other desirable characteristics."

Stanley thought her a little cryptic and oddly clinical.

"And what are those?" asked Stanley.

"The characteristics?"

"No, the skills and background."

"You have deep experience and knowledge in specialized underground engineering and construction," she said.

"So do a thousand others."

"True, but you have experience in deep shaft specialized containment."

"So do a hundred others."

"Again, true. But you also are a metallurgical expert. That is important to us. And despite your age and position in your own company, you keep working. And you prefer to work alone, virtually

unassisted. You don't even use others for your drawings and models."
Now how does she know that? he wondered.

"I love my work, yes. I like the doing part. I like to think and draw. I haven't tired of it."

"And you have no family."

"I am a widower. I have no children or nieces or nephews. I have no siblings. Neither did my wife." He paused and looked over the faces in the room. "Is that a qualification?"

"It's a characteristic, a desirable one," said Susan McShane.

"How is that? I don't consider it a great thing." His wife had been dead nine years, and it seemed like yesterday to Stanley. He missed her deeply, still sadly.

"I am sorry," said McShane. "I did not mean it that way."

It was true that the CIA planner had not meant to imply that it was a good thing for Stanley that he was a childless widower without any family. But it was also true that the murders of Ruth and Melinda Morgenthal and Leo Kinz, the murders that occasioned the candidacy of Stanley Bigelow in the first place, were still raw in McShane's mind. In retrospect, it was clear that too little thought had been given to the risk of using a mother in such a covert operation. Ruth had been told not to disclose her involvement with anyone, including her family. But the instructions were not explicit enough. Ruth had not told her daughter that she was in Washington to work with the CIA and the Department of Defense. But she did tell her it was related to the government, and she had disclosed to McShane that her college-bound daughter would be staying with her for a month, which—regrettably, so regrettably—McShane had approved. Who knew how the killers had learned of Ruth and her whereabouts? Jack Renfro had interviewed Ruth's ex-husband and Melinda's father, a Lockheed engineer living in Rockville, to rule him out as a suspect. It was not difficult to do. He was devastated by the loss, in brutal fashion, of his only daughter and his former wife. Melinda had emailed him to say she was coming to live for a month with her mother at Dupont Circle. Her mother had been recruited for a government job of some kind. "Some secret thing, I think," she had said to her father. Could he take her to college for orientation in August?

"He was thrilled by his daughter's request," Renfro reported to McShane. "And crushed by my visit. Believe me, crushed. This was a professional hit. Nothing domestic about it."

McShane leaned forward and looked across the table at Stanley. "Really, Mr. Bigelow, I did not mean to say it is good that you are alone. The thing is that in this circumstance, it is better that an operative not be distracted by personal commitments."

Operative, Stanley thought. *Now we* are *getting clinical.*

"And better to have no one to talk to, I assume," he said. "You know, this security thing."

"Yes, that is a consideration."

"And what other 'characteristics' make me suitable to you?" He looked again at each of them around the table.

"Frankly, your age. You are seventy, right?"

"Barely, but let's not quibble," he said, nodding.

"With no military service or law enforcement employment in your background."

"Correct."

"From Pittsburgh."

"All my life. So far."

"Moderate in your drinking."

"When I want to be."

The undersecretary interjected. "We assume your health is all right? We have to ask. You have no illness that you are aware of?"

"No, except that apparently I'm lonely with no one to talk to and I work all of the time for no good reason." Everyone smiled, except the black Navy SEAL.

"Well," said Steeden, "you probably have the picture now on the qualities we are looking for. We can't talk yet about the project in specific terms, except to say that it involves unusual underground construction that will have to be undertaken in complete secrecy. To ensure it is not discovered, the least number of individuals possible must be involved, from first drawing to final completion. And the design and construction professional must be someone who does not attract notice, for the same reason. That rules out any of the global firms that have installed military infrastructure, especially in the Middle East or Africa."

Oh brother, thought Stanley.

"We don't think an engineer of your age from Pittsburgh who has never worked abroad for the United States government is likely to attract attention," said the undersecretary. He rose and reached toward the carafe of coffee. "Would you like more coffee?"

"None for me, thanks," Stanley said. "You know that I have done military projects in this country."

"Of course. But we don't think those should attract interest. They were pretty minor."

"The Wright-Patterson project was a two-hundred-million-dollar contract."

"As I said, pretty minor."

Stanley shrugged slightly. McShane stepped in.

"There are some other things that would be involved, Mr. Bigelow. We need to be sure you understand them before we go any further."

"That sounds ominous."

"Some of them will seem a little scary. Most will just seem intrusive, irritating," she replied.

"Let's start with the intrusive," said Stanley, smiling.

"Yes. Well, you saw the precautions that were taken transporting you here today. That's old-school stuff, elementary. It still works and is useful. There will be plenty of that going forward if you do this. But there will also be newer technology and methods. We will need to install monitoring devices in your home, your cars, and your company offices. Your email traffic from any device will be surveilled in real time. Any person who has contact with you about the project, no matter how minor, will be watched also, sometimes for a long time, including your own employees."

"And we will need your agreement for all this, in advance," interrupted the undersecretary. "We need to be able to move immediately at any time. You email some supplier in Detroit with a technical question, we must immediately watch that person's communications until we are satisfied that nothing about your interaction has caused a possible compromise. We can't come to you each time with a request."

"Is that legal?" asked Stanley.

"I am afraid that is above our pay grades," Steeden said. "I can tell you, though, that the project and our methods are known—in detail—at the highest levels of our government. Even the president. They will be reviewed regularly."

"Does that cover the 'intrusive' part?" Stanley asked.

"More or less," said Ms. McShane.

"Then what is the scary part about?"

"We used to say the television shows and movies about these things were wild exaggerations, unrealistic. We don't say that anymore." McShane had been leaning back in her chair, but now she leaned forward toward him and placed her hands on the table. "When—if—this project is more fully explained to you, you will see that there are many moving parts. Related operations. There will be dozens of individuals involved, including military people and logistical elements. Many will have small roles, only brief involvement. But every element presents risk, and the more elements, the greater the risk."

"Susan means," said the undersecretary, "that we assume there will be breaches and breakdowns. These plans never go without a hitch, no matter how careful we try to be."

"I am not surprised," Stanley responded. "I've never done a complicated design that didn't require changes to make it work."

"Do people get killed when you make a change?" These were the first words out of the Navy SEAL's mouth. His tone was not kind. Steeden looked at Captain Brew coolly but, Stanley noticed, not disapprovingly.

"God, no," Stanley answered.

McShane resumed. "In this work, sometimes they do. Often they do. Of course, we don't like that. We don't want it. We hate it. But we must accept it, and accept it as more than an extreme unlikelihood."

"And if I accept this work, I do too," said the seventy-year-old engineer from Pittsburgh who lived a lonely comfortable life.

"Yes, you do."

13

FROM ONE GENERAL TO ANOTHER

★ ★ ★ Hitting last in the group, Henry Winters drew his tee shot on the sixteenth hole well into the left rough. It was dense six-inch-high grass dotted with clumps of fescue. He shrugged and hit another, a so-called "provisional," in case he could not find the first. "Don't spend forever looking for it over there," called out his daughter as she strode up the center of the fairway toward her well-placed drive of 170 yards.

Henry was not grateful for the suggestion. He flashed a darting look at his caddie, and another at the Secret Service agent who had trotted over to assist in the search.

"Don't listen to that," Henry told them. "By rule, we have ten minutes to find the damn thing."

He would need that and more. General Williamson's ball was better struck than his friend's, and he found himself with the president as they stood in the fairway leaning against golf clubs, watching Henry moving his foot like a broom through the grasses.

"Is that legal?" she asked the general.

"Is what legal?"

"Using the agent to look for the ball. Your caddie can help, but I don't think you can get help from others," she said.

"You can't be serious."

"I am completely serious. He wouldn't let me get away with that. He is a total stickler."

"Well, I wouldn't make a point of it now. He won't find that ball with a dozen helpers. You know what the stuff is like in there. He'll have to use the provisional anyway."

"I suppose you're right," she said. "If it doesn't matter, why push it?"

"It's the smart choice, if you ask me," said Williamson. Henry was still flinging through the high rough, and now the caddie and the agent were using clubs to explore the patches of fescue. "There's another thing I wonder if we could talk about, Madam President."

"'Madam President'?" she echoed. "Please, Ben. That's a little formal, isn't it?"

"I think so too, actually," he replied. "And it's pretty much what I wanted to mention to you."

"Now you've lost me."

"I don't think you should have dressed down Lazar this morning when he didn't call Jennings by her military rank," he said.

"I noticed you seemed uncomfortable."

"He is a civilian and he is my boss. You are his boss. I am pretty sure he was a lot more uncomfortable than I was about being called out on that in front of all of us."

"I see your point," she said.

"The point is really a little broader. I've been in meetings with four presidents. Your father has too. Anyone who meets in the Oval Office remembers every word, every encounter with the president. The president doesn't, but they do. Scorecards are kept. People can't help but have a sense of self-importance in those moments, even if the truth is that they are not important moments at all. And they never forget them."

He told her that Lazar would not forget what had happened earlier that morning, that it was not just about egos and bruised feelings. He said she needed to be careful. Rivalries for her attention could be induced. It wasn't healthy. It was damaging to trust. And trust, he told her, especially in the line of command, was critical in the clutch. There were always problems that came up suddenly, sometimes terrible things. And when they did, there was no time to be bothered with hints of distrust or envy.

"And reprimanding him in front of you isn't helpful for that?"

"Even gently, as you did."

"Well, this is the kind of advice I need, Ben," she said sincerely. "How could I make this right?"

"Nixon used to have William Rogers up to the White House residence for drinks when Rogers was his secretary of state," recalled the general. "It made others envious, especially Kissinger. But it made Rogers feel good, and he needed it because he knew that Kissinger, Laird, and Haig did not consider him their intellectual equals. Nixon did the right thing singling him out for attention. He just shouldn't have let the others know he was having those drinks alone with Rogers."

"And what do you think of Mr. Lazar?" she asked. "His abilities."

"I think he is the most qualified defense secretary since James Mattis. And I think he likes scotch."

Her father emerged from the rough, looking frustrated and resigned, almost like a child giving up on a darkened doorstep on Halloween night, and plodded to his provisional drive, laying—painfully—three.

"Too bad, Dad" called Del. Then quietly she said to the general, "Reprimand averted."

14

LARGE AND A LITTLE LONELY

★ ★ ★ In the Pentagon conference room, the vetting of Stanley Bigelow descended into the details of the visitor's personal lifestyle and his business activities. Without family, what did he do for a social life? Did he have hobbies? charitable interests? a church life?

Stanley said there wasn't much to tell them. He had no lady friends and was disinterested in dating. He did have a poker group, and was fond of all of its members. It was an eclectic bunch, and he was probably the tie that bound them, as he had known each for decades: his barber; a funeral director he had grown up with in Pittsburgh; the tobacconist from whom he had for years purchased his cigars (Captain Brew raised a brow); and a retired otolaryngologist he had met as an undergraduate. They played at Stanley's apartment on the last Thursday night of every month, except for November and December, which were skipped on account of the holidays. He did not play golf and belonged to no country club. He had been a visible member at the Commerce Club for businessmen downtown for seemingly forever, but had eschewed any attempt to place him in leadership there. He was not interested in titles, he liked to say, just the bourbon, about which the pub staff was expert, and attentive to his preferences. If classical music could be called a hobby, he would admit to it as one. He tried never to miss a performance of the Pittsburgh Symphony and was a substantial donor to it, at his insistence anonymously. But again, he had evaded any position within the organization. He made annual gifts to several nonprofit service organizations, including the small hospice that had touched him with its tenderness toward his dying wife nine years ago.

Religiosity? His wife had been a practicing Catholic of Irish descent, but it had never connected meaningfully in him. After her death, he had dabbled with Mass attendance, and appreciated the parish pastor's interest in him, which he thought sincere and kind, but after a year or so he concluded it was no use—it just wasn't him, and he believed his wife would understand.

He could say that if he had a religion, it was baseball. He was not just a regular fan. In fact, he really wasn't much of a fan at all in the deeply partisan sense, though he preferred the Pirates in the National League, out of civic duty, he said, and the Indians in the American, out of sympathy, his friends said teasingly. More than a rooter, he was a student. Most people watched baseball; Stanley absorbed it. Perhaps it was the engineer's impulse. He loved the minutiae that most people did not care about or even know existed. He analyzed strategies, skills, and statistics. He developed novel statistical theories of performance for his own amusement. For a given pitcher, what was the ratio of foul balls to pitches thrown and to walks issued? A lower ratio reflected more efficiency, he theorized, and was predictive of fewer extra-base hits allowed. He considered the aversion of pitchers and their managers to walks as overblown and misguided. "Nobody ever cleared the bases with a walk!" he declared, supremely confident in his position. Better to issue, within limits, more walks than to yield an excessive number of foul balls. His friends were too polite to ask whether anyone ever cleared the bases with a foul ball. His assessments and theories rarely went further than the poker table, but they kept him occupied and impassioned.

Then there were questions about his workplace. He was the sole owner of his company? Did he intend to keep it that way? Did he plan to sell the business? There must have been business suitors, perhaps private equity groups or other engineering firms?

He explained that while he was sole owner of the one thousand shares of his corporation, he had for years been parsing out "share promises" to employees—most of them—in relation to their length of service and contributions to the business. While not stock shares in the usual sense, they amounted to a promise by him to reward these employees, in proportion to their named percentage, with the proceeds of the sale of the business when it occurred. If they retired before the company was sold, he agreed to redeem or, in a sense, "buy back" their shares, if they wanted him to do that, for a price based on a reasonable estimate of the value of the business at that time. Or they could hold their ownership position until the company was sold off. He was seventy, but he loved his work and what he had built. Until he stopped enjoying it, or until he became infirm, he had no intention of selling CSB Engineering. Though when the time came, he was certain there would be buyers. The company would be valuable with or without him personally because he had accumulated a cadre of strong engineers and industrial architects, most much younger than him, who worked cohesively on projects too complex and specialized for most other firms.

Finally, Wilson Bryce, the technical operations officer, participated too. How did Stanley use technology in his work, and personally? How many apps did he own, and how often did he use them? There was a long exchange between Bryce and Stanley about different kinds of engineering software and one particular technology that enabled the encryption and reconstruction of blueprints and drawings. Stanley was familiar with it but had not used it. His drawings had never been so sensitive, he said.

A knock at the door announced that lunch had arrived. A navy seaman wheeled it in on a walnut cart. The conversation continued as everyone served themselves. Steeden motioned to Stanley that he should go first. He took a generous portion of salad and, after quickly tallying the tray of sandwiches, two of the ham and cheese. He glanced at Captain Brew. He was pleased that the military man showed no reaction to his choices.

Stanley was amused that his hosts were disappointed with the luncheon fare. Wilson Bryce blurted, "What the hell is it with these carrots?" He stood over the salad platter like a raptor displeased with his prey. "Look at those carrot strips. They're all dried up and shriveled. They're not even really orange anymore! Those things were peeled two weeks ago. They always do this!"

The oddity of the comment in its context seemed lost on Steeden, who chimed in too. "It's terrible," he said. "Why do they even put them on there! Now I have to load up on the dressing because they're so dry."

Stanley made a comment that a little suspect produce ought not get in the way of national security. "You probably have more questions for me?" he asked.

But as it happened, they didn't. There were a few moments of small talk at the end, which was striking to Stanley because there had been none when one would have expected it, at the beginning.

"Mr. Bigelow, thank you again," Steeden said. "Captain Brew will take you up and explain your departure."

So, Stanley and the Navy SEAL left the room and headed down the long corridor to the elevators. The sailor walked ahead of him. His posture was perfect as he strode, his arms hanging nearly motionless from his strong shoulders. Stanley thought him a small man for such a job, five ten at the most, a compact build. And still, after three hours together, the man was not overly friendly; in truth, he was not friendly at all.

He directed Stanley into a small caucus room near the lobby entrance. There were three armchairs and a coffee table and a generous surplus of white noise. The two men did not sit down. Brew produced a bank card and handed it to Stanley.

"The same driver who delivered you here this morning will take you back to the hotel in the same car. Sit in the front seat, just as you did getting here. He will pull directly into the garage and go to the lower level. You and the first driver will part. Wait a minute or two and then take the elevator up to the lobby. Go into the bar and buy a drink."

"I am ready for one," said Stanley. Brew did not smile, but at least he didn't appear annoyed either.

"Pay for your drink with that card. It's a twenty-five-dollar debit card from Fifth Republic Bank in Pittsburgh. Then give the card to your second driver, who will be waiting for you at the front entrance thirty minutes later."

"Why do I do all this?"

"That hotel is popular for foreign intelligence operatives because of its location. We don't think you were monitored today, but we want to be sure. It's kind of a stress test. If you aren't observed there, you are a pretty clean risk for surveillance."

"In other words, I am uninteresting."

"That would be a good thing," said Brew. "We like uninteresting. If there is any action on that card after you leave, we know we have a problem."

"What kind of 'action' could there be? You told me to give the card to your man."

"But its number will be in play because you will have used it. If you are being watched, an attempt will be made to learn more about that card and who used it. Someone calls and says they lost their debit card, that kind of thing. The bank works with us. If there are any inquiries, by internet or phone, we will know."

"Really?" said Stanley. "It certainly is a new world." Brew opened the door of the small room. "How will I know the driver who will take me from the hotel to the airport?" Stanley asked. Brew quickly closed the door again.

"Black BMW 6 Series with an Uber decal on the passenger side of the windshield. Approach the car on that side. He will call you

'Mr. Morris.' If he doesn't, don't get in. Just walk back into the lobby. We will have people there for you."

The two men stood silently as Stanley took it all in. He felt strange to be standing so large and old and uncertain over the smaller, athletic, confident military man. The door to the little room remained closed.

"I wonder if I am up to this," said Stanley.

"I wonder too," said Brew, as he opened the door. "Here is your phone," he said, handing it to Stanley. A wave, a startle, ran quickly, disarmingly, through Stanley. He had been so absorbed in the events of the unusual day that he had completely forgotten about the phone.

At the Pentagon entrance, he recognized the second driver from the morning, the more communicative one. He extended his hand to Stanley, a gesture that Stanley inordinately welcomed. He grasped the nameless driver's hand firmly. As they pulled away from the entrance, the driver looked at him.

"Well, I guess you have the answer to your question," he said.

"What do you mean?" asked Stanley.

"Somebody still cares about you."

15

PRESIDENTIAL APOLOGY

★ ★ ★ As Vern Lazar reached the doorway of the residence study, he saw Henry Winters just rising from his comfortable chair near the fireplace. As if on cue, the First Father walked past the defense secretary, nodding as he did so, and left the room. The president remained in her chair and motioned Lazar over with a smile, jabbing a hand toward the seat her father had just vacated.

"Thanks for joining me, Vern," she said warmly. "I hear you're a scotch man. I have Macallan 12 for you." She poured him a double, neat. "I wish we had 15, but the taxpayers might find out."

"It's very nice of you, Madam President. You know, I've never been up here to the residence."

"I haven't made a practice of inviting people up. Maybe I shouldn't be so concerned about hurting people's feelings."

"Oh?"

"My dad says it's like a grandpa having one child on his knee and not the others. They notice those things."

"I suppose he's right."

"I would be grateful if you didn't mention it downstairs."

"You have my word."

"Thank you. Your word is important to me. That's really why I asked you up." She adjusted herself in her chair and looked into the fire. "The other day in our meeting with Williamson and Hastings, I was not kind when you didn't call Meryl Jennings 'Admiral.' It was rude of me. I apologize."

"You needn't."

"But it irritated you."

"Yes."

"I think you were right to be irritated. I know you respect her, and I know she respects you. So, it was uncalled for."

"There is no question that I respect her, and I hope the feeling is mutual."

"I can tell you it is. And I don't want anybody inhibited. It's important that we are free with each other. Because we disagree and we argue. We're supposed to. It's good to do it. But only when it's complete. If someone holds back, it's not complete."

"I could not agree more," said Lazar. "In the military, that's a problem. Very often, I am afraid. Rank and hierarchy. Line of command. At the very top, they talk freely. Getting a junior officer to speak up and challenge a senior? That's a challenge."

"And the junior may be the one who's right," she said.

"Almost as often as not."

"Well, I was talking to one of those senior officers about you, and I think *he* was right, though I will say that no junior was there to challenge him."

"Oh?"

"Ben Williamson." She poured herself a small amount more of the Macallan. "He says you're the most capable defense secretary since Jim Mattis. Quite a compliment."

"That's kind of you to share with me."

"And do you want to know what my father has to say?"

"I don't think so."

"Good, because I haven't asked him."

She raised her glass to his as they leaned in front of the fire, smiling. "He's consulted enough," she said.

16

STANLEY GOES COVERT

★ ★ ★ Stanley loped to the bar in the vast lobby of the JW Marriott. He took a stool near the middle with three open seats on either side. The stools were too close together for his liking—as he usually found barstools to be—so he moved one out and shifted it behind another one down the line, creating a broad berth for his own. A person listening closely might have heard a self-comforting sigh as he lowered his ample backside onto it. But it did not seem to him that anyone was.

He stared straight ahead, motionless, moments of the strange day reappearing in his head like postcards in mail slots. One after another, he retracted them, reconsidered them, and returned them to the pigeonholes of his memory.

In a few minutes, a bartender of unusual mixed nationality presented him with a glass of water and a cocktail napkin. *Perhaps Indian and Japanese?* Stanley wondered. The bartender didn't say anything, just stood in front of Stanley with raised quizzical eyebrows that asked his question for him.

"The Jefferson Reserve. Double. On the rocks, please." Wordlessly, the waiter turned away.

Stanley felt out of sorts hunched over a hotel bar knowing he was being watched in order to see if he was being watched. It all seemed so implausible. The aging engineer from Pittsburgh who'd thought he was merely visiting the military to hear about a routine business proposal was seemingly one foot into perilous duty as a covert operative. And without any careful thought! If engineers were anything, they were careful, for God's sake. How had he gotten into this?

He left the debit card, as instructed, on the bar top in front of his napkin.

The bar was L-shaped. Two persons sat on each flank. Stanley, unable to tell if either pair were together, did not want to look at them long enough to determine if they were. He turned on his stool and quickly surveyed the lobby. But what could you glean from such a glance? There were small groups gathered near the automatic foyer doors and two men in golf jackets standing, just a little suspiciously he told himself, between the registration desk and the bar area. Brew's people?

He sipped his bourbon sparingly. May as well let everyone have a good, long look. Maybe, as Brew said, someone would signal an interest in his presence and that would be the end of this business.

The bartender returned and—curiously, to Stanley—pointed to his near empty glass and repeated, without a word, a questioning look that could only be asking one question. *Is this guy mute?* he wondered. Not likely.

"No," Stanley answered the bartender's wordless question, a little emphatically. He pointed to the debit card, and the bartender swept it up silently, with a "have it your way" expression.

Stanley was looking around from his stool once more when the bartender came back with the leather folio, card protruding, and left it on the bar top. Stanley took the card and left three dollars in cash for a tip.

He strode past the men in golf jackets and out through the automatic sliding doors. The black BMW 6 Series was there. It had the Uber decal. He walked to the front passenger side and the window slid down.

"Mr. Morris," the driver said, without making eye contact.

Stanley said nothing in reply, just climbed into the front seat, unfurling his long legs and dragging in his briefcase, placing it on his lap. He handed the debit card to the driver. The deep leather seat felt soothing to his lower back. *Well, that was not too bad,* he thought. What a day it had been. His blood seemed heated to him. He flicked down the sun visor and saw that his ears looked red in its mirror. They were warm to his touch. His heart was quick, but now slowing. Sitting above the mixture of all these sensations was an umbrella of mild exhilaration. Maybe the idea of this assignment was growing on him.

As the comfortable sedan cruised passed the monuments en route to Reagan National, Stanley knew that he was concluding, without really wanting to acknowledge, that it was good to be cared about.

17

MOMENT OF DECISIONS, DECISIONS OF MOMENT

★ ★ ★ The president was late.

Admiral Meryl Jennings, the NSA chief, waited with the others in the personal conference room of CIA director Jack Hastings. His office was in the Eisenhower Executive Office Building adjoining the White House. The president had suggested they meet there instead of in the Oval Office. She liked to get out of the West Wing and could move about the old building with only a small security detail. Besides, Ben Williamson had shared another kernel of wisdom that she was finding to be true: advisors tended to be more candid outside of the Oval Office than in it. Something about that storied room produced an air of deference so imposing that things that should be said sometimes were not. The general had told her that was the reason, as much as security and technology, that presidents had so often in times of special stress assembled senior advisors in the Situation Room downstairs in the West Wing, instead of in the Oval Office.

"What's your view on the Pittsburgh asset?" Jennings asked her CIA counterpart while they waited.

"I am fine with him, but Brew is dubious."

"Why?"

"His physical condition, his inexperience in covert activity."

"Well, we're not going to find a trained spy who knows how to build something like this in the desert," said Jennings.

"You know Brew," said Hastings. He explained the SEAL's objections. Brew was the quintessential planner, he said, and his concern was not without reason. It was not so much the Pittsburgh man's inexperience in secretive behavior as it was the combination of that inexperience with his poor physical condition. On his tall frame, Stanley Bigelow carried 290 pounds, a good bit of the surplus around the waist. He was seventy years old and unathletic. Especially in view of the murder of Ruth Morgenthal, the initial choice for the engineering work, Hastings agreed with Brew's view that it was only prudent to assume a secrecy breach somewhere along the way. An extraction might be required. "He's worried we won't be able to protect him because of his poor mobility. And if we can't protect him, we can't protect the program."

Jennings paged through the binder sitting on the table at her spot. There was one of the same at each place, atop a leather desk pad and next to a water glass filled with ice. She found the page of photos showing Stanley Bigelow. There were two of him raising his large abdomen from his seat in the Pentagon meeting room, a zoomed profile that exposed his abundant jowl and double chin, and three as he walked down the corridor after the meeting, trailing Brew with an uneven gait and slouching shoulders. She passed the open binder to General Williamson. He looked at the photos without comment, but Jennings saw a glint of concerned surprise in his eyes. It was his first look at the new prospective asset.

"I'm not saying the captain's worries are illegitimate," Jennings said. "But everything else about Bigelow is a dream."

She related Steeden's opinion from the defense department. Bigelow's engineering history was rock-solid. He did difficult projects with speed and, despite his age, was still a "do-it-yourselfer," even doing his own drawings and material specifications down to the minutest details. The NSA chief thought his unusual work habits were a significant advantage because it reduced the risks necessarily incurred when staff and assistants were used. And she reported that her technical czar, Wilson Bryce, adjudged the Pittsburgher amply tech-savvy to work with new encryption devices and software despite his age.

"But can he climb into a moving extraction vehicle?" pondered Hastings. "Or run to a pickup point?"

The door opened and the president entered with Defense Secretary Lazar. Everyone rose. She and Williamson exchanged salutes.

"How late are we?" she asked. She didn't wear a watch. Funny how few people did anymore. If anyone would, you would think it would be the president. A typical president's daily diary scheduled appointments every twenty-two minutes.

"Just ten minutes?" She'd answered her own question, glancing at her secure cell phone. "Hardly worth an apology, but you have it anyway."

She poured her own coffee and took the seat always reserved for her, in the middle of one side of the conference table. She motioned Lazar to sit next to her. The NSA and CIA leaders took the chairs at the head and foot of the table. The SOCOM commander Williamson sat directly across from Lazar.

"I wanted to wait until Admiral Jennings could be with us to discuss security implications, so we didn't go there when we met last week," said the president. "But now we have a quorum." She nodded to Jennings, her signal to begin.

Jennings talked without interruption for over ten minutes. She had made her way to the top of the navy as an intelligence and technology officer before being tapped to head the NSA. She was a brilliant communicator. Del thought it an irony that her career roles had all been in the secret shadowy world of security and intelligence, when her natural gifts, as the president's own, befitted political life. Six years ago, Del herself could walk into the Starbucks next to the White House and be unrecognized. Jennings still could.

The admiral detailed the measures that had already been implemented to make Eaglets' Nest as secure as possible. The work was formidable. A secure "intra-intranetwork" had been constructed to house all email communications between anyone working on any aspect of the program. If Mr. X, a nuclear engineer in the Talon warhead group, sent a message to Ms. Y, overseeing logistical movement of components for the new missiles between air force bases, that communication stayed rigidly within the confines of a cyberarena that could not be penetrated from the outside unless, first, the existence of the outer ring arena was known and, second, herculean hacking skills were applied in a constant barrage that would take days, if not weeks, to accomplish penetration. Even then, it would have access only to the outer area, and not the inner ring in which the communications occurred and were held—all while attempts to hack the special arena's walls were monitored every second of every day. In the eight months since its completion, not a single "insult," or attempted breach of the outer ring, had occurred. This meant that, for now at least, its existence was unknown.

In the two parts of the program that were essentially finished—the downsized Eaglet drones and their Talon nuclear missiles—a total of 286 individuals were working. This was a substantial number of people, and it presented inherent risk. They had been selected with great care, however. Nearly all were career military or long-term civilian specialists working for the air force or the Department of Defense. The rest were trusted technicians within Grumman, Lockheed, and Raytheon who had passed repeated clearances on earlier projects. Further, the knowledge of each person was isolated as strictly as possible to the specific part of the project on which he or she worked. An air force engineer designing rivets for the small drone wings saw only the drawings for the specific wing assemblies to which he or she was assigned. This meant that in the unlikely event someone was solicited for information by a foreign intelligence asset, no single individual had a volume of knowledge that could bring much value. No participant knew who was designing any other assembly, or their specifications, even generally. Jennings described the protocol as "need-to-know on steroids."

But the security challenges implicated by the remaining leg of the stool—the Eaglets' Nest deployment base—were far more demanding. The Army Corps of Engineers and their air force counterparts could build an airport faster than anyone in the world. But the Nest was nothing like an airport. It was to be a subterranean—perhaps deeply subterranean—containment facility that had to be designed and then constructed in complete secrecy. Not only must it not be detected during its construction, but also it had to be designed in such a way as to be undetectable by satellite, airborne intelligence aircraft, and hopefully even x-rays *after* its construction.

And then, of course, there was the separate set of security issues that arose out of the purpose of the facility and what it would hold. There was nothing in the US nuclear arsenal remotely like it: short-range mini nuclear weapons that could produce physical destruction that was total and uncompromising but predictable and containable in reach. You surely could not call them surgical. One of President Winters's predecessors, secretly discussing his phase of the program's development, called that "an inhuman understatement." And no president had harbored the notion that even the smallest nuclear weapon could be deployed without the probable large loss of innocent life. It was reported that Kissinger had studied, and revisited, the idea that nuclear weapons might be used "tactically"—in other words, on a limited basis. Be he ultimately concluded, insofar as anyone knew, that there was no practical way of stopping a chain reaction of use once the initial deployment occurred, leading almost certainly to unacceptable global consequences. Pentagon planners,

however, had never given up on the idea, and there was good reason
to believe that other world powers had not either. Russian leader
Putin, for one, had uttered publicly, at least since 2015, that tactical
nuclear weapons should be on the table in dealing with regional
crises—unsettling words, to say the least, to NATO leaders and
many others. And, as everyone in the room knew, but few others
knew, each US president since George W. Bush had continued his
initial covert development of the Eaglets' Nest program.

American nuclear capability, it was ultimately concluded, could
not be frozen as threats grew. The so-called "triad" of the United
States nuclear arsenal—land-based intercontinental missiles resting
in silos in Wyoming and North Dakota, submarine- launched
medium-range missiles cruising the world's oceans, and large nuclear
bombs delivered by airborne bombers—remained essential to the
defense of the country against major power threats such as Iran,
North Korea, and the old nemesis, Russia. But it was essentially still
rooted in the unthinkable—but necessary—strategy that nuclear
force of devastating measure could be deployed only to avert or
counter massive destruction of the homeland. There was no one who
believed that the triad was suited to deal with regional threats or even
the ugliest nation-state dictators or regimes. As to those, diplomacy,
coalition building, and, where finally necessary, conventional military
forces must continue to be the options. But the terrorist clusters, as
they grew to become occupying forces and as they demonstrated
inhuman violence not seen since Hitler's extermination of the Jews in
Europe and Russia, presented the most ominous of questions. Where
reason is absent—and therefore diplomacy futile and unavailable—is
the use of circumscribed nuclear ordnance possible and justified? The
answer to that question had not been decided. But the need to be
able to ask it had been. When it came to major world powers and the
largest questions of world order, options were everything. A nation
could measure its strength by the depth of its toolbox, whether it used
the contents or not.

Hence, Eaglets' Nest.

Jennings turned to the third program component: the deployment facility. She reviewed the work that had been done to narrow down candidate locations. There were many factors. The Nest needed to be in a place where essential construction steps, especially excavation and earth blasting, would not seem unusual or, alternatively, could be effectively hidden from observation. It also needed to be a place that could be defended on extremely short notice by a small protection force. This meant that strategic natural barriers were both an advantage and a problem. Positioning the base in a mountain range would make it easier to defend physically but could hinder the sending of emergency defense forces. It was important too that it not be sited close to population centers. It was foreseeable—frightening as it was—that at some time the base might be infiltrated and nuclear warheads stolen. In such a case, it was vital that infiltrators be required to transport their stolen cargo over a reasonably long distance of terrain flat enough to facilitate rapid observation, interception, and destruction by pursuing forces on land and in the air. This was a critical concern of Israel, the only country yet consulted by the Pentagon planners. As the Israeli intelligence chief had said to Jennings, "Saddam's Scuds were a nuisance. Your little nukes could be annihilation."

Three options had been settled on for presentation to the president, Jennings told the group. One was in northern Afghanistan, two hundred miles from the Russian border. It had the advantage of intimate terrain knowledge by US Special Forces derived from hundreds of prior deployments. Its natural barriers were the best of any option. But it was terrain that also was well-known to Russian operatives and under their microscopic surveillance. It was inconceivable that it could be selected unless the president were willing to bring Russia into the circle of knowledge.

"That's out," President Winters declared flatly.

A second option was Syrian territory near Turkey where United

Nations Peacekeeping Forces had been situated for several years. It was not mountainous, but there was one elevated area planners deemed suitable. Construction activity would not seem out of the ordinary, and the project could be described as a storage facility for humanitarian supplies. There were two downsides. First, nongovernmental agencies, so-called NGOs, were prevalent in the region, and the CIA and Defense Intelligence Agency both believed many were the targets of intelligence infiltration by foreign operatives. Second, the United Nations obviously could not be advised.

"How could we build it there without their knowledge?" asked the president.

"We couldn't," said Jennings. "They would know it was there. But they would not have to know what it really was. We could do it under the cover of a new NGO that would look like any other international NGO but that would actually be staffed exclusively by our own operatives."

The third option was an area in Kuwait adjoining a large oil-production field. The construction could be described as a storage facility for production equipment and supplies, designed to protect them from assault. Kuwaiti leadership was trustworthy, and military cooperation with the Pentagon had been deep since the First Gulf War directed by the first President Bush in 1990. Knowledge of the project could be confined to a very few individuals, and its true nature could be hidden from all. And the facility could in truth also store some of the equipment and supplies it would be explained as holding.

"But would it be defendable?" asked the president. She knew that the small country of Kuwait was remarkably flat without any mountainous areas at all.

"That is its weakness. It would be vulnerable to attack on all sides in a flat zone. It would require a substantial intervention force at the ready at all times."

"But that is something we can do with planning and budget?" the president said.

"Yes, we can," said Lazar, speaking for the first time. "It does not have to be another Benghazi," he said. "We could have a large enough defense force in the area at all times. It could be there in an hour."

Jennings concluded with cost estimates and required force levels for each of the options. She passed ground and satellite maps of each to everyone.

The president looked at the CIA chief. "You've been quiet, Jack," she said. There was always something a little different about spymasters in a room of policymakers. Accustomed to the shadows, they tended to dislike attention. They did not jockey for agenda time and were not prone to self-assertion. Maybe for that reason, they were listened to when they did speak. It was no exception this day. Hastings spoke unemotionally, in terms so direct and concise that one might conclude he was allergic to adjectives. He said the United Nations site was impractical; it housed NGO staffers you could not trust. They had "eyes and ears for others," he said. Afghanistan was all right from the intelligence perspective because it was sparsely populated and movement in and out could be monitored. But he agreed it would be necessary to clue in the Russians on account of their own intelligence prowess there. He personally could live with them knowing, but he was not the president of the United States, and she had ruled it out. Kuwait was doable. They were good people who would cooperate without asking to know everything. But, he concluded, no matter where the deployment base was built, the concept was, in the end, an enormous risk.

"No one can tell you honestly that the base will be kept a secret for years and years," Hastings said.

The president then turned to Lazar and his general. "Are you two of one mind or not?" she asked.

They said they were. General Williamson recalled that he fought in Afghanistan, having led men there as a young officer. He hoped the country would never send a large force there again. "Except for small teams of Special Forces, it's just a hell of a place to operate," he said. He and the defense secretary favored Kuwait.

There was a long pause. The president looked from face to face, her expression inviting further comment. None came. She made her decision. The civilian presence in the UN zone was disqualifying, she said, even if the problem of intelligence infiltration of the NGOs were set aside. The day could come when a terrible firefight would be needed to protect the base or to retrieve its contents. A location exposing civilians in numbers could not be justified on moral grounds. Despite its vulnerability in flat terrain, Kuwait was the best option. "There will never be a perfect choice," she said to the group. "Kuwait it is."

Admiral Jennings raised the matter of the engineering resource. Actually, she said, it was more than a matter of only engineering. It was design, materials procurement, construction training, everything. It was best to consolidate all those functions in the same asset. Lazar challenged that view, asking why. The CIA's Hastings answered that the old expression "security in numbers" was anathema to covert activities. The smaller the circle, the better it could be protected. It was preferable—he allowed himself one adverb, "highly"—that a single resource perform all acts necessary to develop the base, save for its actual assembly on-site by soldiers.

"Which is why finding the right contractor for this has been difficult," Hastings said. He explained that a search had been made of information from every governmental organization with experience in land-based construction and engineering. The Army Corps of Engineers had been most helpful. It had a database on thousands of contractors and professionals evaluated over the years, as far back as Vietnam. "We worked it down to two hundred and looked at each of those closely," the CIA chief said.

"Who did the winnowing down?" asked the president.

"A joint team from the CIA, the DIA, and the FBI. When we reached the finalists, NSA came in to vet their communications—to see if there were red flags on the personal side."

"I'm not sure I want to hear how they did that," the president mused.

President Winters, and for that matter all of them, knew that the decades-long tension in the country between privacy rights and the problem of finding terrorist activity had evolved to a place of grudging acceptance that the latter must hold sway over the former. Safeguards against wholesale eavesdropping had been arranged, principally a requirement that each invasion into a citizen's phone or internet communications had to be logged and submitted to scrutiny, albeit after the fact, by judicial review courts established in every metropolitan area of the country. The privacy invasions needed to pass muster as prompted by a genuine concern directly related to suspected terrorist activity or US government action to prevent it, and not for any other reason, not even strong suspicion of other criminal behavior. The meetings of the regional privacy courts were all held in secrecy, but each court produced a semiannual public report detailing the numbers of "monitoring or intervention instances" occurring in its region, the initiating governmental agencies, and the number of such instances deemed by the court to have been "improvidently conducted." No remedy was provided to a person improperly monitored, and no such person's identity was even made public. But the reasoning was that the public and Congress would ultimately be the judge as to whether the number of privacy intrusions was growing too large, or conversely could continue to be tolerated in the interest of stanching terrorism.

"And after all that, it comes down to this gentleman from Pittsburgh?" surmised the president.

"At first it did not, Madam President," said Hastings, the CIA chief.

"Explain," the president said.

"Our initial choice was an engineer from Chicago," Hastings said. "Ruth Morgenthal. Superb skills and a lot of work in underground construction. But maybe we should have been more careful. She had done several overseas projects for defense, including a couple in the Middle East. We brought her in for final vetting about seven weeks ago. It was just a formality. We knew we wanted her. Before we could even finish her security clearance and tell her details of the program, she was murdered in her Dupont Circle apartment. With her daughter. And a pizza delivery man."

"I saw that in the paper," the president said. "Terrible. But the story said she had come to work at the Library of Congress. A presumed robbery. Why wasn't I briefed?"

"I take responsibility for that," Hastings said.

"I do too," said Admiral Jennings. "We talked it over and thought nothing good could come from informing you. The Metro police were very cooperative. We knew you had scheduled a press conference for the next week. You could have been asked about it."

"I wasn't."

"But we couldn't know that. We thought you would want to be able to truthfully say you knew nothing about the incident," Jennings said. "If you knew, how could you answer questions about it?"

"I understand," the president said. "It was a good decision. It would have been awkward, to say the least. Do we know who killed them?"

"No. But it was professional," said Hastings. "We can't be sure, but my people think it was probably foreign intelligence operatives. Ruth Morgenthal's former husband works at Lockheed. He may have been tapped or hacked. We know the murdered daughter had told him her mother was starting a new job for the government. It would not take them long to learn she had done engineering for the military before."

"My God," the president said. She paused. All were silent, as if in an announced moment of silence for someone fallen, until she spoke again.

"So, I guess I go back to my original question. After all of this, it comes down to this gentleman from Pittsburgh?"

"Yes. C. Stanley Bigelow," said Hastings.

"What's the *C* stand for?" asked Jennings.

"Cyril. He goes by Stanley."

"Vern tells me there are some concerns about him," said the president. "Physically."

"Brew has heartburn," said Hastings.

The president knew Navy SEAL captain Tyler Brew well. In private ceremonies when she was vice president, she had observed him awarded for valor on assignments that could not be made public, and even in her own young presidency she had singled him out for special achievement in covert service. In consultation with the SOCOM chief, she had personally recruited him to quarterback the real-time activities for the completion of Project Eaglets' Nest, convincing him that his many years and hundreds of missions involving covert intelligence and execution made him more qualified than even more senior military men or CIA operatives. It was not easy for Brew to accept her request. It was a little like asking a good ball player to leave the field and take a business job in the front office. But, of course, he would not refuse the president of the United States.

"What doesn't Brew like?" the president asked.

"He'd prefer a younger man," said Jennings.

"Who wouldn't?" replied the president. There was laughter. From Ben Williamson, a little too much. But the president smiled warmly at him.

"And one who is more fit."

"How bad can it be?" asked the president.

"If he's not clinically obese, he' awfully close to it," said the NSA chief. "He's uncoordinated. He's big and he's seventy. Sedentary."

"How is his attitude about this?"

"Well, it all came completely out of left field for him. We brought him in under less than open premises."

"You mean under false pretenses," said the president.

"Not false, exactly. But not very informative either. He certainly had no idea he would be solicited for a global security mission presenting personal risk. And we didn't tell him about Ruth Morgenthal."

"And?"

"Well, there were a few stiff hours at the Pentagon," said Defense Secretary Lazar. He said the screeners had not held back on the security issues, the privacy inconveniences, or the potential danger. He told how measures had been taken to be sure Bigelow wasn't seen going to the Pentagon or leaving it. He described them as "'now you see him, now you don't' maneuvers" that must have struck the old civilian as strange, probably a little upsetting. But Lazar said the man from Pittsburgh had handled them well.

"We changed out his phone while he was at the Pentagon so we could tap his calls after his visit," said Jennings. "Of course we didn't tell him that. But after Ruth, we thought we needed to, for his benefit as much as ours. It's been seven days. He hasn't mentioned a word to anyone about his trip, about us, anything. We've watched his email too. Same thing. Nobody has asked him about his trip, which means he likely has not told anyone. As we asked."

"All good signs," said the president. She said she had read the binder and seen the photos. She felt he was a rare person and, despite appearances, right for the role. He had the brain and temperament needed. She said she shared, however, Brew's concerns about his physical condition. "But I can tell you, my father would be just as overweight if he didn't walk that dog of his," she said.

"What are you telling us?" asked Lazar.

"Sign him up. And get him a dog."

"Are you serious? I mean about the dog?"

"Yes, I am. Let's get this lonely overweight man a dog and see to it that he walks him. Or her. And I'm sure Jack and Brew can put the dog to other good use too. To help protect the man. I wish the Morgenthal woman had had a dog."

Lazar had a further suggestion. He felt the president should call the civilian from Pittsburgh herself to request his service. They were asking a great deal of him, and it might be that he was feeling somewhat manipulated, what with the phone tapping and the way he had been induced to come to Washington for the vetting. Surely a call from her would send a powerful message of the importance and confidentiality of the project.

"And he has not yet really said yes or no," added Jennings. "Because we haven't made the formal ask. But the truth is that we have no alternative candidate nearly as suitable on the technical side. It would be back to the drawing board to find another if he said no. And it is awfully hard to say no to the president."

"I assume we've encrypted his cell phone?" asked the president.

"Yes."

"Get me the number. I'll call him tonight."

She rose from the conference table. At the doorway, she motioned General Williamson toward her.

"Ben," she said to him alone. "What I said about my father? You didn't hear it, did you?"

"Hear what?" he answered.

18

A CALL AT DINNERTIME

★ ★ ★ In his eighth-floor luxury residence at RiverBridge Place on Fort Duquesne Boulevard in downtown Pittsburgh, Stanley cleared the clutter from the coffee table and arranged a plate and silverware for the dinner that was expected to arrive at the door momentarily. He adjusted the angle of the television. Its position, suitable for his own the evening before as he lay across the leather sofa watching the late-night replay of the public television news, needed correction for the serious viewing to begin in half an hour, the Pirates game against the Reds.

His apartment overlooked the Allegheny River, between the Roberto Clemente and Andy Warhol Bridges, iron weavings that immortalized two of the city's cultural luminaries. Stanley always felt that the expansive steel bridges and their surprisingly juxtaposed namesakes gave good witness to the city's character. Strong. Basic. Complex in its own way. Diverse. He had a splendid view of both bridges and, beyond the Clemente Bridge to the west, of PNC Park, home to the Pirates.

It was early days in the new season to be sure. But Stanley knew the importance of a reasonably good start, and the role even the first games played in year-end standings. Even for more casual observers, opening day was always of great interest, commanding a brimming stadium and pregame anticipation. Then interest and attendance typically fell like a marble from a table's edge, at least until school was out. But for the deep lover of the game named Stanley Bigelow, *every* game held high significance. He was like an orchestra conductor to whom every measure of a long score was important unto itself and to the whole.

And not only every game, but every inning of every game, and every pitch of every inning. He found a software program that allowed him to keep score on his laptop. Its off-the-shelf capacity accommodated the simplistic essentials well enough, but he'd adjudged it lacking in its ability to document the true details needed for deep analysis. A table of icons on either side of a graphic playing field displayed the obvious selections. The left side for batting and base running listed single, double, triple, home run, walk, run batted in, and so on. The right side displayed basic selections for pitching and defense: ball, strike, ground out, pop-up, strikeout, etc. But what of check swings, pickoff throws to the bases, defensive infield shifts, and that underrated bugaboo, the foul ball? Stanley tormented the software company's help desk for weeks, modifying the program repeatedly, "tweaking it to death" as an exasperated Javi Patel on the other end of the help line finally declared. But at last, acceptable utility was reached, and just in time for opening day two weeks earlier. Stanley took the day off and watched the game from his couch, wielding his laptop cursor like a conductor's baton.

When his cell phone buzzed, he reflexively checked the time. Still plenty of time before the opening pitch. No reason to be irritated by an interrupting call.

"Hello," he answered.

"This is the White House switchboard," came the male voice. "Could you please hold for the president?" *My God,* he thought. *They* really *have a switchboard?* And in fact they did, but an ordinary observer could not likely guess its function. It was not actually in the White House at all, and instead was a wall of monitors blocks away in a nondescript building, tracking and logging every communication in and out of every line and cell phone in the hub of the executive branch. Neither incoming nor outgoing calls were routinely recorded, but a select number of senior officials could, with a simple digital command, instantly order an encrypted recording, as the president had just done.

"Mr. Bigelow, this is President Winters."

His first thought was how casual and matter-of-fact she sounded. It was as if nothing was out of the ordinary and there was no reason in the world for either of them to think there was.

"Thank you for coming to Washington last week. I realize the trip was surprising to you. Sometimes we are just not able to be as upfront as we wish we could be."

"It wasn't as surprising as getting this phone call," Stanley said. "Is this safe?" He instantly regretted his question. Here he was questioning the attention paid by the president of the United States to communications security.

"Actually, it is entirely safe. Before Captain Brew returned your phone to you, it was equipped with encryption technology. And some other things."

"Really? What kind of other things?" Stanley asked. His tone was more wonderment than resentment.

"I hope you will understand that this matter is beyond any notion of confidentiality. The slightest crack in the secrecy of it could have enormous implications."

"I don't even know what the project is," he said.

"You will soon, very soon. That is, if you are willing to undertake this for us, for your country. That is why I called." Stanley thought her expression calm, oddly calm in comparison to his racing heart. "I can tell you now that if you do this, it will require all of your attention for months," she continued. "It will require you to put up with much inconvenience and intrusion into your personal life."

"I do have employees to pay."

"Of course. You will be compensated. The way funds are provided to you—the channels used—will be unusual for you, but you will receive them. And without questions. If we did not trust you, we would not be having this conversation. You will be forgoing other business revenue. You tell us what the number is and you will receive it from us. And maybe then some."

"I would not want anything more than I would have earned. That would not be right."

"Your fairness is noted and appreciated. But you need to understand that there is more to consider. This could not be further from business as usual. I am told that you were advised at the Pentagon that your personal safety could be at risk. Is that true?"

"Oh, yes."

"And even knowing that, you are willing you do this?"

"I am willing to do it if I am qualified to do it. I am a particular kind of civil engineer. I cannot tell you that I am really competent to do something that hasn't been described to me."

"Again, if we believed there was any possible question about your professional suitability, we would not be having this conversation." She still spoke with the same level tone. No single word seemed to be emphasized more or less than any other. "But I cannot describe it for you unless I know that I have your firm commitment to do it, even with knowledge of the time involved, the bother to your life, and the personal risk involved."

There was the first meaningful pause in the conversation. Stanley hoped that she might say something more, but he realized that her last words amounted to the central question. He looked down at his dinner plate and remembered that the delivery person could be at the door any moment. Here he was, about to embark on a frightening journey, talking to the president of the United States, and concerned that the Dinner-for-U delivery person might interrupt. Perhaps fifteen seconds elapsed.

"I give you that commitment," he told her.

"I am very grateful to you, Mr. Bigelow," she responded immediately. For the first time Stanley detected an uplifted expression in her voice. "Your country is very grateful to you. Would you like me to give you a description of the project now? I could call back if you prefer."

"No, please tell me something. But I am expecting my dinner to be delivered any minute."

"And the Pirates game begins in fifteen minutes too," said the president.

These people are unreal, thought Stanley. *Even my baseball habits.*

"Are you a fan too?" he asked.

"Not like my father is. I hope you meet him someday. He thinks he's a master of baseball statistics. He was talking *Moneyball* language before the movie. Before the book, for that matter. You really should meet him. You might be good for his modesty."

"That would be a great honor."

"If someone does come to your door, just hang up. And please don't refer to me when you do. I'll call back—after the game. But here is the Cliff Notes version of the project."

He listened as she explained the development of the new drones with the miniaturized nuclear missiles. She described their ability to hover, ascend, and descend. She explained that they would be deployed from an underground containment facility to be located in Kuwait. The design, and then the construction, of this facility had to be conducted in secrecy. It was not desirable to involve many contractors or other engineering professionals. A small circle of knowledge was vital. He would have to create the design and train the installers. It needed to be designed with simplicity so that military personnel, rather than skilled laborers, could install it with limited training, to be provided by him. Further, once completed, the base needed to be as invisible as possible to surveillance or detection technologies. She explained that the secret program had been under development for two and a half decades and that the unmanned aircraft and the new warheads were ready for deployment.

"But you have not even started the design of the containment base? Why not?" he asked.

"Because you were a hard man to find, Stanley," she replied. For some reason, he believed her.

"I can't be the perfect candidate," he said.

"All things considered, you are near perfect," she said. "There are a few concerns, though."

"With what?"

"Frankly, with your physical condition. You are not a fit forty-year-old."

"I am not a fit seventy-year-old."

She did not laugh. After a pause, she replied, "I am actually happy you said that. No one is kidding anyone. We are going to need you to work with us to improve your physical condition. Not only to keep you in good health so that you can complete the project, but also to reduce your personal risk in the event we need to get you out of danger in an emergency. You may have to run a distance to find waiting help; you may have to get into a vehicle very rapidly. That sort of thing." She was back to an expressionless tone. But his heart raced even more.

The lobby buzzer sounded.

"Dinner has arrived," he said.

"Thank you again, Stanley. You will be contacted by one of the agencies soon. Just hang up." He did. It was not lost on him that she'd called him by name.

It was one of the regular delivery people from Dinner-for-U. Stanley was suddenly energized and voraciously hungry.

"Here's your order, Mr. Bigelow," the deliveryman said, reaching into a thick paper bag with rigid cord handles. "Short ribs, mashed potatoes, and cheesecake." Then he looked down into the bag, puzzled. "Oh. They put an extra side of mashed potatoes in here. You didn't order that, did you?"

"No, but they will come in handy. Gravy for them too?"

"Yes, sir!"

He tipped the deliveryman lavishly, and gave him five extra dollars for the unordered side. He enjoyed his meal through the third inning, taking some pleasure in the fact that despite the excitement running through his veins, he continued to record his usual minutiae. He even made a note that he ought to be documenting whether the third baseman was playing even with the base, playing deeper toward the outfield grass, or hugging the line. He already recorded such data for the first baseman. *Have to call Javi Patel about that tomorrow, as there must be a way,* he thought. Between innings he cleared the coffee table. He poured his first bourbon in the top of the fifth. A second, more generous in volume, followed in the eighth inning. As the game wound down, he sensed his emotions calming and fatigue coming on. When the game was finished, he entered his customary summary notes for future reference. The Reds' starting pitcher had been very effective, throwing only seventy-two pitches over six innings, but had nonetheless been removed. There was no indication of injury. Stanley could have looked right then to see what his average pitch count had been in his first two starts and his final ten starts of last season. Perhaps a managerial trend under way? But he was tired and that could wait till tomorrow. He showered, as he always did, pulled on a loose-fitting long-sleeved T-shirt, and climbed in his big bed. He reached across his large abdomen to turn off the bedside lamp, its switch irritatingly high and hard to locate, as they always seem to be. But on this night, Stanley was not irritated, even though the Pirates had lost the game four to one. Suddenly, without appreciating it, and surely without seeking it, Stanley's life seemed to be taking on new meaning. For heaven's sake, the president had called. He had made a commitment.

Thinking back the next morning, he was surprised to recall that he'd drifted off within minutes to a deep sleep.

PART II

PART II

19

WATCHING STANLEY

★ ★ ★ Tyler Brew and the NSA technician stood outside RiverBridge Place. Brew wore a blue blazer over an open-collared pinstriped shirt; the NSA technician, a Schindler Elevator Company uniform. They spoke briefly under the entrance awning, black with yellow accents, reminiscent of the Steelers' colors. Then the technician entered the lobby, carrying a small work duffel. Brew stepped back out onto the sidewalk and walked casually around the building. His left arm hung still at his side. A microsized video camera with a wide-angle lens, secured between his left thumb and ring finger, filmed the building and its details as he walked. In the rear of the building Brew made two passes, one from the rear perimeter line, another close in to the building so that he could film the areas partially blocked by vehicles and refuse dumpsters. After circling the entire building, he crossed the wide boulevard at the front entrance. He took long looks in each direction as the digital recording rolled.

As he had assumed, there were multiple points of road access to the building—an oversized hived-out valet area at the front entrance on Fort Duquesne Boulevard and two winding driveways at either side. The driveways passed through small parking lots before descending to underground parking garage entrances on each flank. He did not like it that there were double garage entrances, but he was pleased that there was no road access from the rear. The rear property line backed up to a decorative brick fence he calculated to be about eight feet high, behind it only the wide river.

He checked the quality of his video recording and was satisfied. He scrolled to the frames showing the garage entrances and zoomed to the doorjambs. There were identical logos on each: Three Rivers Door Company. Another uniform was needed for the NSA technician.

He crossed back to the main entrance, walked in, and rang unit 820. Stanley promptly buzzed him into the first-floor elevator lobby without answering through the intercom. Just forty seconds later, when Brew emerged directly across from his front door, Stanley was standing in his doorway.

"Hello, Captain," he said.

"Why didn't you use the intercom to identify me?" Brew asked, a bit sternly it seemed to Stanley.

"I knew you were coming."

"No. You always use the intercom. Please, Stanley, remember that." *At least we are getting to be on a first-name basis,* thought Stanley.

"I'm sorry. I will be more careful."

Brew followed Stanley into his residence and closed the door.

"It locks automatically," Stanley said, nearly with a note of pride. Brew nodded. "Would you like coffee?" Stanley asked.

"That would be good. Just black."

"May I call you Tyler?"

"Sure."

Stanley moved to his kitchen to fetch two cups of coffee. Brew stayed behind in the foyer and asked if he could walk around the residence. Stanley said that of course he could. The residence was certainly not small, nearly twenty-four hundred square feet, but he was still surprised at how long Brew took for his inspection. When Brew was finished, Stanley was sitting on his main room sofa, nearly finished with his own coffee. Brew moved to the comfortable leather wingback chair, in reaching distance from the coffee table.

"Nice digs," Brew said as he sat down.

"I like it. I've been here since shortly after my wife died. She helped pick it out. We always lived out to the north. She was a gardener. Avid, avid gardener. But she knew I would want to be somewhere else after she was gone. Said I would get fat and sad if I stayed alone out there." Stanley paused for his coffee. "At least here I am not too sad."

For the first time in their admittedly brief relationship, Brew smiled.

"And I hear *you're* worried about my weight too," Stanley said.

"You could lose a few and everyone would be better off," Brew answered.

"I told the president she could count on me."

"Don't take anything the wrong way." Brew paused as he sipped his coffee. "She is grateful for your service. We all are. And we all need to get used to how unusual this situation is. Maybe me most of all."

Brew explained his background as a Special Forces operative; that as a soldier so much depended on physical skills and precision. He told Stanley how the SEALs and Rangers had conducted many hundreds of missions and how hardly any of them ever came to the public's attention because the secrecy of each—with precious few exceptions—was vital to the success of future ones. The disclosure of a mission could be authorized only by the president, and rarely was this done. Exceptions had been the mission for bin Laden, and for the infrequent Medal of Honor recipient, such as the one President Obama had singled out in 2016 for the rescue of the US aid doctor Dilip Joseph from Taliban captors in Afghanistan. Brew said he was used to either picking his own team or knowing for dead certain that every member was unquestionably qualified—and not only qualified, but also skilled and practiced in their specialty to an almost incomprehensible degree.

"Well, I am a little surprised that I wouldn't make your starting lineup," Stanley said. "But I am not in the slightest offended, Tyler." Stanley sat up straighter on the couch. "I am wondering, though. What do you think the chances really are that something will go haywire making my fitness an issue anyway?"

"The odds are time-driven. If your involvement lasted a brief time, say a month or two, unlikely. But every month beyond that increases the risk. Our military programs are the target of nonstop intelligence assault from a raft of other countries, friends and foes alike. And the attacks of even the friends, especially cyberspying, is a big problem, because they learn it and then *they* are hacked."

"Well, I am only beginning the design, but I can tell you we are talking at least five months, maybe as many as seven, before the facility is complete," Stanley said. "If it takes that long, what are the odds?"

"At five months, one in five. Seven months, one in three."

"One in five what? One in three what?"

"That you will be identified by a hostile and an attempt will be made to abduct you."

"To learn from me what this is all about?"

"Yes. And if they get you, they will." It was a sobering comment, delivered unvarnished, elaboration unnecessary.

Brew's cell phone vibrated in his pocket. It was a text message from the NSA technician. Stanley knew nothing about his involvement.

"I need you to check the rear service elevator in the hallway outside your kitchen," Brew instructed him. "Try to open it as if you were going down with your trash. It shouldn't work. We think it's been disabled by our agent, but we need to be sure. I'm going to do the same for the two in the main entrance hall."

"You'll turn them back on, won't you?"

"Of course. But we need the ability to disable them remotely in an emergency."

"Did you get permission for this?"

"Yes, but not from the building. Please, just go check the rear elevator."

Stanley walked briskly through the kitchen and into the service hall. He jabbed the elevator button repeatedly. It illuminated, but the door did not open. He returned to the living room as Brew reentered too.

"Are we cool?" Brew asked.

"If that's what you call it," said Stanley. "The light came on, but the door wouldn't open."

"That's cool, then. Same out front."

Brew texted a very short message, Stanley thought only two characters, three at most. "Now, try it again."

This time the elevator door opened as usual, following its usual mild binging chime. *These people are amazing,* Stanley thought.

"Part of your security plan, I guess?" he asked Brew.

"Yes. Your residence will always be under watch whenever you are here. Often when you are not here. If we believe you are at risk by someone who enters the building, we want to be able to stop them in an elevator if they use one."

"My."

The doorbell rang. Stanley was startled because no one had buzzed up from the lobby. He rose from the couch and took a step away from the door.

"You can relax," said Brew. "It should be the agent I brought for the elevator work. And some other things. But that's good thinking. I'll make sure it is him." He moved to the wall next to the door and sent another two or three-character text. Instantly his phone hummed, and he opened the door. The man in the Schindler Elevator Company uniform came in.

"Mr. Captain Brew," he greeted Brew.

"It's just 'Captain' to you," Brew replied.

"Well, you're almost a civilian now, so I'm covering all the bases."

Stanley could see that they knew each other well. Then Brew explained that his agent would be installing monitoring devices in the residence.

"Cameras?" asked Stanley.

"Yes, and audio and motion sensors too."

"Not everywhere, I hope."

"In the bathrooms we will have audio only."

"Kind of you."

"It's all miniaturized. If you didn't know it was there, you probably couldn't even find it. You'll get used to it quickly—won't even think about it."

The man in the Schindler Elevator Company uniform moved from room to room and made notes into an iPhone. It took him less time to inspect the place than Brew had spent. In only a few minutes he rejoined Stanley and Brew in the living room.

"I have what I need. I can do it right now."

"Go ahead," said Brew, looking toward Stanley with raised brows, seeking approval. Stanley nodded.

"But for the neighbor, I'll need more. It's larger than I expected."

"Fine," said Brew. "Come back for that one. You have to anyway for the garage doors."

Brew and Stanley sat down again. Almost immediately there were sounds of a thin drill, more like a dental instrument than a power tool, coming from the next rooms.

"What neighbor are you talking about?" asked Stanley. "The apartment next door is vacant. Harry moved to assisted living three months ago."

"We've rented it," said Brew. "Don't want you to be alone here. We need as much physical presence as we can have. It's better for everybody."

"When will I meet this new neighbor?"

"Very soon."

20

THE NEW NEIGHBORS

★ ★ ★ Captain Brew was a man of his word. At eight forty-five the next morning, as Stanley reviewed his scorekeeping from the Pirates game the night before, a buzz came over the intercom from the residence lobby.

"Yes?" Stanley answered.

"Captain Brew sent me. I'm your new neighbor. Can I come up?" It was a female voice. Fairly young, Stanley thought.

"What is your name?"

"L.T. Kitt."

"Just a moment." Stanley was not suspicious, but he deemed this an opportunity to show his diligence to the cautious Navy SEAL. He texted Brew. "Woman has buzzed. Says she is L.T. Kitt."

Instantly, Brew replied: "Legit. Let her up."

"Okay, come up," Stanley spoke over the intercom, as he buzzed her in.

He bent over his laptop and finished the note he had started before the buzzer had rung, namely that the three relief pitchers used last night had thrown forty-two pitches in all, thirty-three for strikes. But how many were first-pitch strikes to a batter? He checked quickly and approvingly noted that nine of eleven were strikes. Good data for a new theory he was probing, that first-pitch strikes were more predictive of success for a reliever than strikeouts per appearance.

A minute later, the doorbell rang. "Who is it?" he called as he approached the door.

"L.T. Kitt. And Augie."

"Augie?" he asked, peering through the eye viewer.

"Our dog."

Stanley opened the door gingerly, about a foot or so, and leaned out. L.T. Kitt stood in the center of the hallway. She was medium height, sturdy but not heavy. She wore black jeans, black ankle-high boots, and a thick bluish sweater. Her complexion was fair, her hair auburn and cropped stylishly above the collar. Her face was pretty, carrying little or no makeup, Stanley judged, and just the slightest weathered, like a person of the outdoors. Her head seemed a little small above the fulsome cowl of her sweater. He thought her not yet forty years old but close to it. Beside her sat what seemed, at that moment to Stanley, an enormous German shepherd, looking up straight into his eyes.

"Brew didn't mention a dog."

"Well, let me introduce you. This is Augie. He also answers to August." She bent, just slightly, toward the dog. Stanley saw that while the dog's paws moved not at all, his head pivoted to look her in the eye. "Augie, this is Stanley. You may also hear him called Bigelow. You're going to be friends." She stood straight again and the dog returned his gaze to Stanley's eyes, as if in acknowledgement. Augie's mouth was open, a long red tongue extending over and between white teeth. His feet did not budge, but Stanley thought his long tail moved a little behind him, scraping the hallway carpeting.

"Brew didn't mention a dog," Stanley said again.

"I gather."

"Whose idea was this, anyway?"

"From what I understand, the president of the United States."

"You're kidding."

"I'm not. But I suppose you could tell her you disagree."

"I'm not really a 'dog person.'"

And as soon as he said it, feelings rushed into him—regret, even a measure of guilt, shame. His wife, his dear wife who'd asked for so little, so little over all those years, *she* was the dog person. Without fail on the street she would stop and talk to every dog that would have her, and nearly all did. "Isn't she a beautiful creature, Stanley?" she would say. "Isn't he well-behaved, Stanley?" she would say. And when the owner praised and petted the beast, she would invariably say, "Now there's a lucky dog. Lovely thing." And all the while Stanley would stand safely away, not following her lead and rarely, oh so rarely, bending to touch the dogs himself.

The new neighbor lady looked at Stanley and paused until he returned her eye contact. "Well, Stanley," she said, "maybe you'll learn something new. Augie here, maybe he wasn't always a 'people person' either. I don't know, maybe when he was a puppy. But he is now. He is *really* a people person now. So long as it's the right person. And we need you to be that right person."

"What are you getting at?"

"I should have introduced myself as *Agent* L.T. Kitt," she said. She explained she was an FBI agent and dog handler assigned for years to its witness protection service. She told Stanley she had done her work in dozens of settings, from cities to farms to safe houses. The dog helped her keep people safe. He was highly trained in specialized personal protection. At six years, he was in his prime; she had been his handler for four. She looked at the dog fondly as she spoke, still standing in the hall. "Did I tell you he answers to August too?"

"Yes, you did."

"You should use both names. It builds trust."

"That seems odd," he said. "I thought dogs usually had one name."

"Not if you think about it. To him, August is a term of

endearment. When you care about someone, you never call them the same thing *all* of the time."

"I never thought of it that way," said Stanley. "But I guess I see what you mean."

"May we come in now?"

"Yes, Agent Kitt. Come in." He looked down at the dog, skeptically. But he said, "Come in, August."

21

SO FAR AND YET SO CLOSE

★ ★ ★ The night before, Sven Hemelstaan hunched over a wide curved monitor in a plain concrete building in Kista, a northwestern suburb of the municipality of Stockholm, intently watching the multicolored lines that moved irregularly across the screen. It was late evening in Sweden, but the spring sunsets were coming later every day; it had been dark only an hour. In the American Midwest, it was late afternoon, another business day winding down.

He knew that outgoing internet communications from manufacturing companies spiked between four and five o'clock in the afternoon, user time. The morning hours brought more incoming internet traffic—customer inquiries, purchase orders, and the like—and volume slowed in the middle of the business day when most internal meetings occurred. As regular as rain, the traffic, especially outgoing, picked up at about four o'clock when companies responded to order inquiries, confirmed shipments, and sent price quotations. So, Hemelstaan made certain that he was always ready at that hour for his midwestern targets. He followed his usual routine this night, taking a short walk in the brisk evening air, then preparing a strong double espresso to bring to his monitor.

He had no idea why these particular companies were of interest, and he truly did not care. He did not know what they produced or how their products were used. And he didn't know to what purpose his own reports were put. He knew only that his handler in the Russian Embassy in Berlin paid him handsomely to infiltrate their IT systems and then to monitor and report on traffic in and out. He was supplied the names of the companies he was to infiltrate and the ISP identifiers of persons and companies of interest in the event of communications to or from them. Trend identification was especially important, as were anomalies too, such as communications of unusual length, a sudden discontinuation of traffic in a period of otherwise highly predictable exchange, and new relationships. He was to report expansively and to err on the side of overinclusion. "Don't decide that something is unimportant" was the way it had been expressed to him. "Consider anything important."

The companies targeted for infiltration were not well-known, and some of them were quite small and specialized. Hemelstaan did not recognize the name of a single target when the list arrived from Berlin. TriConic Equipment Films in Saint Louis, Missouri. Spellinger Flange in Hammond, Indiana. Precision Beryllium Company in Milwaukee. But when he researched the ISP identifiers of the "correspondents," as Berlin called them—the entities whose communications to and from the targets he was to chart—the names were instantly recognizable: Boeing, General Dynamics, Lockheed Martin, Northrup Grumman, and others. And—Hemelstaan could not say he was surprised—he was ordered also to look for any communication that included a "us.mil" domain in its email address, signifying a US military affiliation. It didn't take a sophisticated hacker to surmise that the Russian Embassy in Berlin was trying to monitor communications between major American defense contractors and their specialty suppliers.

Sven Hemelstaan *was* a sophisticated hacker, however, and he knew that he was. He was neither overly proud of his work nor ashamed of it. He avoided self-judgment. It was just his work, what he did, what he could do well. In his mind, surveillance was a profession and a business. Computer surveillance was just one specialty within it that happened to pay well because there were not many people who were proficient at it and also willing do it. He was apolitical and made no value judgments. Anyway, as he told himself, he was not a thief. He stole nothing. He harmed no one. All he did was glimpse into commercial computer networks in ways that targets did not observe or detect—not when he intruded, and often never at all. Their systems were not even physically damaged. Why should he feel remorse? Besides, he followed the rules of his handler that forbade taking advantage of his access for any other purpose, such as taking batches of personal identification numbers and selling them on the "dark markets," which he easily could have done. These were the qualities that made him valuable to Berlin and trusted by them.

A special keyboard allowed him, with only a few strokes, to flag and log any email communication he selected from the streams moving across his monitor. Every message was encrypted on creation with sophisticated host site technology, so he could not see the content of any transmission, only its baseline data: the ISP address of any message, whether incoming or outgoing; time of transmission; size of the message and anything attached in kilobytes or megabytes; and the document format of those attachments, such as photo, PDF file, or spreadsheet. Why this data, without the text of the messages, was even useful, he didn't know, and he was smart enough not to ask. But he assumed his Berlin handler furnished it, or some of it, to other specialists for further analysis or cyphering. Perhaps other hackers, he knew not where, were infiltrating the Lockheeds of the world and using his reports as access indicators. Who knew?

This April night seemed pretty much like most nights, the Swedish hacker concluded. He continued his monitoring, marking messages every few seconds, until one in the morning, Kista time. By then, the traffic at the three targets had slowed to a drip. He used his report software to summarize the night's data. A quiet evening, he considered. Only one item of note, which he described in his encrypted end-of-session report to Berlin.

Precision Beryllium Company of Milwaukee had exchanged three messages between four fifteen and five thirty Central Standard Time with a correspondent with whom it had not had any other communications in the year and a half of his monitoring. He closed his report by noting that the ISP address of the correspondent indicated, according to his coding directory, that the transmissions came from and were returned to "somewhere called Pennsylvania."

22
THE START OF SOMETHING

★ ★ ★ As soon as Agent Kitt was inside the foyer, she released the dog's leash. The agent, Stanley guessed, was about five foot six, neither thin nor heavy; strong looking but feminine; attractive; fair-skinned. Her light brown hair was thick and cropped above the neckline. Unsnapping the leash was almost effortless for her, as she barely needed to bend to reach the large animal's collar. Stanley noticed that the same hand that released the leash swept gently and naturally over the dog's head and ears as the action was completed and that the dog's eyes darted up briefly, as if in appreciation. He stood next to her, contented. A well-practiced routine, Stanley thought.

"Is that a good idea? Unhooking him?" Stanley asked. His tone was unsettled. "I mean, shouldn't you show him around first? Will he get into anything?"

L.T. smiled at Stanley, as if showing gentle patience.

"Yes, he needs to be shown around," she said. "But not by me. Better that you do it, so that he understands this is your space and that you are in charge here." She looked down at the dog. He seemed to be paying attention, looking from one to the other of them. "But no leash in here. The leash is only for outdoors."

"Why?"

"You and Augie don't communicate through that leash."

"Well, I wouldn't expect him to say much to me with or without a leash."

"Oh, he'll talk to you, Stanley. You'll see. You'll talk to him too. Your words will be important, but not as much as your tone and body language."

"But why does he have to run free around here right away?"

"So that he knows you trust him."

"I don't trust him."

"Watch your tone." She was no longer smiling.

Augie sat directly next to L.T. He looked straight ahead, making eye contact with neither of them, as if now ignoring the conversation.

"And he doesn't trust *you* either, yet," she said. "He is relaxed right now because I am here and he trusts me. Believe me, if I *weren't* here, he'd be in a different posture."

Stanley's expression grew slightly grave. "Well, I certainly want him to be relaxed."

"Good."

"So how do I do that?"

"Give him a tour. Keep your hands down. Just let them hang at your side. Look him in the eye and tell him to come with you. Just a conversational tone. Kind. Like you were calling a grandchild to follow you around the house."

Stanley may have revealed a wince in his eye, reacting to her comment. He thought he might as well clear the air. "I don't have any grandchildren, Ms. Kitt. I don't have any children."

"Oh," said L.T. She shifted her weight, a little nervously. "Then, you will *really* appreciate Augie." She wasn't sure if that was a good thing to say to this seemingly nice older man whom she had just met minutes earlier, this man who was willing to turn his life upside down for some clandestine project she knew only the slightest about. Who was she to suggest that this canine could meet any of his needs? She wished she had not said it.

Stanley did not take it harshly. He didn't see how this dog could make a difference to anything, but what was the point of taking it any further? Besides, he liked Agent Kitt already, her positive air, her sincerity. Surely, she had not meant to sadden him by speaking of grandchildren.

"Well, let's see how this goes. Come, August," he said, calmly he considered, given the circumstances. "Let's have a look around."

He started walking through the main room at his usual gait. Immediately he heard the dog's steps following him. He moved on to the kitchen, after stopping briefly at the coffee table. There was a salad plate on the coffee table and, on it, half a slice of toast with jam. The dog peered at the food, showed no interest, and continued on pace directly behind Stanley. He moved with the dog from room to room. At the small bathroom off the study, Stanley opened the door and said, "It's okay, Augie. Go in." The dog went in immediately, turned his large body around in the small space, and sat down. He stayed there even as Stanley moved away.

"He's sitting in the bathroom," Stanley called out to L.T., who'd remained behind in the main room. "He's just sitting there looking out at me."

"You told him to go in, but you didn't tell him he could come out," the FBI agent called back. "He's very literal."

Really, thought Stanley. "Okay, Augie, come out," he said. At once the dog stood, stepped out of the bathroom, and followed him through the other rooms. In the master bedroom, as an experiment, Stanley opened the closet door and pushed aside the clothing to form a small opening. "In, August." The dog stepped in, turned around in the cramped area, and sat facing Stanley, who was looking down at him from outside the closet. Stanley glanced at his watch to measure fifteen seconds. Then he moved away from the closet door toward the bathroom. Another fifteen seconds passed before he returned to the front of the closet. The dog remained sitting, his tall ears erect but otherwise appearing relaxed.

Stanley looked in his eyes. The dog might have seen the slightest hint of a smile on Stanley's large face. "Out now, Augie."

The dog stepped out quickly and stood by his side, his upturned head well above Stanley's pants pocket. And it was then that he received his first touch from the engineer from Pittsburgh. It was only a quick, light pat on the head at the base of his high dark ears. But it was a start.

23

STANLEY'S FIRST DRAWINGS

★ ★ ★ Captain Brew was to return to Pittsburgh in a few days to provide Stanley with more information, needed to begin his design work in earnest. He knew Brew was a soldier, not an engineer, so he asked the Navy SEAL if he would bring with him a technical person. True to secretive form, Brew would not say. And he did not expound much on what the president had told Stanley in her call to him: the facility would base small aircraft below ground in Kuwait and needed to be designed so as to be capable of very rapid installation by soldiers instead of tradesmen. It needed to be virtually undetectable once constructed, even by the latest and emerging surveillance technologies.

It was not a lot to go on. Still, Stanley had some immediate thoughts.

He did some research on the Kuwaiti climate and was surprised to learn that average temperatures were not as astronomically high as he'd expected. Ambient surface temperatures rarely exceeded ninety-five degrees Fahrenheit. Subsurface temperatures would be materially lower. Ventilation would be required, but not as much of it as he had feared. This was important because ventilation added to space requirements and, more troublesome, detection challenges arising out of the noise and vibration that conventional systems produced, especially large ones. He was pleased that he could use less space and a smaller system for temperature and humidity control.

Stanley was traditional enough to reserve to himself, as the firm's founder, by far the largest and best-appointed accommodations at CSB Engineering's downtown Pittsburgh office on Oliver Street, an easy walk from his high-rise home. Arranged to satisfy his own preferences, his office featured a set of twin stand-up drawing desks connected by a rack of circular holding tubes made of antiqued brass that looked to uninitiated visitors like a broad wine rack. Actually, the tubes were meant to hold rolled blueprints and drawing sheets, and nearly every tube was typically occupied by his current projects. But just to keep things interesting, he always kept three or four bottles of quality cabernet or chardonnay on hand in the rack. It was an office tradition having to do with reward. When an engineer's meeting produced a piece of work that Stanley thought particularly inspired, he would spring from his favored wingback office chair and, without comment other than "well done," withdraw a bottle of the good stuff and present it to the awarded. Younger engineers, anxious to discern his reaction to drawings submitted the day before, learned to watch for his arrival in the morning to see if he was lugging in wine bottles. A believer in encouragement and praise, he often was.

Before her illness, his wife had been a frequent visitor to the office. She liked to walk the halls and duck into the offices of the engineers and the staff members. She was well-liked and talkative with everyone. She knew the names of everyone's children and always asked about them, delighting in the latest reports from the parents. An advocate of sorts for the staff, she thought their workspaces too spartan and was critical of Stanley's attitude toward the subject.

"Those offices are cramped and the furniture looks cheap," she told him. "Yours is as big as a basketball court and everything is top drawer. It's not becoming, Stanley."

"I don't deny them anything," he replied. "But I need to set an example of thrift. Remember Ben Franklin's code! Industry and thrift!"

"But *you* don't set that example," she said, standing in his office. "Look at these things. They must have cost a fortune. And why *two* televisions?"

"If I had only one, how could I watch the game when I'm standing at the board?" Knowing his sincere preoccupation with baseball, it did seem, even to her, a reasonable excuse. "And besides, there is no better example of the benefit of thrift than a fat paycheck. These engineers are the best paid in Pittsburgh. Ask them."

She knew better than to take it any further, and she did know that his last contention was true. Despite their lack of apparent creature comforts at the office, they were well paid. She knew the employees enjoyed Stanley's attentions and were deeply committed to him. It moved her that so many came to her during company functions to say—sincerely, she judged—that working for Stanley was wonderful. He was kind, they said. Fair. Such a teacher. And generous, too. "My husband said that the wine he gave me was *stupid* expensive!" one told her.

And for his part, Stanley experienced their affection in a painful way when she had died nearly a decade ago. They didn't just seem to grieve *with* him; they seemed also to grieve *for* him, their concern for him so deep and apparent. He could not bring himself to use her name when recalling her, they'd noticed. It was just too sensitive to him. And even as the years passed, it stayed that way. He never used her name aloud, so they didn't either. One of the older engineers patronized Stanley's barber and poker group friend, and asked him if Stanley talked of his wife and called her by name.

"Oh, all the time. But only to himself," he said. "He has that in a private place inside just for him. He keeps her name in there. It's like if he keeps her there, he still has her with him. That's what we figure, anyway. We all respect it."

A week earlier, Stanley had emailed Precision Beryllium

Corporation in Milwaukee for some preliminary information on its capacities. Could it process pure beryllium into the form of large sheets, say, for example, a surface dimension of twenty-four inches by ten feet? And, if it could, how thick could those sheets be? His previous uses of the unusual metal had all been for thin films, but could these large sheets be far thicker, say, three-eighths of an inch, or even a full half inch? He received answers later that same day. Yes, but the cost would be very high. He acknowledged the response, saying he likely would be in further contact in coming weeks. He made, of course, no reference to the end use of the products or the nature of his project.

His first impulse was to use beryllium because of its highly unusual properties, and because those properties seemed to align with the peculiar requirements of the project, insofar as he understood them. Beryllium was an odd substance. You could say it was used in almost nothing and used in almost everything. Most people, other than chemists and metallurgists, had never heard of it. But it was a basic element, the fourth element on the periodic table, signified as "Be." It was by far the lightest of the metals. Aluminum was also a very light metal, but beryllium was just one-third its weight per equal mass or, to the layperson, three times lighter than aluminum. Like aluminum and copper, it was nonmagnetic. But very unlike those metals, beryllium was not flexible. In fact, it was stiffer and more rigid than even steel—stiffer than any metal or metal alloy. And on top of those characteristics, it possessed another property that occurred to Stanley immediately: it did not vibrate. You could tap a hollow tube of it with a ball peen hammer and hear no ring or chime at all. It had stealth potential. And Brew liked stealth, Stanley knew.

Stanley knew that beryllium was almost always used in very small physical applications, such as in high-end electronics and cell phones, as razor-thin film to protect resistors and chips from— among other things—magnetic contamination or physical wear caused by vibration. Medical devices, and especially medical imaging equipment, incorporated it because of its transparency to x-rays. Its unique properties, including its ultralight weight, made it ideal, notwithstanding its high cost compared to other possible, but underperforming, substitutes. But he was unsure whether it realistically could be processed into what amounted, in his mind's eye, to interlocking building panels, each one of substantial size.

Unlike basic steel or even widely produced metal alloys, beryllium was almost the definitional opposite of a commodity. For one thing, while it was common in the earth, commercial availability of the element in usable form was extremely limited. It was found in minor concentrations as veins in rock. But there was only one place in North America, a mine in Utah, where such rock was brought up in any significant volume. And even when that rock was mined, extracting the pure beryllium out of it was a severe challenge of chemical and physical processing. The rock had to be crushed and filtered, and then subjected to extreme temperatures and pressures in the presence of sulfuric acid, an unfriendly substance to say the least. At the end of this difficult, multiday process, the pure beryllium output was in the form of tiny whitish pellets, hardly larger than kosher sea salt. A large amount of starting rock produced a small amount of pure beryllium pellets. Production was not measured in metric tons but in simple pounds, and not many of those. Any given twenty-four hours of production might produce a few drums of material, and only that. But its extreme lightness meant that a little could go a long way and sell for a very high price. A pound of pellets could be melted and then fabricated into tiny parts for a hundred thousand cell phones or laptop computers. And so the little pellets were processed, nearly as quickly as they could be produced, into finished pieces of beryllium of every shape and configuration imaginable, each a special design intended for a particular industrial or product application.

Precision Beryllium Company was the only US company with

the know-how, and some said the courage, to do it. It was a mainstay of the Milwaukee industrial community, but it kept a low profile. Its activities and products were essentially unobserved, even in its own backyard, because it made and sold nothing for direct consumer purchase. All its work—in seemingly limitless shapes and forms—went into the components of finished devices sold by others.

As Stanley would come to learn, the Wisconsin company was much better known to the United States military than it was to the general public, because one of the first industrial uses ever put to this odd fourth element of the periodic table was in the making of the initial atomic bombs—and virtually every nuclear warhead since. Its extreme hardness, extreme stiffness, and wildly high melting point of 2,745 degrees Fahrenheit made it uniquely suitable to harness fissile material before and during detonation—to contain the building force within the warhead until the time of desired release and to maximize it when it did occur.

Stanley stood at the left side of the double drawing desk. He moved his instruments with ease and sketched a three-dimensional side elevation of a long panel that he scaled, for the moment, at three-eighths of an inch in thickness with a surface dimension, outside edge to outside edge, of twenty-seven inches wide by one hundred twenty inches long. He stood over his simple drawing for a few minutes. He remembered the instruction that unskilled workers—soldiers, really—would have to install his design. He adjusted the position of the drawing paper on the slanted board and clamped it. He penciled in a three-dimensional raised edge on one side of the long edge of the panel. He carefully scaled it so that it would form a three-inch overlap over an abutting panel placed in a reversed position. It was a wider overlap than he would have usually prescribed, but it would be forgiving for the soldiers, who would be prepared with only marginal training and would be working under pressure to install the underground walls quickly, often without aid of good lighting.

Stanley knew that he could be working directly from a keyboard making digital entries into a large monitor, as was the norm nowadays. He had such devices stationed at the companion stand-up desk five feet to his right. Nearly all his engineers, even most of the seasoned ones, would do it that way. Stanley, though, still preferred his protractors, slide rules, and hand liners, and a lighted magnifier to see his etchings. For heaven's sake, erasers! He understood they were all old-school. Call them obsolete; he wouldn't argue. But still, this was his way and he felt no compunction to defend it. The lead tip of his drawing pencil meeting paper was, for Stanley, a moment of conception. Its movement down the edge of his just so calibrated straight edge was his statement on the matter, his decision, if only for that moment. He did not want to surrender his own first judgment—Stanley Bigelow's first impression—to some cyberspace purgatory inside a computer without a stop first on paper that he could feel and smooth his fingers over and adjudge for himself and only himself, without aid of machine, to be satisfactory.

He would take it to the computer at the right time for the finished copy, to be sure. Usually it was not long after. He found then that his manual draft expedited the keyboard inputting and facilitated a digital drawing in short order. He knew this might be something of a justification on his part against the observation that he was, in reality, doing every drawing twice. But no one made that observation, though it was known by all at the firm that Stanley still did every drawing by hand and *then* produced a digital version.

In truth, the other engineers fell into two camps: the more senior ones who admired Stanley's discipline and regretted, however slightly, that they lacked the will to still do it as he did, and the younger ones who marveled at the old man's manual skills and regretted that they would never have them.

Stanley pondered his drawing of the overlapping flange. To help the soldiers align the sheets accurately, he added a slim vertical protrusion running from top to bottom in the center of the back side of the flange, and a corresponding slot in the female side of the flange of its reversed mate. When the panels "slotted in," the soldiers would be assured that alignment was proper and could move to the next panel. Now satisfied with it as a preliminary drawing, he moved to the other desk and made the digital entries needed to produce the electronic version. He had to remind himself to use the special software he had received from the NSA specialist Bryce Wilson, automatically encrypting the illustrations and the dimensional data, then sending it securely to Brew's data archive, accessible only to Brew and to him. Per his agreement with Wilson and Brew, once his drawings were sent via Wilson's software, his original paper drawings went straight to the shredder beside his desk.

The Pirates were off that evening. Stanley's wall clock showed seven fifteen. He was the last one in the office. He left his briefcase on the office sofa and walked out the dimly lit entrance past the reception desk. His key card produced the usual heavy metallic clunk, ensuring the locks, top and bottom, had engaged. He rode the elevator down the twenty-six floors alone. Agent L.T. Kitt and Augie awaited him on the sidewalk on Oliver Street.

"There's no game tonight," said Kitt, handing him the leash immediately. It was crisp but pleasant outside, with little wind.

"Regrettably," he answered. He took the leash and reached to pet the sitting dog that followed their words with his eyes.

"So we have time for a longer walk tonight," she said in a tone that anticipated, incorrectly, shared enthusiasm.

"I suppose," Stanley said.

They crossed the river and walked most of the North Shore neighborhood around the ballpark and Heinz Field, the football stadium. A large loop took the distance to three miles. Augie walked with Stanley the entire route. The dog strode confidently and, initially, a little too quickly for Stanley. But the big engineer soon adjusted and kept up in reasonable comfort, the dog at his side, head high and tail up. Approaching home, they stopped at a deli that Stanley liked. Stanley went in and brought out sandwiches for Kitt and himself.

"You know, I have to ask, Stanley," she said when he came out with the sack of food.

"I didn't get the grilled Reuben again, if that's what you're asking. Lean corned beef on rye, a little low-fat mayo. Put that in your report to Brew."

"How many orders of potato salad?"

"Oh, please, L.T."

"How many, Stanley?"

He didn't answer. She let it go.

24

TERRORISTS WITHOUT BORDERS

★ ★ ★ President Winters was in the White House residence when the evening call came from her secretary of defense and General Williamson, the SOCOM chief. She was reading a draft speech in the study, to be delivered in a few days to the Detroit Economic Club. Her father sat near her with a book and his usual bourbon. When the switchboard operator said over the speaker that it was Mr. Lazar and the general calling from separate locations, her father looked at her with questioning eyes, his way of offering to step out. She shook her head and motioned that he should stay. She rose to close the door to the study and then punched the phone.

Lazar's tone was that of a person doing his best to appear calm. He told the president that a British physician on the staff of Doctors without Borders in Afghanistan had, at great risk to himself, slipped out of a hospital in Turj, a small city not far from Kabul. He had contacted friendly Afghan forces that in turn informed Special Forces in the area. A large unit of Hasikan Jahideen terrorists had entered the hospital under cover of darkness, he reported. A small force of Afghan security guards had resisted them, but all were quickly slaughtered, even before they could contact reinforcements. The terrorists were occupying the hospital basement and freely moving in armaments and explosives. All the hospital staff had been herded onto the second floor. Their phones were collected and they were told all would be killed if there were attempts to leave or even call out to the street. The patients from the first floor, many of them children and elderly, were brought to the second floor with the others, where they remained in cramped quarters. In a brutal and seemingly gratuitous act, a volunteer doctor from Finland, showing no apparent resistance, was executed in front of them. And then a patient too. The British doctor witnessed the scene through the window in a door as he returned to the hospital from the rear. He had left the building to fetch medicines stored in a warehouse a few blocks away. He had been away just twenty minutes, he estimated, and the takeover of the hospital had occurred in that interim. When he saw the events inside, he escaped down a stairwell unnoticed and ran for his life.

"How many hostiles? How many civilians?" These were the president's first questions.

"The doctor estimates twenty terrorists," replied the general. "First estimates are usually understatements, so we assume up to forty. The civilian count he is sure of. Staff numbers eighteen. Then there are sixty patients, a third of them not ambulatory."

"Americans?" the president asked.

"One," the general said. "Interesting, she is a patient in the hospital, working for an NGO that purifies drinking water in the city. Admitted to the hospital three days ago with a blood infection."

Lazar described the military resources available. Joint Base Bagram was not far away, which was fortunate. Evacuation equipment, both overground and aerial, was available there, as were air force fighter jets and armed helicopters to provide support. There were two outposts in the general region where Special Forces were presently stationed. One housed several platoons of Army Rangers, the other four Navy SEAL teams of twelve warriors each. And from the Bagram base, a large force of ground troops could be mobilized to hold and defend the hospital, if the terrorists could be first removed.

Williamson outlined the tactical response options. In any scenario, it would be necessary to get special operations forces in on the ground to take the building with speed and, hopefully, stealth. It was not practical to use ground troops in large numbers to take control of the hospital through a frontal assault. That would be a bloodbath for the hostages. But special ops might be able to get inside and take control of the building; ground forces could then immediately be parachuted in to hold the facility until reinforcements and evacuation vehicles arrived over land.

The special operations teams could be dropped from helicopters at a landing area a sufficient distance from the hospital to avoid immediate detection. The regional commander was already doing aerial surveillance sweeps of the region, ruling out drop zones where hostile presence was suspected. He should have at least two good options within hours.

The real question was how to prioritize the mission's objectives. Should the priority be to destroy the terrorists while also trying to save as many of the hostages as possible? Or should the priority be the protection and extraction of the hostages, and the killing of the terrorists a secondary objective? There was no question that an attack led by skilled Special Forces—thirty would probably be sufficient— could root out and kill all of the terrorists, if that was the principal objective. But there surely would be casualties, and the hostiles could be expected to kill some, many, or even all of the innocents inside the building before they could be eliminated. On the other hand, if saving the hospital staff and patients, and the facility itself, was more important than destroying the terrorists on-site, a more complex tactical plan was needed, and far more additional resources.

The decision was not difficult for President Winters. She said the location of the terrorist band was known and would remain known no matter what ensued in the assault to take back the hospital.

Even if some eluded the Special Forces on account of attention to the protection of the civilians, they would not be at large for long. Surveillance drones could track their movement. Other forces could be dispatched to deal with them. She authorized Lazar and Williamson to use any and all resources to move on the hospital as soon as possible, with mission priority given to rescuing the hostages and preserving the hospital.

Her father listened but said nothing during the call. But when it was ending, he gestured to his daughter that he wanted to speak to her. He put a finger to his lips to show that he meant it for her ears only. She pressed the mute button.

"You told them to move as soon as possible," he said.

"Of course."

"Make it clear they should move when they believe all of the resources are truly ready, all the tactical information confirmed. Remember Kunduz."

Kunduz. The tragedy at Kunduz. The mistakes at Kunduz. She did remember it, as if it were yesterday. In November 2015, another Doctors without Borders hospital in Afghanistan, also not far from Kabul, had been accidentally—but many said negligently—obliterated by American airpower called in by Special Forces on the ground. Forty-two were killed, including many hospital staff members. The humanitarian organization in Kunduz had registered its GPS coordinates exactly as it was supposed to do, and in that case, the organization had not reported the presence of terrorists in the facility—and there were none. But Special Forces found themselves engaged with Taliban fighters in an adjoining neighborhood. The ground forces called for bombing support. The logistical instructions to the fighter and drone pilots were, at best, ambiguous. Del Winters, then the lawyer in the Special Forces command, was deeply involved in the review that followed the heart-sickening assault. There were many causative factors, errors both human and mechanical. But senior command knew that the overarching cause was simply too much hurry and too little certainty.

She released the mute button.

"I want to be clear," she said to them. "I told you to act as soon as possible. Don't read that as an order to execute under suboptimal conditions. The situation is urgent, but you should send your people only when your tactical plan is in place—with confirmed intel—not before. I understand this could result in something horrible happening in there before your teams arrive. I take that responsibility."

"I am glad you said that, Madam President," said the general. "We understand."

"Godspeed," she said, and hung up.

25

NAVY COOKING

★ ★ ★ The text from Captain Brew buzzed on Stanley's cell phone at three in the afternoon. It was, as usual, terse. "Get your walk early. Be home by six. Don't eat." Stanley saw that Agent Kitt was copied on the message.

Stanley thought it fortunate that there was much to admire about Brew—mainly, his record of brave service to his country—because he was so often irritating. Nothing ever seemed to be asked. Everything was ordered. There seemed never to be room for discussion. The president of the United States spoke to Stanley more warmly than Brew did. But when Stanley brought it up on one of their long nightly walks with Augie, Kitt urged patience. She reminded him that Brew was purely military in his orientation. He was a warrior and probably not keen to have been pulled from field missions.

"In the FBI, they send us to charm school during training. From what I hear, these special ops guys are taught to kill first and be charming after," she told Stanley. "I can't imagine what they see out there, much less what they have to do."

Augie, leashed now, as always, by Stanley, seemed to look up in agreement. "He treats me well enough," Kitt added. "There is a person in there somewhere. Give him a chance."

Stanley noticed that Kitt never asked him anything about the work he was doing with Brew. On a few occasions, he forgot Brew's admonition to share nothing about the project with anyone, including Kitt, and began to say something about the kind of material he was working with or a drawing he had done that day. She instantly interrupted and stopped him from going on. "I'm not in the circle," she reminded him. But she could tell Stanley about her own work, and he welcomed her stories of past assignments and how she came to be placed in witness and protective services.

She told him how after 9/11, the ranks of the FBI were broadened, with a new emphasis on counterterrorism. Some in law enforcement thought that once bin Laden was finally eliminated, the threats would die down. But it didn't turn out that way. Plots and plans continued to spread, often insipiently. Agent recruiting was boosted even further, and women were aggressively sought, with the hope that they would be effective in penetrating domestic terror cells. Perhaps female agents could induce male hostiles to let down their guard, or at least relate to their women.

"I said, that's me," said Kitt. "Terrorist slayer. One tough girl. Bring 'em on."

"So, that's what you went in for?" asked Stanley on one long walk.

"Yeah. But it turned out I didn't test well."

"On what? You seem very athletic."

"Oh, I am plenty athletic. And was then. Just a lousy shot."

"You're kidding."

"Well, I wasn't *that* bad," she said. "I mean, I qualified at Quantico and everything. But you had to be a lot better for the terror work. Basically, sniper quality. They made a big deal of it. I wasn't even close to good enough. It was hard when they told me. I understood, but it was hard. I thought about leaving. I didn't want to do desk work for a career."

"So you went to the dogs, so to speak?" Stanley said. It did make her laugh.

"To canines and protection pretty much at the same time. I loved the canine training at Quantico. There's a lot of it there. I was training dogs full time for a couple of years."

"For this kind of work?"

"No, mainly detection. Substances, explosives, cadavers. Protection work was most always done by human field personnel, usually two-agent teams, at least. And somewhere the light bulb went on and somebody realized an agent with a dog might be as good as and cheaper than two agents for protection duty. They sent me to Tucson with a shepherd—not Augie, before him—to stay with a woman who was going to testify against a drug gang. And it never stopped from there."

He asked her if she had ever worked with Brew before. No, she said. Assignments involving military personnel used to be unheard of in the bureau. She knew that some units within the FBI began to be sent overseas after 9/11 to assist in investigative work, mainly forensic, and that those agents often worked in contact with special operations forces. But she herself had always worked in canine training and personal protection, and always domestically. As to what soldiers like Brew did, she only knew what she'd heard. And what she'd heard was that it was usually pretty brutal.

Stanley texted Kitt at four o'clock to say he would be on the street in fifteen minutes. She replied that she and the dog were already on the way. Before leaving his office, he checked his email to see if there was anything from Precision Beryllium Company. He had sent an inquiry in the morning asking whether the large sheets of beryllium he had previously written about could be alloyed with eight-tenths of 1 percent copper. He wanted to soften the material ever so slightly so that its edges and grooving might be easier to manipulate during assembly on-site, without sacrificing the extreme tensile rigidity of the panels, though he did not disclose that as the reason for his question.

There was indeed a reply. Yes, copper could be alloyed in his specified concentration and machined into such thick panels. Nickel could also be alloyed as an alternative, the reply stated. He was tempted to respond by asking for specific data on how the rigidity and melting point of the panels would be altered if the material were alloyed with such a minor amount of copper, and not pure beryllium, but he refrained. It might trigger curiosity. He could do the computations himself, and preferred to anyway. And he knew nickel was out of the question, as it was magnetic and easily detected by x-rays and magnetometers.

The daily walks with Kitt and Augie were now stretching to ninety minutes. Kitt selected routes that avoided frequent corner stops and provided long uninterrupted stretches. A bike path along the Allegheny River was becoming a favorite. Augie quickened his pace, and therefore Stanley's, along that route. By the time they made the turn off the path and back toward RiverBridge Place, the old engineer was usually in a modest sweat. But Kitt noticed, and he did too, that his breathing was materially less labored than it had been at less distance and lighter pace just weeks earlier.

"I kind of like being a personal trainer," she said as they neared the apartment residences. "Usually, my job is just to keep the person alive. I don't have to get them in shape too."

"Don't forget about the first part," Stanley answered.

She wasn't forgetting. Before entering the building, she checked her phone app to see if any motion had been detected inside of Stanley's apartment in the time since her departure from her own to meet him for the walk. None had been.

They took the elevator to the eighth floor. As always, Kitt led the way into his apartment, while Augie stayed back, on all fours, attentive, in front of Stanley. She went in alone, to see that it was clear.

"Come on in," she called after a few moments, Augie's signal that he should lead Stanley in. It was ten minutes before six.

"Care for a drink?" Stanley asked her.

"If I can take it to go," she answered.

"Suit yourself," he said. "I was hoping you would wait until Brew gets here. You could tell him how fit I am becoming."

"I've already told him you're taking it all very seriously, that you're being a real sport about it, and that you like Augie."

Stanley moved to the butler's pantry off the kitchen where he housed his liquor and wine. Augie followed, keeping a convenient distance, then lay down on the cool kitchen tiles.

"Well, the last part is true," he said. "He is a beautiful creature and, I must say, good company."

"For someone who is not a dog person," Kitt said. She had stayed near the foyer until Stanley returned with her drink. He hadn't bothered to ask what she wanted. She had asked for the same thing every other time: Grey Goose on the rocks with an olive. She nodded as she took the glass from Stanley's hand. Then she walked over to pet the dog and left.

Stanley remembered Brew's directive not to eat before his arrival. He wondered where they would be dining, and what say he would have in the matter, if any. But before becoming too negative, he remembered what Kitt had urged about giving Brew some allowances. And, happily to his credit, Brew had not said not to *drink* until he arrived. Stanley retreated to his bar and perused his stock of red wines. He spotted a favorite, a Cakebread Cellars cabernet, and deftly uncorked it with the speed of a veteran Manhattan waiter. He reached up to the cabinet above the bar top and fished out first one, then two suitable thin-rimmed red wine glasses. He poured just a swirl into one and slowly reviewed it with nose and tongue. More than satisfied, he poured more into the glass and took the bottle and the second glass to the kitchen counter.

There was a single perfunctory knock on the apartment door

before it instantly opened, revealing Brew, holding a large paper grocery bag. Augie launched to his feet and stood in a braced footing in front of Stanley. The dog recognized the captain and relaxed at once, returning to his position on the floor. Stanley looked startled and visibly displeased that the Navy SEAL had allowed himself in. He gave the sailor an unkind look from across the room.

"This is still my home, you know."

Brew was taken aback, then immediately appreciated that he should not be. "I am sorry, Stanley," he said.

Stanley sensed his sincerity, which was oddly surprising to him, since the rude entry seemed just another in the line of presumptuous behaviors by the brave Captain Brew toward the servant engineer. Why did he not resent Brew's self-entry more? Why was he, even as he stood glaring at the sailor, affording him the benefit of the doubt on the sincerity of his apology? It may have been the bag of groceries.

"What have you got there?" asked Stanley.

"Food for dinner."

"I don't cook."

"I know you don't. L.T. told me." He walked to the kitchen with the groceries. "I do. It's my hobby," he said.

"*Really?*" It seemed incongruous to Stanley that the tough warrior would have culinary interests.

"Been doing it for fifteen years," Brew said. "There aren't many golf courses or tennis courts where they send the SEALs. But there's always a camp stove."

He arrayed the groceries on the counter. There were four large beef tenderloin filets, a sack of small red-skinned potatoes, and an array of fresh vegetables, including collard greens.

"You don't mind if I cook for us, do you?" Brew asked. "Instead of going out."

"Why, no." Stanley moved over and inspected the items. "If you've gone to all this trouble."

"Kitt says you like beef."

"True, but normally I order a rib eye. Something … more marbled, I think they call it."

"Well, see what you think of my filet."

Brew went to the refrigerator and confirmed what Kitt had reported. Stanley did keep butter in there, and a lemon or two. Then he opened the upper cupboard left of the gas range top. Vinegar, salt, and pepper. It was all there, as she had said.

"I just opened a nice red," Stanley said.

"Perfect."

"Should I pour you a glass now?"

"Sure." He was arranging all of the items in some kind of sequence on the workspace near the range.

"You're not in a hurry, are you? I'd like to get the filets to room temp before I sear them."

"No, that's fine," said Stanley. "I usually don't eat anyway until the game is under way. The Pirates are playing in Philadelphia tonight. Seven-ten start."

Stanley had more or less assumed, when he'd received the afternoon text from Brew, that he would be pulled from his ball game. But Brew surprised him, pleasantly.

"Put it on anytime, Stanley," Brew said. "We can talk between innings. And after, if we need to."

Stanley brought over the bottle of the Cakebread Cellars and poured Brew's wine as the navy man put on a pot of water for the potatoes.

Brew quickly examined the bottle.

"Nice label," he said.

The evening was improving, Stanley considered. Lying comfortably, head on paws on the kitchen floor, halfway to the door, Augie seemed to agree.

26

NEW ORDERS IN STOCKHOLM

★ ★ ★ At his desk in the Stockholm suburb of Kista, Sven Hemelstaan opened his encrypted laptop to read the latest instructions from his Russian handler in Berlin. His report on the traffic between Precision Beryllium Company and its new correspondent from Pennsylvania was of interest. Another cyber contractor in Berlin had been trying to penetrate the content of the emails and determine the identity of the correspondent. So far he had been unsuccessful. The encryption embedded in the Pennsylvanian's text was too deep. It was not commercial grade. Perhaps military. Did Hemelstaan think he could penetrate the Precision Beryllium internal network in such a way as to see the content of individual transmissions, in addition to the digital traffic identifiers?

"Maybe, with some time," Hemelstaan wrote back.

The reply was immediate: "Proceed and report."

He began at once. Progress was slow. In the first few hours, all his attempts were futile. He tried the routes he had used in other infiltrations, but none of them took him to the pathway of the email server needed to see any information beyond the ISP address of the correspondent and the time and size of the transmission. No names, no content. But Hemelstaan was an experienced hacker and knew better, even at his young age, than to allow frustration to disarm him. He took a break. He left the building for a walk and a cigarette in the night air, turning possibilities in his mind. It came to him.

He had been trying to penetrate the server at Precision Beryllium that was directly receiving and replying to the messages from Pennsylvania. The firewalls and encryption measures protecting that server were too strong. Continued attempts to penetrate it would be detected before long, and the firewalls would probably grow even deeper. But he knew that large companies made backup copies, usually daily, of all email communications so that they would not be lost in the event of a serious malfunction or electrical outage. The Pennsylvania emails were stored, at least for some period of time, somewhere other than on the originating server. And those storage devices might not be as well protected. What he needed to do was stop his infiltration attempts on the well-guarded primary server. He needed to find a less secure server outside of the network but with access to it, and infiltrate *it*. Perhaps a smaller vendor that did business with Precision Beryllium. If he could get inside that vendor's system, he could use it to penetrate the defense contractor's network and navigate through it until he found a hallway to a server where the targeted emails might be exposed in a less secure environment, such as in the backup drives.

He cut his walk short and returned to his desk. Making educated guesses from the coding of the various messages he had already monitored, he inched his way into a vendor's portal on the Precision Beryllium Company's network. It was a portal set up to allow a landscaping contractor to use online scheduling for its visits to the headquarters building in Milwaukee. The Precision Beryllium facility superintendent enjoyed the ability to go online and see when the lawn crews were coming. And Sven Hemelstaan, the hacker in Kista, Sweden, enjoyed the ability to enter the flimsily firewalled portal and from there travel to the backup servers holding the company's recent emails. It turned out they were, as he hoped, just down the cyberspace hall in the basement IT center of the Milwaukee company.

The transmissions to and from Pennsylvania carried unique numerical identifiers that he had already recorded, so it did not take Hemelstaan long to execute search queries for them. Within minutes, the email threads appeared on his screen in Sweden. He made screen prints of each page, then used a hacker's malware application called ReturnMal to send the exposed emails back to their places in the backup drives in the Milwaukee basement. Hackers said it worked like a broom sweeping away rabbit tracks in the snow, or the way you used to patch a nail hole in a tire with rubber cement on a bristled probe. It was unlikely—highly unlikely—that Precision Beryllium Company would ever know of his unauthorized visit.

Hemelstaan read the emails. Then he read them again. The names meant nothing to him. And though his English was fair, the content read like Greek to him. That didn't matter. He had done his job in extracting the messages. Satisfied, he forwarded them immediately to Berlin.

What the Swedish hacker did not know was that thousands of miles away, in a gloomy industrial complex south of Pyongyang, a North Korean intelligence operative was also satisfied. In real time, he had just observed each of Hemelstaan's moves, as if he were physically present with the Swede, standing unseen at his shoulder. He had hacked not into the American company's network but into Hemelstaan's own computer. The Koreans had been monitoring the Swedish hacker for weeks. A girlfriend of the Swede's had told a coworker at the Stockholm Park Hyatt that she thought her boyfriend worked at night as a hacker for some foreign government. The coworker was a North Korean operative passing as a South Korean learning the hospitality industry.

It was a favored tactic of the Koreans. Land surreptitiously—and ever so gently—on the back of someone else's operative and use what they are learning for your own benefit. It was spy craft by piggyback—effective and inexpensive. Why go to the trouble of penetrating sophisticated corporate networks with their deep security devices when you could let someone else do it, and then break into their simpler machines? The Koreans had been making a meal of it for years.

The Korean agent took the information to his supervisor at once. The older career officer studied the transmissions intently.

"Stay with him," the supervisor instructed his hacker.

"How closely?"

"Like glue," he answered.

27

DINNER IS SERVED

★ ★ ★ Stanley had not watched anyone cook since his wife gave up the kitchen a few months before she died. It felt strange, but a little pleasurable too, to sit on a counter stool and observe the Navy SEAL doing his thing. Stanley and his wife used to talk about the day as she cooked in the kitchen of the old house outside of town. She was a light drinker, but normally sipped a glass of wine as she chopped and sautéed, listening to Stanley relate the day's events at CSB Engineering. She enjoyed his watching her in her element, and his genuine praise and gratitude for the aromas, tastes, and lovely presentations she routinely conceived. Oh, Stanley remembered, what an excellent cook she was. And how he missed her and their married life, the routine comforts, the ordinary moments.

Brew prepared the four large filets on an ample cutting board, seasoning each side, more generous with the salt than Stanley would have guessed. He gave the seasoning a few minutes to saturate as he retrieved a twelve-inch cast-iron skillet from the drawer beneath the gas cooktop. He examined it carefully, surprised to find no sign of rust. He rubbed its insides with a paper towel drizzled with canola oil and placed it over a suitable burner set to high heat.

"L.T. is joining us?" Stanley asked.

"No, hers is to go," Brew said.

151

"Seems a little unkind."

"She understands. She's not in the loop."

Stanley was puzzled. He motioned inexactly toward the ceiling. "She can hear us anyway," he said.

"Not tonight she can't," replied the sailor. He pointed to his cell phone on the counter. "She's shut down while I'm here. I'll reconnect her when I leave."

"I see," said Stanley. He eyed the fourth filet, hoping it might be divided between the two of them. An extra portion would be welcomed.

As he moved between the ingredients, Brew began asking about Stanley's thoughts for the design of the deployment base. He told Stanley that it would be best if the facility could house at least six of the drones, though it was likely that it would normally base only three or four. He recited the dimensions of the drones, asking Stanley to commit them to memory and not write anything down at home. Brew said also that it would be important to deal with sand and dust. The drones would be able to ascend vertically on departure from the facility and to descend into the base upon return, but the thrust to do so would be great and fair amounts of sand and debris would be cast into the holding area. This was new information for Stanley. He knew it meant that a strong vacuum system would be required to pull this material out during takeoff and landing, perhaps by shunting it through sidewall vents to cavities on the other side of the underground walls. Vibration and noise control would be difficult, but he had some thoughts on how to manage it.

The little potatoes put a pleasant smell in the air as they boiled. Brew eyed them carefully and compressed one of them with a heavy fork against the side of the roiling pot, measuring its doneness. He removed them from the pot with a large slotted spoon, put them into a bowl, and returned the hot water to its burner, adjusting the setting to its lowest notch. Stanley asked if he would be browning the potatoes in a pan. He loved hash browns. No, Brew said, they would be simmered with a little butter and chopped onion, and served with fresh-cut parsley. Stanley withheld protest.

Brew lightly buttered each side of the filets, then placed them into the hot skillet. The sizzle was instantaneous and high-pitched. He studied his watch, tracking the time closely. In just forty-five seconds he turned them. Stanley looked on, surprised that each was already richly charred.

"You don't move them at all. No pressing with a spatula, no nudging," the captain said. "It disturbs the searing."

In just another forty-five seconds, the filets were resting on a baking sheet next to the range top.

"They can't be cooked enough, can they?"

"After they rest, we finish them in a hot oven. Five minutes at four hundred fifty degrees. Rare center."

The "we" was not lost on Stanley. "Can I help in some way?" he asked.

"You could set the table if you like. We'll need a salad plate too. Put L.T.'s up here on the counter."

To Stanley, the Navy SEAL seemed a different man in the kitchen, not so hard or directorial; more collaborative, friendlier. And he was surely in his element, thought Stanley. Brew was as at home with his cooking tools and ingredients as Stanley was with his laptop score sheet. He spoke about his upbringing in Alabama in the nineties, and his parents' influence. His father drove a fuel oil truck in Birmingham, delivering for the same company for nearly forty years. For a long time, he delivered the heavy fuel oil that went only to commercial sites and manufacturing plants to fuel grimy furnaces. Most of the company's business, though, was selling propane to homeowners. White drivers delivered to them in cleaner, more modern trucks. And those drivers received clean uniforms at the end of each shift to take home and wear the next day. That changed, Brew told Stanley, when the company owner's daughter came of age and began to manage the business.

"My dad's name was Foster," Brew told Stanley. "The daughter comes up to him when he's punching in one day and says, 'Foster, why do you suppose you only deliver to factories?' And he says, 'Some things you stop wondering about.' And she asks, 'It doesn't bother you?' And he says, 'I said I don't wonder about it anymore. Don't need to wonder. I didn't say it doesn't bother me.' And the next day they gave him a propane truck. From then on, he came home in a better mood, talking about the kids and dogs he'd seen that day in the Birmingham neighborhoods."

"In his own way," said Stanley, "he got there."

"Yeah. It took two things, he told me. That woman coming in, and him speaking up when she did."

They kept talking as they worked, their conversation moving between the construction project and the culinary one. Brew asked how many soldiers would be needed to install the foundation and walls of the underground facility, and how quickly could they do it. Stanley said that once the cavity was prepared and its foundation cured, a dozen workers could probably assemble all the prefabricated components over seventy-two hours if they worked continuously in three teams working eight-hour shifts. Stanley asked what the eggs were for, and Brew said he would be poaching three of them to top the salads and would find a good use for the others. Would cranes be needed to lift or lower parts or beams? No, but a cement mixer would be necessary on-site to pour the subsurface footings and the vertical support posts to which the wall panels would be attached. And the collard greens? His Alabama grandmother's recipe, the captain said, with chopped tomato and crushed garlic. Nothing like them, he said.

Stanley poured more wine and studied Brew's dexterity on the chopping board as he prepared the salad on one side of it and the collards on the other. He found a large serving bowl in a cupboard, lifted the chopping board above it, and pushed all the salad vegetables, except for a corner's worth of diced tomato, into it with a single sweep of the cook's knife, sharp side up so as not to dull its blade. He moved immediately to the cooktop, where the pot of potato water waited at a near boil. He swiftly swept the trimmed collard greens into it and turned off the heat. The diced tomatoes hung on their corner of the cutting board like the tires of a race car in a banked curve. A minute later he drained the blanched greens in a colander at the sink and used a rubber spatula to transfer them to a large sautéing pan over medium heat that he had stocked in the interim with chopped bacon, onion, garlic, and a few tablespoons of water. Good smells wafted in the underused kitchen of Stanley Bigelow.

It was nearly time for the Pirates game when Brew's work was done. He texted the agent next door, so quickly that Stanley surmised it must have been a single word. Almost instantly, there was a knock at the door.

"It's L.T.," said the recognized voiced.

Stanley opened the door and Agent Kitt stepped into the foyer. She was barefoot and wearing gym shorts, a T-shirt, and a ball cap with her hair pulled through the back of the headband. She was slimmer than Stanley had thought. She smiled warmly at the navy man at the counter, who walked over with her plated dinner. She looked admiringly at the two plates he handed her. Her filet rested in a pool of demi-glace he had prepared in the cast-iron skillet with the tenderloin jus, a small dollop of butter, and a few tablespoons of the cabernet. The little redskins and his grandmother's collards flanked it. The salad plate was colorful, generously covered with Parmesan, and topped with the poached egg.

"They teach you this in warrior school?" she asked. "Who knew?"

Augie stood in the kitchen corner where Stanley kept his water and food bowls. Tonight, a dinner plate was positioned with them, holding what had been, until a few moments earlier, the fourth filet and a side of scrambled eggs the dog was finishing. L.T. saw it and laughed mildly.

"We can't make a habit of that," she said. "But I guess it's okay once in a while."

"Enjoy," Brew said. He motioned, not rudely, toward the hall, her signal to leave.

"Do you do dishes too?" she asked as she stepped into the hall.

"The enlisted engineers do that," he said.

"I didn't enlist," said Stanley. "I was abducted."

"Not yet, you haven't been," said Brew.

28
A PLAN COMES TOGETHER

★ ★ ★ The Navy SEAL teams moved rapidly through darkness toward Turj. Two bomb-sniffing dogs preceded them across the scruffy terrain. The men ran two by two in a narrow path in the dogs' trail. Their pace concerned General Williamson, who watched a satellite feed in real time with his command team, including Captain Tyler Brew, from MacDill Air Force Base in Florida. He thought their pace was too brisk. The aerial surveillance sweeps all had been conducted in the past thirty-six hours and the SEALs were moving on land where no human activity had been recorded. But any improvised explosive devices, so-called IEDs, that had been planted earlier would not have been observed.

"They're moving too fast," Williamson said. "Tell them to back it down, and not so close to the dogs. Give the dogs a chance to react to something."

His order went out immediately, and at once the SEALs slowed noticeably. The dogs' lead grew in front of them. The specialists numbered twenty-four, a large contingent by usual mission standards, and they were now just three miles from the small city center of Turj and the hospital that stood on its southern flank. They had already traveled nearly five miles from the drop zone where they had landed three hours before first light. The teams would have preferred a shorter approach on land, but stealth was essential and the chance too great that noise from the aircraft, if closer, might alert the terrorists. They would approach from the south, hopefully undetected, and assess the best entry point to the building when they reached it. It depended on the positions of the terrorists at that time. The plan was to take control of the hospital building just before dawn and secure the civilians. A holding force of three hundred would arrive then in swift waves: first a hundred paratroopers dropped at low altitude at the town border, followed immediately by the rest of the force arriving by convoy from the Bagram base. The armored vehicles bringing the soldiers would be used to get the civilians out, except for any with acute medical needs. Those would be airlifted out on Apache helicopters.

That was the plan.

Each of the SEAL teams carried dual sniper teams, comprised of two riflemen and two spotters each, so that all sides of the hospital could be examined and threats eliminated wherever they appeared as the SEALs approached the complex. This required three of the four sniper teams to break off from the approaching stream to take up positions on the other three sides. Except for the direct engagement of the terrorists inside the building, it was the most dangerous part of the mission, because the departing sniper teams were unguided by dogs and it was entirely possible that the terrorists had planted explosives around the hospital perimeter when they entered three days earlier.

When the advance was just a third of a mile from the hospital, the sniper split was commenced. There were still no signs of detection or visible activity, even as the hospital came into view of the approaching forces.

Suddenly, the sniper team heading to the western flank saw headlights on a moving vehicle. The team's spotter immediately called the one-word signal to all of the headsets: "Ditch." Each of the SEALs dropped instantaneously to a prone position. The headlights of the vehicle, ironically a US-made Jeep Wrangler, swept across the ground in front of the SEALs as it moved away from the hospital and onto a road running southeasterly. The SEALs' commander on the ground, his headset tied live to the Central Command, watched it intently. The Jeep accelerated normally and proceeded away from the hospital. He gave his assessment.

"Hostile blind." The SEALs had not been observed.

"How many in the Jeep?" Williamson asked from Command.

"Two."

"We'll track it from above. Resume when you're ready."

Williamson and his MacDill team conferred quickly. Armed drones were airborne and readily available in the area. They could allow the Jeep to travel a suitable distance and then destroy it easily without alerting the other terrorists in Turj. Brew had a different notion.

"Let them run," he said flatly. "Follow them high, but let them run."

"He's right," said the general. "Let's see where they go."

The SEAL teams on the ground waited motionlessly for several minutes to be sure the Jeep was not turning back and that no sign of movement appeared in the building in front of them. The captain of the forward team signaled. Three of the snipers and their spotters rose and diverged toward their intended positions on the sides and front of the hospital. Without dogs to lead them, they moved more slowly and crouched close to the earth, looking for hazards. The fourth sniper team took its position in front of the larger group on the south side. The captains waited for the snipers to report in. The protection provided by the snipers was important at all times but especially vital at the beginning of a surprise attack. It was their job to take out the sentries who would otherwise see the SEALs first and alert the larger force of hostiles inside. There could be no further advance until the sniper teams were in place and until any hostiles guarding it were removed, as silently as possible.

The spotters checked in sequentially, clockwise. A single armed hostile stood near the front entrance. Another sat on a deck off the west side of the second floor. A third leaned against a ventilation pipe rising from the east side of the roof. No hostiles were visible at the rear side, where the balance of the SEALs waited to advance. The captains agreed that entry would be made simultaneously through the unguarded rear entrance and through exit doors on the east and west sides. An equal number of SEALs would take each vector.

The communications between the captains and the snipers were prearranged. Each was to use one word—"clear"—when they possessed line of sight to a clear lethal head shot, but was to hold fire from the suppressed rifle until all had a clean shot at the same time. The Team One captain would then issue the kill order. If a sight line became impaired before the order for simultaneous fire was issued from the captain, the sniper was to report "hold," and the wait for clarity on each target would begin again.

The signals came in within seconds. "Clear"; "clear"; "clear." The captain spoke at once: "Kill." With muffled single shots, the three terrorist guards fell in unison. The SEAL teams raced toward the doors, fanning out into three streams—one each to the left and right sides, the third, led by the dogs, straight on to the rear side of the building they faced. Unexpectedly—and perhaps it should not have been—the advance dogs suddenly pulled up short, about thirty feet from the building. They stopped all forward movement, almost like a neighborhood dog reaching an electric fence line. They pranced laterally, back and forth. They did not bark. The racing SEALs, still in a two-by-two formation behind the dogs, knew what this meant. The rear of the complex was laced with land mines, probably the reason it was unguarded by a hostile. The captain at their lead did not hesitate.

"Split and join," he said into their headsets.

The SEALs divided like a stream around an island to join the other two lines of advancing specialists. At MacDill, Brew and Williamson watched and listened.

"Those damned dogs," said the general. "Those beautiful damned dogs."

29
NUTS AND BOLTS

★ ★ ★ For weeks Stanley worked steadily on the project drawings. He completed the specifications for the wall panels first, and then he designed the floor flanges to which they would be secured. Every side and angle was separately drawn. Nothing was left to interpretation. The pages mounted. He sketched elevations of the completed "box in the ground," as he described it to Brew, and experimented with different options for the ground-level roof structure.

The roof was the most difficult design challenge. His first thought had been a laterally sliding roof, powered by electric motors that would function like a double pocket door lying on its side. When the containment base needed to open, two sections opening from the center would retract to the sides into slots built into the ground just below the surface. Once the aircraft had ascended, the roof sections would slide back. He asked Brew to get him information about the volume of sand and dust that would be displaced during takeoff and landing by the vertical thrust mechanisms of the aircraft. Brew's report convinced Stanley that a roof that slid laterally was not practical. The volume of moving sand around the open pit was too great. A huge removal system would be needed, and even then the aircraft remaining in the base below would probably be damaged.

He settled instead on roof flaps that would rise like the four

161

sides of a cardboard box. Like the interior walls, they would be fabricated from beryllium. Unbelievably light for their size, they could be raised and lowered with a small hydraulic system. And when opening during the drones' ascent, and raised during their descent, the upright sections would act to shield the open pit from much of the swirling sand and dust. The debris that did enter the container could be managed and removed with a reasonable vacuum system once the flaps closed.

Stanley considered every detail of each component piece needed for the facility. To make for speedy assembly, he decided to attach all the wall panel sections with the same size machine screws, to be self-tapping and tightened with simple tools. He knew this was not the most cost-effective means, because it meant that smaller parts were being held together with fasteners much larger than necessary. But it meant the soldiers would not need to select from various sizes and keep changing tools and driver bits.

Over their next dinner in his Pittsburgh apartment, Brew nodded approvingly as Stanley showed him his sketches and explained his reasoning.

There was one aspect of the construction that worried Stanley. The concrete foundation and cement support stanchions, the first components to be installed after excavation, needed perfect placement. The entire design concept of the beryllium overlapping panels for the walls, floor, and roof depended on their matching alignment. The stanchions were to function like vertical wall studs rising from the foundation every thirty-six inches around the perimeter. Formed by pouring concrete into precisely calibrated forms, the interior side of each stanchion would be faced with a strip of beryllium machined with threaded holes to accept the self-tapping bolts that would pass through the wall panels to secure them. Stanley looked at the installation as in two phases. Phase two, essentially the bolting and assembly of the panels and other components, could be performed well enough by the soldier crew he would train in a location that Brew was working to identify. But phase one was another matter. The spacing and alignment of the support stanchions could not be just "close enough for government work," he told Brew.

"Once the support frame is installed, your soldiers will pretty much be playing with an erector set," he said to Brew. "But the underground support frame will require skills. People don't know what goes into civil engineering."

He told Brew that digital leveling devices would be needed to set the posts accurately. The equipment resembled that used nowadays by land surveyors, but was far more exacting, relating the position of one object to a virtually unlimited number of others. He reminded Brew that the critical attributes of beryllium that made it such a good choice for the walls and roof—its extreme rigidity and strength, even compared to steel—meant also that tolerances for assembly would be extremely close.

"The walls and roof flaps are not going to bend into place. They will be stiff as hell. All surfaces and connection points will need to line up perfectly," he told Brew. "I can alloy the beryllium with a small amount of copper, which will make it just a tiny amount softer for machining and slotting without measurably changing its stiffness. But it will give only small relief."

Brew asked why alloying the beryllium with a large amount of copper was not a good idea. Stanley said there were a lot of reasons. The beryllium was much lighter and harder, and the rigidity was needed for the stability of the roof flaps when they were opening, closing, or extended. More copper content meant more flex and less rigidity. And copper was not invisible to x-rays, he explained. Only a small amount could be incorporated without comprising the detection-proof quality of the walls. And, importantly, increasing the copper percentage would materially lower the melting point. In the event of an accident in the pit or, heaven help them, a nuclear release, the high melting point of the beryllium could be vital.

Brew did not know whether he could find military personnel experienced with the digital measuring equipment that Stanley described, but he would try. "There may be reserves with that kind of training," he said.

They discussed timing. Stanley's communications with Precision Beryllium had been extensive and, he thought, had gone well. He had deflected all questions about the end use of the panels, flanges, and machine screws, but before long, he told Brew, he would need some cover story. He had told the supplier that he would need delivery of all the components at the same time, but did not yet have a delivery location. This was unusual. He told Brew that eventually there would be questions.

"Have you decided where we will do the training?" he asked Brew.

"Getting close," Brew replied. "Maybe the low country."

"The Southeast?"

"Near Charleston."

"In July? The heat will be terrible."

"About like Kuwait," Brew said.

30

OCCUPATIONAL HAZARDS

★ ★ ★ At the Russian Embassy in Berlin, Hemelstaan's handler followed the Swede's daily reports from Kista. He had begun passing on the information about Precision Beryllium and its Pittsburgh correspondent to Moscow Central. Analysts there saw more in the communications than he had. The volume of beryllium discussed was extraordinary. True, the material was used in many commercial applications, and increasingly so in small electronics, but the odd earth metal was also a key component in nuclear devices and weaponry.

"Moscow interested in Milwaukee reports," the handler emailed Hemelstaan. "Expand window of monitoring. You will be compensated. Confirm."

The young hacker understood the request and welcomed it. The Russians wanted him at his screen for extended hours to collect more of the Precision Beryllium communications if there were any. The timing was convenient. Matters with his girlfriend were getting more serious. She had secured a future weekend off from her job in the events department at the Stockholm Park Hyatt. She wanted to go to Zurich with him. She wanted to divide the costs, the way nowadays. But now he could afford one of the better villas he had been looking for and insist on paying the entire cost. She would be impressed. He immediately confirmed to Berlin that he would add three additional hours daily to his network surveillance of the Milwaukee company.

In Pyongyang, the intelligence officer and his own hacker observing Hemelstaan's communications were impressed too. The Swedish hacker was very good at his job, they considered. But then he proved to be too good. That evening Hemelstaan downloaded an update to his ReturnMal software. A pause occurred in the synchronization during the download. It concerned him. He aborted the download and performed an emergency virus scan on his own laptop and, simultaneously, on the larger unit and monitor in front of him. The files scrolled. Clean, clean, clean, clean. Until a file was *not* clean. He stopped the screen as his blood rushed. He had been infiltrated. And—worse—by a live feed. He entered a series of commands to identify the feed. Then he removed it and immediately emailed his Berlin handler.

"Machines compromised," he wrote. "Live feed to Pyongyang detected. Feed now removed, but must assume indefinite prior presence."

Was it a lapse arising from the stress of the moment? Or perhaps he'd been distracted by pleasant thoughts of his intended trip with his girlfriend to Zurich. But whichever it was, Hemelstaan had made a serious omission. After finding the penetrated file, he had stopped scrolling the remaining ones. The North Koreans had inserted not one feed but duplicate feeds. The second, placed in a file further down the scroll, was left unimpaired. It permitted the agents in Pyongyang to continue to spy in real time. His communication to the Russian in Berlin announcing the infiltration had been observed as clearly as all his other reports.

The supervisor in Pyongyang studied the email with a flat expression. He knew it was only a matter of time, and probably a short span, before the Russians' hired hacker realized his mistake and found the second infiltration. He texted two of his field operatives. They appeared in his plain office within minutes. He showed them

Hemelstaan's email to Berlin, and handed them a photo of the young hacker, standing with his girlfriend in the Park Hyatt lobby. The North Korean operative working undercover at the hotel had taken the photo. The boyish Swede had long straggly hair and tortoiseshell glasses with round lenses. The street address of the cement building in Kista was written on the back of the photo.

"Go to Stockholm," he instructed them. "End him. And take his machines."

"Why the machines?" one asked. He knew his superiors possessed their contents and had total access from the successful infiltration. "We have them already, don't we?"

"Yes. But we don't want anyone else to have them too."

31

THE DOCTORS ARE IN

★ ★ ★ It was one of those rare briefings when the tone almost could have been jubilant.

Almost.

General Williamson and Brew reported from the SOCOM command room at MacDill; Vernon Lazar and Jack Hastings, the CIA chief, sat with the president in the Situation Room of the White House.

President Winters had just finished her call to the executive director of Doctors without Borders at the organization's headquarters in Paris. She was about to receive full details, she reported, but could confirm that the hospital in Turj had been retaken by United States forces. All doctors, staff, and patients were accounted for and unharmed, except for the Finnish doctor and the patient who had been executed by the terrorists in their original assault. Most of the patients were stable enough to remain in the facility under the care of staff, who had insisted on staying and resuming their duties. Some patients, mostly among those that had been moved from the first floor to the second by the terrorists, had deteriorated. They were airlifted along with military medical personnel, joined by a supervising physician from the organization, to the hospital at Bagram Air Force Base. Their conditions varied, but none were considered critical.

"And the patient whom they killed?" asked the French doctor.

"The American," the president said quietly.

"I am sorry, Madam President."

"We think she was picked out because she was."

"They hate us all, but you have the honor of being hated the most. Let us hope it will not always be so. Let us hope some greater power will win out and change everything."

The foreign doctor's words were more striking to Del Winters than the doctor could have known. She thought of Project Eaglets' Nest, its power—its terrible power—and its potential to change *everything*.

Williamson credited Brew for the tactical planning of the successful raid and rescue. It had been masterful, he said, with options and suboptions to meet every conceivable circumstance that the SEAL teams and follow-on forces might encounter. He singled out Brew's conviction, debated before execution, that once the hospital ground floor was penetrated, rather than immediately engaging and destroying the terrorists in the basement, it was best to hold that floor with one team while the other secured the staff and patients above them and took them away from the building. It was counterintuitive to leave the terrorists below to their own devises, with their armaments and explosives, for the length of time needed for the evacuation. During the planning, Williamson initially thought that risk too great to be sensible. They could blow up the entire complex and everyone above. Brew believed otherwise and spoke up to his senior. The British doctor's initial report was reliable, reinforced by aerial intelligence in the following days. During and since the takeover, truckloads of weapons and explosives had been moved into the building. This was not a suicide mission or one designed to destroy the hospital. The terrorists intended instead to make the hospital a staging base for munitions, believing the Afghan security forces and the Americans would not bomb them when they were shielded by civilians, especially medical ones. They were not there to die themselves, the certain outcome of releasing explosives in their basement quarters. That became a risk only once they were engaged below. If the SEALs raided the basement and killed nearly all of them, a desperate survivor or three might attempt a detonation, but not before. The best course was to evacuate first, then raid with an overwhelming coordinated attack on the basement occupants. Williamson was convinced. He approved the plan.

Perhaps it was the dawn timing and grogginess; perhaps the terrorists were fatigued from their labors moving in supplies. Whatever the reason, the SEALs overwhelmed them within just a few minutes, entering the basement from every stairwell in the building in a vicious assault. No prisoners were taken. Only one SEAL was injured, and not seriously. A grateful Danish physician treated him cheerfully, and he left with the other SEALs in the Apaches. The holding force established a wide perimeter. Within hours, the hospital was functioning again, with only limited physical damage. There was peace again in Turj.

The president thanked the command team. Williamson and Brew were spent; they had gone without sleep for twenty hours. But at the end of the call, the president raised the topic of Eaglets' Nest.

"Captain Brew, are you satisfied with progress on the deployment base?" she asked.

"Bigelow has completed the design for the holding area. He is working on the ventilation and power systems. We will begin training the installers next month near Charleston Air Force Base."

"And what do you think now of Mr. Bigelow?"

"He is a good engineer. And a good eater."

PART III

PART III

32

A CONVENIENT COVER, AND VEGETABLES NO LESS

★ ★ ★ US Highway 17 runs about 120 miles through the low fields and tidal marshes that stretch from Charleston to Savannah. Twenty miles along the way sits a federal research center operated by the United States Department of Agriculture. Known as the United States Vegetable Laboratory, the complex expands for nearly a mile on each side of the highway. The original headquarters building, dating back to the Reconstruction era following the Civil War, resembles an old Southern plantation house. It rests on the left side of the highway as you drive toward Savannah. Many acres of testing fields flank it. Students and faculty of Clemson University often can be seen inspecting the experimental plantings, part of a cooperative education program of long standing between the university and the federal government.

On the other side of the highway stands the new headquarters complex. It was the product of a second reconstruction of sorts, the one that followed the financial markets' collapse of 2008. To brake a deepening recession and spur employment, Presidents George W. Bush and Barack Obama ushered in stimulus legislation to fund public and private works projects across the country. Fifty million dollars later, the taxpayers thus acquired a shiny new vegetable research facility in the low country. Owing to Captain Brew, it was about to be put to new use.

He surmised that the Department of Agriculture site addressed multiple needs for Eaglets' Nest. For one, it provided the cover that Stanley had been asking for—an explanation he could give to suppliers about the end-use application of the materials he was ordering and where they should be shipped. He could identify the project as being for the Department of Agriculture, having to do with long-term storage of perishable foodstuffs in the event of a national catastrophe. The government is always trying expensive new things.

Equally important to Brew, the facility was the closest thing imaginable to a federal installation that was logistically convenient to military bases and yet of distinct disinterest to foreign intelligence assets. The NSA's secret web of countersurveillance technologies continually monitored physical sites operated by the United States. It wanted to know the degree to which each was under surveillance by satellites or other means. It was fundamental national defense practice to understand what assets were watched, by whom, and how often. All military installations were closely observed by world powers. It was just a fact. If you wanted to conceal activity, you didn't conduct it at them. But many mundane federal assets went unobserved: postal distribution centers, national parks, and, as Brew learned after a review performed for him by NSA, the United States Vegetable Laboratory on Highway 17 in South Carolina. The NSA confirmed that it was not the subject of a single surveillance technology other than its own perimeter security camera system. This even though it was located less than fifteen miles from Charleston Air Force Base.

Brew reasoned that all of Stanley's special materials could be shipped to the USDA site unobserved, and the training of the military installers could be conducted there covertly. After the training, the materials could be conveyed by disguised convoy to the air base in

Charleston for flight to Kuwait. Since the Charleston base had for decades been the principal sourcing point for US military assets to the Middle East, Stanley's materials would draw no special attention.

But Brew, ever the cautious planner, did not want the crew of trainees to come from the large air base. Stanley estimated that at least twenty-one days of training would be required. The soldiers would have to come and go from the research center daily, as there were no lodging facilities on-site. A daily transport of the installers from Charleston Air Force Base, especially when followed by the eventual movement of the materials to the same air base, risked detection. Brew designed a work-around.

The marines operated a flight station base at Beaufort, just fifty miles down Highway 17 toward Savannah. The trainees, reserves called up for short-term deployment because of their useful occupational histories, would be temporarily stationed at Beaufort. It would be easy to commute them to the Department of Agriculture site in a disguised supply truck of a kind seen routinely entering and leaving the marine base—a UPS or FedEx truck, perhaps. That way none of the training activities would implicate the large Charleston air base. No red flag would be raised when the building materials were finally sent there.

Brew waited in the parking lot of the new building on Highway 17 until the marine major arrived from Beaufort. Both were out of uniform. Inside, the laboratory's general manager was understandably nervous to be meeting with his two unannounced visitors. Military representatives had never come there before. They all sat in a conference room near the lobby, normally used to begin tours for the public, usually school groups. Brew had barely introduced himself and the major when the manager's assistant opened the conference room door.

"Sir, the secretary is calling from Washington."

"What secretary?" the manager asked.

"*The* secretary," he answered.

"I'll take it in my office." He started to rise.

"He told me to put him through to you in the conference room with the guests."

"Oh." He sat back down.

Howard Dalton, the secretary of agriculture, came over the speaker.

"James," he said, "I will take only a minute." His tone was warm and familiar. In truth, the two men had never met or spoken. "We have an unusual situation here, an unusual opportunity to be of assistance. I don't have the full picture, but I understand the matter is of importance—and sensitivity. Captain Brew and the marine major need your help. Please give them every assistance they need, and don't speak to anyone about their work. Anyone, James." He paused. "If there are budget consequences, present them to Captain Brew and they will be handled. He will leave his contact information."

"Yes, Mr. Secretary."

It took nothing more to arrange Stanley's classroom. The general manager was a good soldier.

33

AUGIE NEEDS PRACTICE

★ ★ ★ Back in Pittsburgh, Stanley's routine continued. He was nearly finished with the designs for the ventilation and vacuum system, and the power system for the retractable lifting roof. To speed the time line for installation, he pored over online catalogues for commercially available motors, fans, and suction devices, studying their specifications and component materials. It would be much faster than custom designs.

The fans for the ventilation modules troubled him. He was worried about their vibration and its close sister—noise—which would be vulnerable to the newest detection technologies. Brew had told him that returning drones would lower into the base with very high engine temperatures. In the confined space of the underground containment box, Stanley knew it would be important to cool them as quickly as possible to prevent damage to the other parts of the craft and to allow soldiers to go down into the container to service them. Cooling fans would need to spin at high speeds, but even at the highest attainable speeds it could take hours before the box was reasonably cool. By then it was foreseeable that detection attempts would be made from the skies above. Fan noise would not do.

He reached the ventilation fabricator by phone.

"You are making the fan blades and housings with stainless steel," he said.

"Yes. They are stable and easy to clean."

"If I arranged to provide you with blades and cast mounting assemblies that were exactly dimensional but made of beryllium, could you use them instead of the stainless?"

"Beryllium? They will be much harder. It will require special presses and milling to attach them."

"We will pay."

"No problem then."

Stanley sent the fan blade specifications to Precision Beryllium the next morning.

"Never heard of such a thing," the engineer at the Milwaukee company said. "Each of these blades will cost at least five thousand dollars."

"Well, they want to spare nothing to keep the produce from spoiling," Stanley said.

He was walking every evening after work with Kitt and Augie. And Kitt, despite his mild complaint, had added a morning walk twice a week. After only a few of the "morning extras," as Kitt called them, he found them unobjectionable, and in truth invigorating.

Brew had told Kitt that Stanley would be working in Charleston soon. He had arranged with the bureau that she would keep her assignment and go with him to the low country. The dog would go too.

"I hear we are going to Charleston," she said on their next morning walk. "Great town. Been there?"

"A few times," Stanley replied. "Never in July, though."

"If Augie can manage it, you can."

"He's going? Brew told me I would be put up in nice hotels." There was the hint of hope in his voice.

"He'll be fine in them. Brew will arrange everything."

"Well, I'm glad he's coming. He really is pretty special."

"And coming from someone who is not a dog person."

"When are you going to stop throwing that back in my face?" Stanley said. Kitt could see that her teasing had drawn a little blood.

"I'm sorry, Stanley," she said. "You two have become a real pair. I assume he's keeping score with you by now."

"He does seem attentive. Lies there listening."

"While you're teaching him new things, we need to get him some practice in what he already knows," the agent said.

Kitt explained that as a personal protection dog, Augie had received extensive training to learn predetermined behaviors and reactions to aggressive stimuli. It was important to reinforce the training with practice on a regular schedule. He was due. The bureau was sending a training cadet from Quantico to stage a simulated attack on Stanley. It would occur later that day on their evening walk. The local police had been notified.

"Augie will do what he's supposed to do. You need to do what you're supposed to do," Kitt told him. Stanley seemed, reasonably, puzzled.

"And what would that be?" he asked.

"Exactly this. Listen carefully."

She explained that in any confrontation out of doors, the dog was trained to perform a specific set of actions. He would engage an assaulter, or more than one, with extreme aggression. He would always direct his teeth to the offensive arm and throat of the attacker.

"How does he know which arm?" Stanley asked.

"He knows it's where the weapon is."

"Of course. What about his leash?"

Kitt reached down and gave a slight pull on the dog's leash near the collar ring. It separated easily.

"It's a release joint. He will break away immediately; you'll feel almost nothing." Stanley lifted the leash and admired the tension-spring fitting.

"He won't stay on top of an aggressor forever," Kitt continued.

"But he will stay on him until he believes he—or she—is disabled, or until he's commanded to get off. While he is working, your job is to move away as fast as you can. When he's done, he will look for you. He will run like hell to find you. So, it's important—really important, Stanley—that you go where you are supposed to go." Kitt had stopped on the sidewalk and looked Stanley straight in the eye as she said it. The dog looked up at him too, as if for emphasis. "Only where you are supposed to go," she repeated.

"And that is?"

"You always run away from the attackers in the direction *you* came from. Never run in the direction *they* came from. They are familiar with that direction. If they pursue, you want them going where they have not been before, and away from their escape vehicle. Often they won't pursue for just that reason. So, you turn around and run straight back in the direction you came from. Always run on the right side of the road. Or the sidewalk, tree lawn, whatever. But always the right side. Drop the leash so you don't trip on it. You'll hear things. Augie will be loud; there may be screams or gunfire. You don't look back, no matter what. You just keep going as fast as you can, straight ahead, until your first opportunity to turn right. It could be the next street, or it might be an alley. But only to the *right*."

"Why not left if it comes first?"

"Because you'd be crossing against traffic, and so would Augie when he follows you. There's no waiting for cars. Always the first right. Unless there is *never* a right and your street is dead-ending with only a left available. Then, only then, do you run left."

Not since the day in the Arlington JW Marriott, when Stanley, following Brew's instructions, had approached the driver calling him "Mr. Morris," had he felt the singe of blood heat that came back to him as Kitt described the protocol. She told him that he should run for at least five minutes, but not more than ten, and then duck into an entrance way; outside a commercial building would be best, if available. If necessary, under an awning or onto a porch. Augie

would expect him to be located in that range, she said, only a two-
to four-minute run for the dog. He would continue to canvass that
range if he did not find Stanley on a first pass.

"And where are you in all of this?" he asked her.

"I stay with Augie and the attacker. If the threat is disabled, I
stay and hold them. If I don't need him, I will send him to you. You
stay with him right there. Don't move any more once he gets to you."

"And if you *do* need him?"

"Then other help will be on its way to you. You'll know they are
FBI or police. They'll be wearing it."

"What if Augie is hurt?" To Stanley, it seemed a real possibility;
he did not want to think it, but he sensed it was almost a likelihood.

"He will come for you anyway, Stanley. If he can come at all,
he will come."

34

ROMANCE, INTERRUPTED

★ ★ ★ It was a beautiful June night in Kista, Sweden.

The Stockholm suburb is the center of Sweden's information technology and telecommunications industries. Ericsson and all of the phone companies occupied large buildings in the sector, providing employment to many thousands and a healthy support economy of eateries, bars, and shops. Even little Schliist Street, running between two of the larger thoroughfares, had its share of them. The two North Korean agents, sitting in their rented Volvo at one end of the block, wished it did not. They had observed Hemelstaan arriving by foot from his regular job at the logistics software company, striding up Schliist Street with his laptop bag. He was fumbling through a pocket of his baggy pants, fishing, they presumed, for his entry card to the plain three-story building in the middle of the block. But a half dozen people were on the street too, and others might pop out of the cafés at any moment. Hemelstaan entered the building unmolested.

Making matters more inconvenient for the foreign agents, the days were growing very long now in Kista. It would be broad daylight until well after ten o'clock.

The agents were unaware of the young hacker's nightly routine. He always booted up his equipment and then walked for a few minutes to smoke a cigarette before beginning his work for the night. They were surprised when he emerged in just ten minutes. Little Schliist Street was still active and in full sun. Hemelstaan walked from one end of the block to the other, then back again, passing directly beside the agents sitting in their car. The walker didn't pause, but he glanced into the car as he passed. The agent in the passenger seat was holding up a city street map, typical of an Asian visitor. The two made brief eye contact, punctuated by slight smiles and small nods. A minute later Hemelstaan reentered the plain building in the middle of the block.

The North Koreans were seasoned professionals. They knew they could not remain parked for too long without the possibility of notice, and one police vehicle had already passed by. They drove the perimeter of the suburb, resisting the temptation to stop for tea at any of the cafés. One of the agents retrieved a cigarette from his jacket and probed the car's console for a lighter. The other blocked his arm.

"No smoke," he said. "Hertz is picky about it." They both knew that lesser indiscretions had sullied assignments such as theirs. It was fundamental tradecraft to leave no reason for notice. The would-be smoker nodded, agreeably, and flicked the unlit cigarette to the street.

It was four hours before Hemelstaan appeared again, stepping out onto Schliist Street for a breath of the evening air. It was deep dusk but not fully dark. It had been a warm day, warmer than typical for June. It was still over seventy degrees Fahrenheit. "Pleasant" would be an understatement. He lit a cigarette and thought ahead to the coming weekend. The online depiction of the villa outside Zurich was enticing. His girlfriend was excited; she was buying a new outfit for nightlife in the city.

The foreign agents were waiting in the Volvo on the other side of the street at the opposite end of their first perch, three hundred feet away. The young Swede leaned against the office building, only a few feet from the plain entrance. The agents stepped from the car in unison, taking care to close the doors silently. One walked on one side the street, the other the opposite, each in the direction of Hemelstaan, each wearing latex gloves.

The agent approaching on the side of the street where the young hacker stood carried the Stockholm street map. A convenient accessory, it might make him familiar to the target, lessen his apprehension to an approach in the lowering light.

"Sir," the Asian agent said in English, the universal language, even of assassins. He held up the street map in the dim light.

"Yes?" Hemelstaan asked benignly. He did recognize the man from the glancing earlier contact, and the small smile. He was taller than the agent and bent slightly to see the map in his hand. He did not observe the second North Korean, now racing across the empty street directly toward his comrade and the young hacker.

Hemelstaan may have taken two more breaths. It could not have been three. The speed was machine-like. The map-holding agent fired his free hand around the Swede's neck, just beneath the Adam's apple, and slammed his head against the concrete facing behind him. The other agent drove a stiletto blade between the hacker's chin and the top of the other assassin's hand, still holding its prey upright against the wall. The knife wielder dragged the deep blade to the young hacker's right ear. The assassins jumped to either side as the lifeless Swede dropped to the sidewalk, avoiding most of his convulsing blood. One reached into his rear pants pocket and removed his wallet. The other quickly located his card key. They pulled him inside the building door and made sure that it locked on closing. They turned on no lights. In only a few minutes they returned to the entrance with Hemelstaan's laptop and the computer drives they had found connected to his large monitor.

One of the killers opened the door of the building and looked down each side of little Schliist Street. Two of the cafés were still open, but no one was entering or leaving them. The other killer rifled through the dead hacker's wallet. He took from it a rail pass with the Swede's photo and dropped it next to his body. He put the wallet, with the rest of its contents, into his own jacket.

"So they have no trouble identifying him," he said to the other. "If we leave nothing, they may bring in Interpol to learn who he is. This way it is just a robbery and a killing."

They went back to their Volvo the same way they had come from it, on opposite sides of the street. They pulled away at normal speed and drove to the Stockholm International Airport—to be exact, to the Hertz rental car return there—odor free.

35

PRACTICE, MORE REAL THAN IMAGINED

★ ★ ★ Kitt was waiting with Augie at the entrance to Stanley's office on Oliver Street when he emerged at six thirty. An afternoon shower had come and gone. The June humidity hung in the warm air. She handed the dog's leash to him. Stanley motioned to the east, toward William Penn Place. The sun was still high enough to look down over the buildings behind them. A warm breeze fell on their backs.

"This way okay?" he asked.

"That's fine," she replied.

"Where will this happen?"

"No cheating," she said.

When they reached William Penn Place, he gently directed the dog south, a right turn. Kitt said nothing. They walked two blocks to Forbes Avenue, then went east again, this time turning left, toward the I-579 expressway in the distance. At the corner of Forbes and Ross Street, Stanley asked if he could light a cigar. He usually did on their evening walks. He thought Kitt might object on account of the difference this night, but she didn't. Stanley attached some significance to this fact. Probably, he thought, the simulated attack would come much later in the walk, when they were nearer their end point, the apartment at RiverBridge Place, at least forty minutes away. He could enjoy his cigar in peace. He brought it to a robust burn and examined it for evenness. Satisfied, he directed Augie left on Ross Street toward Mellon Green, the small park through which Ross Street ran two blocks ahead.

Augie led him at a brisk pace, matching Stanley's long strides. The fit Agent Kitt kept pace effortlessly. L.T. never seemed nervous, but this evening she appeared to Stanley even more relaxed than usual. She asked Stanley if the Pirates were playing away tonight. There did not seem to be much traffic on the streets, she remarked. A late start on the West Coast, Stanley said, an interleague game against the Los Angeles Angels. A traditionalist in such matters, Stanley told her he disfavored interleague play. It queered the symmetry of the schedule. "How so?" she asked, as they continued up Ross Street.

"Each team ends up playing a slightly different group of opponents from the other league," he explained. "It is luck of the draw whether you are pitted against a good or bad team for that difference. Like tonight," he complained, "the Pirates will face the Angels, a very good team with feared pitching, while the Reds have drawn the Indians."

She said she thought he liked the Indians in the American League. He did, he said, but they were laboring near the bottom of their division, their usual location since the end of the Terry Francona era. "No," Stanley said, "interleague play produces dissymmetry, and there should be no dissymmetry in baseball, a game whose entire premise is built on events emanating from a perfectly aligned diamond of ninety-foot sides."

When enjoying a cigar on their walks, Stanley tried to be considerate in the matter of his smoke, navigating the breeze as best he could to avoid it sailing toward L.T. But occasionally, some inevitably did, and he would swat his massive hand in the air to move it away.

"It's okay, Stanley," L.T. said as they progressed up Ross Street and the breeze of a passing electric bus pushed a plume of his cigar smoke toward her face. "My father was a cigar smoker."

"Oh?" She had not mentioned her father before, or hardly anything about her family or her upbringing.

"Maybe the least objectionable thing about him," she said. Stanley, surprised, tried not to reveal it.

"Sorry to hear that," he said. "He didn't treat you well?"

"Me or anybody else."

"He had problems?"

"Well, he never got the memo that the three-martini lunch was a fifties thing."

"I see. What business was he in?"

"Commercial real estate sales."

"I think there's a lot of schmoozing and boozing in that," Stanley said. He thought it might be somehow consoling, and anyway not hurtful.

"And there were other things," L.T. said. Stanley glanced at her. She seemed to be filing things in her mind. "My mom made up for him," she said.

Stanley drew on his cigar and sent his waft of smoke to the side, downwind.

"She's a strong person, my mother," L.T. said. "I know I take after her, but she actually gives him credit for my turning out okay."

"How so?"

"Says he taught me never to take crap from jerks like him."

"What did he say when you went into law enforcement?" Stanley asked.

"I don't know if he ever knew," L.T. said. "The last time I saw him, I was nineteen."

"Well, I can't say I know what it is like to be a father," Stanley said, "never having been one. But if you were my daughter, I would be very proud."

Ross Street divides Mellon Green into two pieces of green space. The larger piece lay to the left as they approached. Two steel benches with flowers behind them lined the left edge of the sidewalk, facing toward the park. He was enjoying his cigar and holding forth on the years when Francona's Indians could always be counted on for a good game. He did not notice the slim man sitting on the farther bench in dark clothing and a ball cap. They had nearly passed him when he rose before them and lunged toward Kitt, who drew her gun from the leather bag on her shoulder, startling Stanley. Augie leaned back on his rear legs, nearly a squat, and then launched himself with unhinged fury at the attacker. Stanley was frightened and shocked at the dog's strength. At the apex of his first leap, Augie flew higher than Stanley's head. He was kicking fiercely with all four of his legs as if he could use them to climb even higher. Stanley would not call what he heard barking; he would not call it growling; he did not know what to call it other than unbridled animal fury. The attacker removed his attention from Kitt and tried to brace himself for the dog's assault. Augie's leap took him across the man's chest to his right arm, in the hand of which he held a dark handgun. The dog took his wrist in his jaws and fired his body and legs into the attacker's midsection. The assailant fell backward, the dog atop him.

Stanley felt the adrenaline sweep over him. He turned and ran with loping long strides back up Ross Street. Kitt's instructions raced in his mind, it seemed to him, almost in time with his strides. *The leash, the leash.* He dropped it, and his cigar too. *Stay right, stay right.* He did. There were gunshots. Were there two or three? Two, he thought. And so loud and deep. Not what he'd expected. He had never been near a firing gun in his life, but he somehow thought the sound would be more muted. It was simulated, he knew, but it seemed so terribly real. Or could it be that it was *not* just practice? Kitt had been so talkative and relaxed. She seemed as surprised as he by the man who rose from the park bench. And why had she drawn her gun? He heard Augie barking wildly as he continued to run, but there was no more gunfire. He had been running nearly a minute when he saw Fifth Avenue ahead of him. *Right, always right.* He turned at the corner with as severe a cut as he could muster. He felt his chest pounding; it was as if his heart would leap from his chest, as Augie had leapt from his stance. He continued running up Fifth Avenue, but he was feeling constriction in his chest. He was panting and his chest was tightening. He had to slow, and he did so. But he didn't stop or slow to a walk. *Five minutes. Run for five minutes. Can I do it?* he asked himself. He looked back over his shoulder. No sign of Kitt. No sign of Augie. A cab appeared and seemed to slow down, then pulled away when Stanley did not motion to it. Sirens wailed in the distance, but his exertion had left him oddly disoriented. He couldn't tell whether the sirens were approaching or retreating.

His legs were heavy and he was sweating torrentially. He crossed over William Penn Place and saw the well-lighted CVS drugstore at the next corner, directly ahead of him on the correct—the right—side of the street. A red canopy hung over its entrance. He chugged to a stop beneath it and stood against the brick facing beside the sliding entry. He bent over and tried to regain his breath, his hands on his knees. A customer came out from the store, carrying her plastic sack of purchases. He startled her with his panting, and she asked, earnestly, if he was all right. "I think so. Yes, I am," he said. "Thank you," he said. But the woman was unconvinced. She moved to her car, parked near, and stood by it, watching him.

He looked at his watch, wondering how much time had passed since the first lunge of the attacker, since the gunshots. It was a meaningless gesture; he had no sense of elapsed time. It was a minute before his breathing slowed enough to allow some degree of comfort. He stood straight and stared back up Fifth. Now his watch was useful, if upsetting. Another minute passed. Then another. Where was Augie? Kitt had promised he would come, that he would always come.

The woman by her car pulled a phone from her purse.

"Are you sure you are okay?" she called out to him. "I could call someone."

And then he saw what he wanted to see. Augie appeared, pounding toward him up Fifth at full gallop and bound. A few pedestrians jumped off the sidewalk or stopped in their tracks, most instinctively raising their arms in weak gestures of avoidance, as the dog flew past them silently. Stanley stepped forward from the wall of the drugstore entrance to be sure that the dog would see him. It was probably not necessary. Without slowing noticeably, Augie seemed to leap to a halt directly in front of him. He sat down immediately, turning to face the path he had just raced, as if still on guard. He panted vigorously, foamy saliva running from his tongue. Stanley stooped to rub his tall ears. He saw Agent Kitt too now, jogging up the avenue toward them, her leather bag draped across her chest. The woman by the car observed all of this.

"Were you running from *him*?" she asked, puzzled, pointing to the dog.

"No," said Stanley. "I think I was running *for* him." This failed to assuage her puzzlement.

Kitt arrived. If she had broken a sweat, it was not apparent. She was smiling broadly. She went first to the dog, kneeling in front of him, praising him, massaging his broad chest. In the violent thrashing in Mellon Green it was impossible to tell whether the dog had been struck with the firearm of the flailing cadet. She looked closely at his eyes and then moved her thumbs gently around each one, pressing lightly to see if he showed any sensitivity. He didn't. Then she pulled a penlight from her pocket and looked into each of his ears. Without fear, she stretched open his jaws and shined the light in and around like a dentist. He was unscratched.

The volunteer cadet had not fared as well. As a precaution, L.T. had arranged for an EMT unit to wait on the other side of the green, hoping it would not be needed. But it was. A strap on the cadet's Kevlar neckband had torn loose when he fell back against the dog's barrage, revealing a thin strip of his skin beneath the collarbone, enough for the dog to find with an incisor and leave a displeasing puncture wound, to which the paramedic had attended after Augie retreated to find Stanley. The agent-in-training was astounded at the dog's strength and precision.

"What do you feed that thing?" he asked, in pain.

"FBI cadets," said the paramedic matter-of-factly.

Stanley watched with concern as Kitt examined Augie.

"He's perfect. Not a mark on him," she declared. "He was great, wasn't he?"

"He was. And me?" asked Stanley.

"Pretty damn good, Stanley. Pretty damn good. Did you think it might have been real?"

"The thought occurred to me. It was awfully violent."

"In that case, you were *very* damn good. You were actually frightened and you still held up and followed the routine. Brew will be pleased."

"Your gun. Why did you fire it? You didn't tell me there would be shooting tonight."

"Not specifically tonight," she said. "But I told you there could be noise and gunfire in an attack. I used my gun tonight because that's part of his exercise too. Nothing excites a dog like gunfire. He's trained not to run from it, but he needs that practice too. They were blanks, of course."

She had picked up the discarded leash and reconnected it to the release clasp.

"Hope you don't mind; I left the cigar," she said.

"I'll put it on my expense report," he said. "Where's the recruit from Quantico?"

"I asked if he wanted to come meet you," Kitt said.

"And?"

"He asked if Augie would be there."

36

A POOR ASSUMPTION

★ ★ ★ The North Korean killers were wrong. The Stockholm police called in Interpol as soon as young Hemelstaan's body was found early the next morning inside the entry of the plain cement building on little Schliist Street by the manager of the upstairs rental suites.

The scene did not look like a simple robbery at all to the police, or to Lars LaToure, the chief investigator of Interpol's Stockholm unit. It might have had the young man's body been left where he was plainly killed, on the sidewalk outside, or if he had been attacked and killed in the foyer where his efficiently murdered body was found. But it was instantly clear to LaToure that the fatal strike to Hemelstaan's neck had been made on the outside pavement, and that he was then dragged inside the entry, presumably using the victim's card key. If just the robbery of a man, why take him inside? And leaving a *single* piece of definitive identification, photo and all, was oddly amateurish. In a mugging, you either take the whole wallet or you take the cash and the credit cards and drop the rest in the rubbish, the detective adduced. It was too obvious. It was intentional. The attackers wanted the man to be identified—unambiguously and without effort. There had to be a reason for that.

LaToure went to the home of Hemelstaan's parents before noon.

They lived in the eastern sector of Kista, a middle-class residential district where many of the workers in the thriving commercial sector of west Kista resided. LaToure knew that uniformed officers from the Stockholm police department had already visited, only an hour earlier, to tell them the shocking news. That is why he hurried. In his experience, it was better to interview a victim's family as soon as possible. Grief deepened in the days that followed a murder. Numbness set in and grew. Memories of loved ones were often arrested before perpetrators were. Communication was difficult. But if you could reach them quickly enough, you might find them still in a state of surprising clarity of thought. You could beat the numbing haze.

That appeared to be the case with the Swedish hacker's parents. They welcomed LaToure in and offered him coffee, which he accepted. Their affect, for the moment, was of great surprise, not of horror or deep emotionality. His father spoke easily about his son. He was proud that Sven had held his job at TransEuro Logistiques for over two years, a duration he considered unusual in these days. Young people seemed to move around in their work so often.

LaToure let them speak about their son at length before starting his gentle questioning. Did they know that he was renting a cubicle space in the shared office floor on Schliist Street? Yes, they said, he was showing industry by taking on extra work as a freelancer for a tourism company. He'd been sought out for the work by a coworker of his girlfriend at the Park Hyatt, they said. He needed a place to do the work because he could not, per company policy, use the equipment of his regular employer. It was technical work he was familiar with.

"And what kind of work was that?" LaToure asked.

Internet security, they told him. It was his area at the trucking logistics company too. The tour company needed help safeguarding the credit cards of its customers. Right up his alley, they said.

Indeed, thought Lars LaToure, *and very possibly the alley that led him to his murder on little Schliist Street the night before.*

"There was no computer in his cubicle when it was searched this morning," the investigator disclosed to them. "I assume he had a laptop or tablet?"

"Yes, he had a Mac laptop. Took it everywhere."

"Just that? No others?"

"Only the one."

"And you are sure it is not here?"

"It isn't. We looked. The other officers asked this morning. Would you like more coffee?"

LaToure said, "Yes, that is very kind." It was the time in interviews such as this that he became uncomfortable, restless with his standing as a visitor, one who could not be refused, even in the worst of circumstances. He decided that he needed only two more pieces of information.

"Are there brothers or sisters to Sven?" he asked.

"No, he was our only."

LaToure grimaced. He was sorry to hear that, for them. "And could you provide the name of his girlfriend at the Park Hyatt?"

"It's Marie. Marie Fisk. Poor girl."

"Fiske with an *e*?"

"No, I don't think so," the father said.

The Interpol man rose to leave. He moved very near to the parents and took the hands of the mother. He marshaled a smile.

"I have asked you many questions," he said. "Do you have any for me?"

He knew enough to allow a long time for an answer. He stood patiently, making no motion toward the door. The parents exchanged looks; the mother finally spoke.

"The other officers said he was killed with a knife. To his throat," she said.

"Yes," said LaToure. "A single strike. It was very rapid."

"Then is it really necessary to perform an autopsy?" she asked. "I do not want him violated any more!" He could see the imploration in her dark eyes. He knew it was not his decision, but he knew also that he could influence it. And he also knew already that this was almost certainly a professional killing by international actors, assassins who would never be found. There would never be a trial or the presentation of evidence, or the droning on of a coroner in formaldehydic tone. There was no true need for an autopsy.

"I think it is clear enough what happened," said the investigator. "I will urge not. I will urge strongly."

And then the Swedish parents broke down and cried.

37

TO KUWAIT OR NOT TO KUWAIT

★ ★ ★ Stanley was in daily communication with the Army Corps of Engineers at the construction site in Kuwait through a secure phone line that Brew had arranged for the purpose. To be doubly sure that the conversations were not heard, the Navy SEAL had NSA specialists tracking each call in real time with devices that could detect any attempt at infiltration and terminate the call at once if any were observed. None was.

The military engineers were pouring the foundation stanchions to Stanley's meticulous specifications. Even they did not know the purpose to which their work would be put. They knew it was a covert project because they were working in civilian worker uniforms at the field adjoining the Kuwaiti petroleum facility and were not permitted to return to the United States military base in the evenings. Instead, they were housed in barracks of an oil field contractor at the site. Each day digital measurements were taken and the data uplinked to a military satellite, then bounced around the globe through numerous reflectors, before their final destination on Stanley's secure office computer in Pittsburgh.

Stanley thought the army corps' work excellent, but he was still uneasy. Never, never had he supervised an underground project from afar. He told Brew he felt like he was stepping around boxes in a dark basement with a poor flashlight. If the support structures were not perfectly aligned with his many pages of drawings, the soldiers installing the beryllium panels and flanges the next month would be at sea. He wanted to go to Kuwait and inspect the foundation work himself.

Brew was opposed. Stanley had now been working more than three months. It had been necessary to involve more component suppliers than pleased Brew, though he trusted Stanley that it was unavoidable to do so. NSA and the FBI cyberteams were watching all of the suppliers around the clock. There were concerning signs. Precision Beryllium in Milwaukee and Depth Ventilation Systems in Naperville were being subjected to so-called "persistent infiltration attacks"; essentially they were being assaulted with nonstop malware penetration attempts. It was almost certain that at least a few cybermissiles had pierced firewalls. Stanley's communications could well have been compromised.

By now, all the suppliers believed—correctly—that their components would be shipped to the federal vegetable laboratory operated by the USDA near Charleston. Brew felt it must be assumed that foreign intelligence operatives, having penetrated the corporate email communications, knew it too. But *no* one, not even Kitt, knew that the ultimate destination of the custom materials was Kuwait, and that their purpose had nothing to do with vegetables or foodstuffs. Travel by Stanley to anyplace other than Charleston risked blowing that cover.

"Well, you have to weigh all of the risks," Stanley told Brew. "But I tell you, from an engineering standpoint, I really should go."

After another of Brew's dinners in RiverBridge Place, they went over it again and again. Stanley showed him laptop video sent by the army corps, and photos of their digital measurements, pointing out blurs and smudges that worried him. They retired to the deck overlooking the river with snifters of B&B from Stanley's shelf.

"I just don't know," said Brew. "Something doesn't feel right. But I will keep thinking about it."

38

A POOR CHOICE AND A CONCLUSION

✳ ✳ ✳ The Park Hyatt in Stockholm resembled the one in Hamburg, where LaToure had attended a conference of Interpol investigative chiefs a few years earlier. Rich dark wood abounded with quality brass trim and hardware, finely machined and brought from Germany. A huge fireplace at one end of the lobby burned real wood, a concession somehow achieved in global environmental accords, or perhaps enjoyed in spite of them. LaToure sat in an armchair near the embers, burning even in June. Marie Fisk, even more lovely, he thought, than young Hemelstaan himself probably imagined her, sat in another.

She had learned of the killing from Sven's father that morning. He had sensed how serious his son was about her. He knew of their upcoming plans for Zurich. He told her the local police had come, and Interpol too. She should expect to be contacted. Probably it would be the Interpol investigator named LaToure. He seemed kind and professional.

So, Lars needed no introduction.

They covered history quickly. She had met Sven at an internet café on the residential side of Kista about a year earlier. He had seemed a little awkward and too studious for her.

"Nerdy, would you say?" asked Lars.

"I thought so at first. He was so tall and skinny, with those glasses with such small round lenses. But then me, I am Swiss, myself," she said, thrusting up her hands.

The investigator had no idea what she meant, but he did not ask.

Besides, she said, the young Swede was gentle, and handsome in his way. He was hardworking. He talked nicely about his parents, and his mother especially. She liked this. He was not pushy physically, though she'd made it a point to put no restriction on matters of sexual affection. At first she considered he must be quite shy. But it turned out he wasn't.

"He wasn't shy *at all*," she said, again thrusting her hands upward.

The investigator had a good idea what she meant, but he did not confirm.

"His parents say he was working nights doing internet security for a travel company," Lars said. "Was he?"

"No, that is not right," she said. "It wasn't for a travel company. He said that because he didn't want to tell them what he was really doing. He thought they would not approve."

"Why would that be?"

"He didn't know whether it was legal or not."

"That seems odd."

"Well, it was government work, but not for Sweden."

"What government?"

"I don't know. He never would tell me. I asked him, but he would only say he was working through Berlin. So, I asked him if he was working for Germany. He said, 'No, but I am working through Berlin, doing internet work.' He asked me to stop asking about it; he said it was nothing important. He said no one was getting hurt by what he did." She paused and began to well up. "And now this."

"If it helps at all, let me say I think he believed what he told you," the investigator said. "He probably had no idea what it was about."

"I told my friends I thought he was hacking for some foreign government," she said. "Somewhere inside, I think it worried me. But I never told him it did." She was wiping tears. "If I had, do you think this would have happened?"

Lars stood to leave. He reached down and touched her shoulder gently.

"He made his own choice, Marie. It was not an informed choice. They are the worst kind. They tend to be poor. It is not on your shoulders."

What a shame, he thought, as he walked out to the early evening air of Stockholm. *A young man with everything to look ahead to. From a good family, now shattered. And a lovely young woman left behind, troubled that she was somehow complicit.*

He decided to assemble his notes and walk to his office to complete his report. Nearing the Interpol office, he stopped at a favorite bar and ordered a whiskey. He often gathered his thoughts there after days like this one.

"Surprise me," he said to the familiar bartender.

"Yeah, right," the bartender replied.

He knew what his Interpol regular always wanted, and poured it: Bushmills Irish Whiskey on ice.

He flipped through his notes. He still used the traditional small spiral pad of an earlier time. He didn't trust cell phone apps. He wanted to turn paper, and turn it again. Back and forth he went through the pages, pausing to sip his whiskey.

Lars LaToure was making up his mind.

The report was back from the forensics team at Schliist Street. No prints—none—in the young Swede's cubicle, other than his own. A poor-quality surveillance camera mounted on the second level of a building down the block showed a grainy image of two men in brimmed hats and dark clothing appearing to enter and shortly later leave the building where the body was discovered, but the angle provided no view of the recessed entryway or what occurred there.

He called home to his wife so that she would not worry.

"I am going back to the office now to prepare a referral sheet. I will take it to Nemrov tomorrow."

His wife knew Nemrov, the attaché at the Russian Embassy in Stockholm. The LaToure and Nemrov sons played suburban hockey together, and the parents shared driving duties.

"Why Nicolas?" she asked.

"I think he will be interested. Him or his colleague in Berlin."

At his office, he prepared his standard referral sheet, merely a page, on his Interpol letterhead. It contained a description of the murder, his conclusion that foreign agents targeting the victim for an undetermined governmental purpose had likely committed it, and a photo of the slain Swede reproduced from an Interpol passport file. He placed it in a brown business-size envelope that he slipped into his slim briefcase, and went home to his waiting wife.

It was odd, he thought. The day had been sadly inconclusive and conclusive at the same time.

39

COMMERCIAL RELATIONS

★ ★ ★ At the Russian Embassy, the clouded glass door to the office of Nicolas Nemrov bore black etched letters: Commercial Relations. The visiting Interpol chief of investigations knew it to be a ruse. But he made a point of *not* making a point of the perfunctory deception. It was one of the many attributes of LaToure that Nemrov appreciated.

They were on such terms that Lars enjoyed kitchen privileges in the beverage area on Nemrov's floor in the embassy. He walked into his friend's office carrying two espressos, sugar in Nemrov's, as he knew he preferred. The Russian greeted him with a wide smile. He reached across his desk, shaking LaToure's hand with one of his own, accepting the espresso with the other.

"So, on what commercial relations business do you come this morning, Lars?" he asked.

The Interpol visitor settled into the only chair across from his host's desk.

"There was a killing on Schliist Street in west Kista the night before last. Did you hear of it?"

It was not an idle question. There had been no press reports of the murder, as Lars and the Stockholm police had agreed to suppress news of the killing for the time being. But LaToure thought it entirely possible that Russian intelligence already knew. He leaned forward in his chair, examining the eyes of his friend closely.

"No, but I suspect I am about to."

Truthful. No doubt truthful, Lars concluded. He could tell a deceiving Russian from twenty meters. Nemrov did not know of the young Swede's killing, he was sure. This was important. It meant, almost certainly, that Hemelstaan's death was not at the hand of the Russians. If it were, Nemrov would have known. It was always his duty to deal with the response to any messy activities of Russian operatives in the city. No, the Russians did not kill the young man or order his killing.

Lars withdrew the brown envelope from his case and handed it across the desk. Nemrov, now serious, put down his espresso cup and opened the clasp of the envelope. He looked up at his friend from Interpol.

"You think I will know this person?" he asked.

"I doubt you *will* know him," Lars said. "But it may be that you *did* know him."

Nemrov pulled out the single sheet and looked at the photo. His face changed from one lacking expression to one of disapproval, a hint of anger.

"You are right, my friend. He is familiar," he said. *Familiar* was a carefully selected word. LaToure understood its meaning and why it was being used. Nemrov could not explicitly confirm that the dead young Swede had been in the service of the Russians, and no such confirmation was therefore to be recorded. But it was permissible for Interpol and Lars to conclude, with discretion, that he was.

"He had a girlfriend," Lars said.

Nemrov nodded.

"She says the boy told her he was working through Berlin," Lars said.

Nemrov nodded again.

"Could she be in danger too?" Lars asked.

"I sincerely hope not," the Russian said.

"Let us not rely on hope," Lars said.

"Agreed," said Nemrov. To show his sincerity, the Russian reached at once for his phone. "You are not hearing this," he said as he punched numbers he knew by heart. His call was answered, it seemed to Lars, almost before the last number was entered.

"Pasha," said Nemrov. "Hemelstaan has been executed. I don't know by whom. Put three people on Marie Fisk. See that at least one is a woman so she can enter bathrooms and such. Make sure no harm comes to her."

Lars heard a deep voice come back over the phone.

"At least a month," Nemrov said to the voice. "If harm is planned for her, it will happen by then." Before ending the call, he looked over to his Interpol friend. His brows were raised, an expression seeking approval. Yes, a month should be sufficient. Lars nodded.

40

THE JEEP FROM TURJ

★ ★ ★ In the stealthy approach to the Turj hospital weeks earlier, General Williamson had ordered his special forces to allow free passage to the Jeep Wrangler carrying two terrorists away from the site. He knew the decision was right when he made it. But he could not have anticipated the value it would later produce.

On his order, a drone high above tracked the Jeep. It traveled six hours through the ridges and valleys toward Kandahar, and then headed west across the Helmand Valley until it reached a small village near Farah, only sixty miles from the Iranian border. On the edge of the village the Jeep pulled into a small compound. The drone captured it all on video. The two hostiles carried crates—one each, about the size of banker's boxes—into the unlit structure. There were no other vehicles at the site, no signs of habitation. They stayed only minutes before returning empty-handed to the Jeep and driving on to nearby Farah.

Williamson's team at MacDill studied the video. Why had the two terrorists made the long drive to deliver just two crates? What was in them? Why was the small compound empty and unguarded? *Unless it was because the terrorists did not want attention called to it,* Williamson thought. Nothing attracted less interest to searching forces than deserted outposts. There were too many such compounds that *were* occupied to worry about those that weren't.

His first instinct was to send a reconnaissance team immediately to check the little compound. But the Iranians were conducting military exercises along the border between Farah and Herat, the larger Afghan city north of it. Despite protests from the Afghan government, the Iranian forces were regularly spilling over the border. There were reports that some Iranian units had even entered the city of Farah itself, intimidating the locals before retreating.

The general issued a preparation order directing that a six-person SEAL team plan and execute a nighttime entry into the compound at the edge of Farah as soon as regional command on the ground deemed it probable that it could be accomplished without detection. That time now came.

The SEALs were dropped in on the western side of the Farah River, only a mile from the compound. But the compound sat to the east of the river; they would have to cross it. "Why not drop you on the other side of the river?" asked the army helicopter pilot.

"Because we are SEALs" was the answer. But in truth, there was a good reason. The city sat on an elevated plain above the river, dotted by numerous small villages. Any approach from the elevated land would be visible from three directions. But a drop on the eastern bank of the river would permit an unwitnessed approach up the steep bank on its other side. The compound sat only a thousand yards beyond the top of the riverbank.

As planned, their approach and entry was unobserved. The rear door to the empty compound was secured by two large padlocks, but its frame was not well reinforced. They were able to knock it in without use of an explosive charge. At first they saw nothing of interest as they combed the interior with helmet and hand lights. The place was barren, except for a few sleeping cots and tattered woven floor mats. They kicked the floorboards to see if there were any hollow spaces below. There weren't. Until there was. In one corner, the farthest from the front entry on the first floor, a section of the floor answered their feet like a bass drum. They kicked away a soiled mat and exposed a recessed handgrip. It lifted easily, like the hatch to a crawl space, with a three-step ladder attached to one side of the hole. The compartment measured about three feet by four feet, sided all around with plywood. Fiberglass insulation was stapled to the plywood. A plastic pot of dehumidification chemical sat in the center of the space, between two large fruit crates. The SEAL leader lay on the floor over the compartment and ran his light carefully around the edge of each crate lid; then, leaning in, he ran his finger gently around the underside of one of them. He motioned to the others to move well away. Then he reached in and removed the lid he had examined.

"We may be here awhile," he said. "Look at this."

Inside the first crate were at least a dozen detachable HP hard drives. Ever careful, he did not immediately lift the lid of the second crate. He ran his finger around its underside, as gently and slowly as he had the first. When lifted, it produced the same result; it too was filled with hard drives.

The other SEALs knew what their team leader had meant by his comment about a longer visit to the compound. In their mission briefing, they had been told not to disturb any electronic equipment they might find. They understood why. For years, such devices had been seized on-site and taken back for technical analysis for the intelligence they could—and often did—provide. But it turned out there was a disadvantage in taking the devices in that way, and even a dark side. Once the terrorists learned that the information had been compromised, they often rendered the intelligence useless by changing the plans and tactics that it disclosed. Worse, in more than a few instances, attempts to capitalize on information—when known by the terrorists to have been compromised—were met with ambushes, booby traps, and severe losses.

The Special Forces command on the ground was prepared for

these situations now. The SEALs' leader called in the discovery. Was a technology specialist available to come and copy the drives so the originals could be left in place, apparently undisturbed? Yes, there was a rested ranger at Bagram with the skills, he was told. He would be sent immediately and dropped at the same landing zone. But there was another problem, the SEAL leader reported.

"We knocked in a door to get in," he told command. "It's banged up good, even though we didn't blow it. It needs repair if you want to leave this place the way we found it."

"We'll send someone for that too," the officer at command said.

"You mean a carpenter?"

"Yes, we'll find one. Send pictures of the damage—both sides of the door and frame. Wait near the landing zone until they get there. Engage no one unless you have to. Don't be seen."

"We're good at that," the SEAL replied.

They moved silently away, the same way they had come. When they reached the river, they slid in, enjoying the cooler water. Only their helmets, eyes, and noses could be seen above the water, and then only to a trained eye. They looked like turtles waiting in the moonlight.

Waiting, as it were, for a computer specialist and a carpenter.

41

THE STYLE TO WHICH HE
WAS ACCUSTOMED

★ ★ ★ He was still undecided about sending Stanley to Kuwait
to inspect the foundation work, but Brew's preparations for the
training of the soldier installers were complete. He texted Stanley
and Kitt and told them to be ready to leave for Charleston within
a week, probably immediately after the Fourth of July weekend.
Finding the personnel had not been as difficult as Brew had feared.
The information in the Army Reserve's database was well organized.
Reserve soldiers with construction experience were easily identified.
To reduce the risk of personality problems, Brew restricted his
selections to soldiers with at least one previous overseas deployment,
but not more than two. He was surprised how many there were,
and how detailed the deployment records were. After the problem
of high suicide rates in the military had come to light during the
prolonged war in Iraq, it had become standard practice to conduct
psychiatric examinations of soldiers serving overseas deployments.
Brew found the psychiatrists' reports especially helpful, both in
eliminating candidates with histories of personal conflict and in
highlighting those who demonstrated composure under stress and
positive interpersonal traits.

e searched also for someone with civil engineering credentials
ar with the digital leveling and measurement devices Stanley
would bring to Charleston. Two were found. Brew called each to
discuss their backgrounds. Each seemed eager for the assignment
and equally qualified. But Brew ruled one out on humanitarian
grounds; he had a child in treatment at Saint Jude's. He chose the
other, who turned out to be the senior-most in rank for the entire
group of call-ups. She was Colonel Helen Ames, attached to the
Reserve Army Corps of Engineers in Saint Louis. She was also the
oldest at fifty-eight.

Kitt secured a late-model Suburban from the FBI livery in
Pittsburgh. Stanley told her he was not accustomed to driving such
a large vehicle, but she insisted it was the best choice, all things
considered. It had been used mostly for canine work and was fitted
with an ample crate for Augie in the rear. And she would do most
of the driving.

They left early on the first workday after the holiday, taking
Interstate 79 south out of Pittsburgh into West Virginia; then
I-77 through the southwestern slice of Virginia; and finally, down
through North Carolina, picking up I-26 to Charleston. "Good old
Ike," commented Stanley. Kitt didn't know it was Eisenhower who
pushed through the interstate highway system. The great general
had masterfully moved Allied troops around and across several
continents and the high seas. But perhaps his signature achievement
as president was in moving Americans around their own nation.

The stretch through the hills of West Virginia was filled
with frequent steep descents and perilous curves. L.T. drove not
unreasonably, but the grade was so extreme in places that it was
difficult to keep the big Suburban to the stated speed. At one point
on a hairpin turn, she left the lane and traveled on the rumble strips
for several seconds.

"Sorry, Stanley," she said.

"No worries," he said. "How are the tires on this thing?"

"Brand new," she said. "I had them change them, after what happened the last time I came down here."

"Oh?"

"You want to know?"

"Sure."

"It wasn't anything recent. Six years ago," she said.

"Well, now you have to tell me." They were still descending an interminable hill.

"It wasn't far from where we are now, really. Did you ever hear of Dudley Lazarus?" she asked.

"Never. That I can think of."

"I wish I'd never heard of him either," she said. "Guy was a creep."

"A criminal?"

"Yes, but more of a witness. He was an undertaker."

Stanley, struck by the description, turned toward her. One didn't hear that term much anymore. "An undertaker?"

"That's what they called him in the county. West Virginia, east of Charleston, maybe an hour or so. Nearest good-sized town is Elkins. He ran a funeral and cremation service outside of town there."

"What did you have to do with him? But stay on the road while you tell me."

"He'd set up this place in an old building left over from the logging business along the Elk River. This father and son are up in a deer hunting blind near the river. It's winter. They're from around there; they know everybody. Late afternoon, they see a van come down the river road and pull into Dudley's place. Looks like bodies are taken into the place. They thought three of them. The guys in the van leave, and pretty soon they see the dark smoke fuming out of the building. Couple hours later, they stop at the gas market to fill up, and the sheriff's there. 'Who died?' he asks the sheriff. 'Nobody,' says the sheriff. 'Well, Lazarus is burning somebody up there,' the hunter tells him. And that's what cracked the Allentown mob case."

That did ring a bell for Stanley.

"The Russian thing?" he asked.

"Serbians," L.T. said. "Versus the Russians. So, I guess you'd say Serbians *and* Russians. But it was the Serb thugs who brought the bodies to him. They'd drive them down in twos and threes, and creepy Dudley did the rest."

"And what does this have to do with new tires?" Stanley asked.

"So, the sheriff goes out there to see Dudley, asks to see the death certificates. The guy breaks down completely, tells the sheriff everything. He's been getting rid of remains for these people for three years. A thousand bucks a corpse. He doesn't want to keep doing it, but he's afraid of them."

"I would say the last part is probably true," said Stanley.

"The bureau gets into it and makes it clear to old Dudley that he's in for a half dozen felonies, even a charge of accomplice to murder. His way out is to testify against the thugs and take his chances in witness protection. Maybe he won't be found. And you know what the guy asks? 'Can I still be an undertaker?'" L.T. and Stanley both laughed.

"Well, he was certainly a morbid thinker," said Stanley.

"So, I'm sent down here in January to protect him until he testifies at the trial. I bring a great dog. Louise. But the place they have for us is in the middle of nowhere. A little house on the same river, upstream twenty miles in Webster Springs. After two days, everything about it is making me nervous, including creepy Dudley. It's dark as hell, there's always wind, I don't think I can hear well enough. I ask for help, and Len Warren, a straight-up agent from Scranton, comes over to join me. It's like the very next night, and we see an old car coming down the mountain road, real slow. It stops for a long time out at the mailbox, then backs up and starts coming in the dirt drive. Len tells me to take the witness out the back to the car and run for it across the yard. He'll stay with the dog and try to get rid of them. All hell breaks loose. Len is firing on them and the dog is going nuts, and one of the thugs gets back in their car and comes after me and Dudley."

Stanley noticed a yellow diamond-shaped sign: six-degree grade, next two miles.

"Maybe you should concentrate on driving," he said apprehensively. She seemed to ignore him.

"It's January, but there's no snow," L.T. continued. "But it's cold and rainy. I'm juicing this Chevy Tahoe around a bend and the damn thing spins a three-sixty, and then some. We slide down off the side of the gravel shoulder and bump, jerk, bump into the woods. How we didn't catch a tree trunk, I'll never know. I cut the lights, and ten seconds later the thug flies past us."

"My God."

"I didn't trust the creep, so I handcuffed him and we walked back to the house."

"Were they okay there?"

"Len killed two of them."

"How many were there?"

"Two."

"And the dog? Louise?"

"She was hit in the chest. We had to put her down the next day."

"Oh," said Stanley. "I am sorry, L.T."

There was silence in the Suburban for a solid five minutes.

"They told me later the tires on the Tahoe were worn," Kitt finally said. "It shouldn't have been in service that way."

There was another long pause.

"Maybe it was a good thing," Stanley said. "Maybe it saved you."

"I've thought of that," she said. "But I learned from it, anyway."

The story put L.T. in a pensive mood. She hardly spoke for the next hundred miles.

As they approached Charleston, Stanley told her this would

have been a three-day drive in the old days. They pulled up to the Meeting Street Inn in Charleston's old section in nine hours and seventeen minutes.

Brew did not want them staying in any one place for too long. And he disfavored larger hotels or national brands. They had too many points of ingress and egress and therefore were difficult to watch with the small team he had arranged with the Charleston FBI field office and its agent-in-charge, Bobby Beach. But he learned that what Kitt had told him was correct. Charleston was blessed with a bevy of small boutique hotels, one more character-rich than the next, catering to ever-growing tourism and the city's signature reputation as a premier venue for destination weddings. They stayed no longer than four nights in any one location.

Brew also required adjoining rooms with pass-through doors, which made reservations a challenge at some of the hotels and in a couple of cases resulted—to Stanley's delight—in luxurious accommodation in special suites, because they were all that was available with pass-through adjoining rooms.

"I must say, Tyler," he said of one such spacious suite at the Andrew Pinckney Inn, "this *is* the style to which I am accustomed." Brew was not humored. Neither were the staff members of any of the hotels about the presence of Augie. A couple of them permitted dogs on a routine basis but limited their size, normally to thirty pounds. Augie's last physical charted him at ninety-five. But Brew had every base covered. Bobby Beach, the local FBI chief, accompanied Kitt and Stanley in to each new reception desk on their arrival date. He discussed the situation—a matter of importance to law enforcement—in low southern tones with each house manager, while Stanley, Kitt, and the dog waited quietly to the side. L.T. handled Augie personally on each arrival. He sat straightly next to her, soundless and motionless, like a statue. It was amazing how FBI credentials influenced hotel policy, especially when extended in the

calm, professional manner of Bobby Beach, supported by a pe
trained canine. Every hotel admitted the whole team.

The Charleston agent-in-charge kept a low profile in town.
Bobby Beach abjured publicity, avoiding the limelight that was his
for the asking in view of his position. It was in keeping with his
natural modesty. Born and raised in Charleston, he'd been sent back
home five years earlier, at age fifty-five, for the final lap of a long
career. He cut the figure of a seasoned agent. He liked to say he was
glad to at last look his age, referring to his full head of thick, neatly
groomed hair that had turned snow white in his thirties. He was
not tall, but he was lean and strong, with thick wrists that served
him well as a long hitter off the tee at Charleston Country Club,
where he was a frequent guest. On his own dime, he was a fixture
at the Municipal, the exceptionally maintained public course on
adjoining James Island that Charlestonians had been enjoying for
one hundred years. He was friendly but not gregarious, selective in
his words but not reticent. Mostly, he was calm and steady in all
weathers. He rarely wore the patented deep blue FBI jacket, even
in the cooler months. He thought it officious. Especially around
other law enforcement officers, he resisted the temptation to assert
the bureau's status and clout. To see him with a group of officers
in uniform, you would think he was one of them and had simply
forgotten to wear his own. He respected them authentically, and
they respected him, in large part because of his respect for them.
And they were happy to help him anytime. If Brew did not know
this immediately about Bobby Beach, he would certainly come to
learn it.

Brew joined Stanley and Kitt for dinner the first night. He
brought a list of the called-up reserves, including information on
the background of each. Stanley had suggested an installation crew
of twelve. Brew added an additional person so that one could be
designated as the chief. Stanley thought that wise. After the training
was under way, they would select a leader from among them.

Stanley ran down Brew's list and made mental notes. Ten men, three women. Most of the reserves were astonishingly young, he thought. Half were under twenty-five. All were under thirty-five. Except one.

"What's this about?" Stanley asked. He pointed to the name in the middle of the list: "Ames, Helen Col. Age fifty-eight."

"I think she's the brains of the outfit," Brew said. "She's a civil engineer, like you."

42

LEFT AS IT WAS FOUND

★ ★ ★ At Special Forces Command at MacDill, Ben Williamson reviewed the reports from Farah, Afghanistan. The discovered storage drives had been copied and returned to their crates as they'd been found. The ranger computer specialist had taken care to leave no indicators of his duplication work. An army sergeant from the maintenance unit, whose regular assignment was the building of plywood barracks at Base Bagram, was wakened in his bunk and told he was needed.

"What do I need to bring?" he asked.

"Whatever you need to make this look the way it used to look," said his commander, holding out pictures of the shattered door sent by the waiting SEALs.

"Piece of cake," he said, blurry-eyed.

In four hours, and fortunately before sunrise, the mission was completed. The hardest part turned out to be getting the sergeant carpenter across the river on arrival and back again on departure. He was a big man and afraid to swim. The SEALs used a procedure intended for taking wounded persons across water, forming a kind of human raft made of four SEALs swimming in a diamond formation, with the passenger riding atop them. The sergeant was plainly embarrassed to require the special help. He apologized repeatedly when they reached the other side. A young SEAL put him at ease.

"Forget it, Sergeant," he said. "We do our thing, you do yours. We couldn't hit a nail in three tries. Glad you're here."

As the group made their way back to the helicopter, the SEAL leader muddied up the new hinges and raked the earth around the compound with fallen branches so that their disruptions would not be noticeable. The closest thing to gunfire were a few muffled spurts from the carpenter sergeant's cordless drill. Farah was left as it was found.

Williamson immediately studied the summaries of what was found on the first drives. He had intended to wait until the rest of the information had been digested before calling the president. But what he read changed his mind. He pulled a small leather folio from the shirt pocket of his uniform and found the special access number he needed.

His call would be diverted immediately by the White House switchboard and given priority over others.

In about a minute, Winters was on the phone.

"What is it, General?" she asked.

"We may need Eaglets' Nest sooner than we hoped," he said.

She told him to call back in ten minutes. She would get the national security team into the Situation Room.

43

JUST FOR VEGETABLES

★ ★ ★ Nicolas Nemrov and his colleagues in Berlin were furious with the killing of their young operative in Stockholm. In the world spy game, there were certain rules that were not broken, certain lines that were not crossed—not among professionals. There were good reasons for these conventions. Efficient intelligence and counterintelligence systems depended on their adherence, especially in these times when alliances were so nuanced, when it could rarely be said that one was clearly an enemy or clearly a friend. The truth was that an enemy today was a friend tomorrow. Sides were always shifting. One thing remained constant: you did not kill operatives involved in noncombative activity. You just didn't. Quite apart from the disrespect it showed, it had other serious repercussions. For one thing, how was anyone going to recruit these young computer braniacs when they were turning up with slashed throats in dingy foyers? No, Pyongyang had made a fine mess of things.

Nemrov and the Berlin handler reviewed all of the fruits of Sven Hemelstaan's hacking labors, including his recent discovery that the North Koreans had observed his own real-time monitoring. With admirable completeness, they had followed the correspondence between Precision Beryllium Company and this engineer from Pittsburgh. Nemrov and his Berlin counterparts knew it was true that beryllium parts were critical to the fabrication of modern nuclear warheads. That was why the company in Milwaukee was monitored in the first place. But beryllium fabrications were used also in thousands of other nonmilitary applications. And the volume and thickness of the panels and parts that were being supplied was wildly outside the parameters for materials used for weapons manufacture. Technical sources in Moscow confirmed this. Also, the engineer's orders were being shipped to a farm science laboratory in South Carolina for a storage installation; so was the ancillary equipment, ventilation fans and small hydraulic power systems he had ordered from other suppliers. They concluded that young Sven Hemelstaan had died for nothing.

"For vegetables they killed him," said Nemrov. "For goddamned vegetables."

"I am afraid so," the Berlin handler agreed.

They decided to recommend to their superiors that the Americans be told what had happened. It was, they considered, a matter both of decency and self-interest. If the killers from Pyongyang could thoughtlessly murder the Swedish hacker, maybe they would pursue this American Bigelow too. One murder on account of vegetables was quite enough. But it was also, they surmised, a good thing to help the Americans from time to time when it was harmless to do so. It was a principle of spy craft to be helpful when you could be. Tallies were kept of such courtesies. It could be useful somewhere down the road.

44

OMINOUS NEWS

★ ★ ★ As the president listened in the Situation Room with Lazar, Jennings, Hastings, and each of their deputies, General Williamson described the information examined so far on the storage drives found in Farah. Much more information would be forthcoming, he told them. Only about half of the drives had been downloaded and translated. But what was learned already was very concerning.

It also presented an opportunity.

For decades, terrorist factions had operated independently of one another in many critical respects. Bin Laden's al-Qaeda had not cooperated with ISIS or more recent players such as Hasikan Jahideen. And the Taliban had never mingled much with any of them, even in Afghanistan where the group was concentrated. Governments in the region, and the Americans too, assessed this fragmentation as both a blessing and a curse. It was a good thing in that it inherently limited the terrorists' critical mass. A hundred terrorists, or even a few thousand, could make short-term gains but could not hold them long against Western military power and the growing competency of Middle East militaries. But it was a bad thing because it meant that large numbers of terrorists could never be eliminated at one time. It was guerilla warfare in the deserts and mountains. Overall progress was excruciatingly slow. Radicals were killed in the tens, twenties, thirties; new terrorists were recruited as quickly as trained ones could be destroyed.

The information retrieved from the small compound near the Iranian border, if real, changed that calculus dramatically. The documents set out strategies of combination, including time lines and locations. Weapons caches were being consolidated in places where they could be defended, or so thought the terrorists. Fighting forces as large as thirty thousand, and more than one of them, were contemplated. There was even evidence that the groups were working together on technical and logistical matters to improve their monetization of oil supplies taken from seized fields and refineries.

"Have you acted on any of this intelligence yet?" the president asked.

"No."

"Good. Take no actions that could be attributed to this discovery. We can't yet know what to do with it, but we certainly do not want any of them to know we have it."

"It is awfully tempting, Madam President," Williamson said. "It says bin Laden's grandson will be in Kabul for a meeting in two weeks. We could pick him off easily."

"No," said the president. "We hold. Do you agree with me?"

"I do," said the general. "Painfully, I do."

President Winters knew well that President Bill Clinton had been second-guessed on his own decision to forgo a missile strike on Osama bin Laden himself when he had the chance to do so years before 9/11, when nary an American had even heard of him or his al-Qaeda organization. Del had discussed it with her father, who had been in the loop on that decision. She had asked him if he thought Clinton made a good decision.

"He did that because the missiles available were not nearly as accurate as what we have today," Henry had told her. "And he knew that innocents, probably dozens or hundreds of them, would be killed if he ordered it. If he knew then what we all learned later, what bin Laden was planning for New York and Washington, he would have ordered it, and a dozen more if needed. He had issues on other things, that's for sure. But on his decision on the bin Laden strike, I didn't fault him them, and I don't now."

Then the president asked everyone to consider whether, as a technical military matter, the new capabilities of Eaglets' Nest, which Brew said might be completed in August, could be used to deal with the new information. In their considerations, no one—no one—was to be consulted who was not already part of the core loop. She said she was not looking, as of now, for views as to whether the new weapons *should* be used or the geopolitical consequences if they were. All that she wanted was their assessments as to whether they would be effective *if* used, and whether they could be deployed so quickly if she so decided.

A serious silence came over the room. She adjourned the meeting.

45

THE DECENT THING FROM MOSCOW

★ ★ ★ CIA director Hastings was surprised by the call coming in to him on his secure line. It was rare to hear directly from Russian intelligence. But he knew the woman who was calling. The Russian president had brought Marraka Yevzelsky to the United States on an official visit a few months earlier, for the purpose of introducing her to Hastings. He felt there should be some level of comity in communications between them. And the US president had agreed. From her military background and knowledge of its history, she knew that even in the furthest depths of the Cold War, back channels were kept open between the two countries' military commands. She concurred with the Russian leader that it should not be different in the intelligence community. It had once been so. While always officially on guard and very private about it, the CIA and the KGB and its progeny had throughout the Cold War, and well after it into the twenty-first century, maintained discreet but reliable avenues of honest information exchange. But following the election of President Trump, and the US intelligence community's belief that Russian agents had conducted elicit technology interventions into American databases for the purpose of undermining national confidence, and even world confidence, in democratic electoral systems, those valves were tightly closed.

The Trump presidency was full of adventure and surprise, in some ways as unpredictable as his rise to national power in the first place. As a billionaire business mogul, he was an unlikely populist. But his unforeseen strategic skill in building an electoral coalition comprised of a mosaic of citizen clusters could not be denied. Nor, as it turned out, could his conviction that government bureaucracy often stifled common sense negotiation and flexibility, even in international matters, and that politicians, and many times the servants they appointed for political reasons were generally poor negotiators. Del Winters had invited the former president to the White House shortly after her inauguration. She wanted most to know how he had conducted himself privately with foreign leaders, especially ones perceived as untrustworthy, even hostile. "A smart enemy is an enemy as long as *you* believe there is no point in seeing him otherwise," he had told her. "That's because he can see your belief. Because he's a *smart* enemy. And if that's what he sees, he will stay that way. But if you can look him in the eye and make him believe that he needs to prove to you he is your *enemy*, not prove to you he is your friend, you can get somewhere." As unlike as she was in demeanor and approach from the former President Trump, Winters thought his counsel wise on this point.

It may have been why, when the Russian president called to suggest an unofficial thawing in communications between the two countries' intelligence relations, she agreed to explore it. But the spies themselves were slow to embrace the idea. When he took Yevzewlsky's call that day, Hastings had spoken with his counterpart just once since her original visit.

"Marraka," he greeted her. "I am pleased to hear from you."

"Yes, Jack," she said, businesslike. "We want you to be aware of something. That's why I am calling."

"What would that be?"

"Mr. Bigelow. Stanley Bigelow. The man from Pittsburgh. Do you know of him?"

"No," Hastings lied.

"I am not surprised," she said. "We don't think he is an intelligence operative. But in our normal activities we have been watching American defense suppliers, which I am sure you realize."

"We assume that, yes."

Though their interaction had been very limited, there was one impression Hastings had already formed about Marraka Yevzelsky: she was direct and to the point. Competent and serious, but not stiff or contriving. There were no frills, no pretensions. She was comfortable in her own skin. All of which was interesting and especially admirable to Hastings, because he knew from his own intelligence that Yevzelsky was not her true family name. Marraka Yevzel*man* had become Marraka Yevzel*sky* to disguise her Jewish heritage and permit her ascendance to the highest ranks of Russian government. Such cultural concealment was fairly common in Russia, in both business and government, but much more so for men in a society that still implicitly repressed both women and Jews. Marraka's secret was safe with Hastings.

"This man Bigelow," she said. "We picked up communications between him and some of those companies. We had installed an operative in Stockholm to do this. At first we were interested. But it turned out our own operative was being hacked by Pyongyang. Through our own man's surveillance, they learned of Bigelow."

"So?"

"Our Stockholm contractor detected the Pyongyang infiltration on his system. He reported the infiltration to us. But the North Koreans saw that report to us too. They knew that he had discovered them. They murdered him in Stockholm the next week, and took his computer."

"Outrageous."

"We thought so too," she said. "It is against all norms, using blood to flex muscles. We are not interested in this Bigelow. We will leave him alone. But the North Koreans may not. They have all the information we had about him. We thought you should know. We assume it is your FBI's job to look after this guy, but we have no channel to them. So, I called you."

"It is appreciated, Marraka. I will inform the right people."

"Maybe you will send the favor back sometime," she said.

"I hope there is that opportunity," Hastings replied.

"Well then. We have done the decent thing. I ask that you make your president aware." She did not wait for his reply or agreement. "Goodbye," she said, and hung up.

Hastings called out to his assistant in the outer office: "Find me Captain Brew."

46

THE DAILY CINTAS DELIVERY

★ ★ ★ It was the first day of formal training at the Department of Agriculture site on Highway 17 in South Carolina. A long Cintas truck entered the facility and pulled into a large warehouse behind the main building. The company provided uniforms, cleaning products, and floor mats to the facility every work day, as it did to thousands of businesses and workplaces across the country. And on this day, and each one after it for three weeks, it also delivered thirteen soldiers from their temporary deployment quarters at the Beaufort Marine flight station base forty-nine miles away.

Tyler Brew and Stanley greeted each of the reserves as they stepped out of the rear of the van. As the ranking officer, Colonel Helen Ames descended the folding stairs first. She looked commanding in every way. Even coming down the infirm steps of the van, her posture was straight and steady. To Stanley's eye, she seemed as fit as Brew and younger than her real age.

"Captain Brew," she spoke first, as she saluted the Navy SEAL, implicitly asserting superior rank. The others waited in the van behind her. "Thank you for your welcome."

Brew was not in the slightest put off, though in truth, in the formal hierarchy of military commissions, his own rank as a navy captain technically equaled hers as an army colonel. Each enjoyed the same service and payroll classification, and few would expect an active duty navy captain to accept deference to a reservist colonel. But Brew was not one to stand on ceremony, and he loved and wanted strength. He was immediately pleased that he had selected her for call-up.

"Colonel, it is an honor to have you," he said.

"Well, it looks like an unusual and interesting deployment," she replied. "I am impressed with the soldiers you've identified." She motioned, only with her head, toward the van behind her. "They are young, but their experience in construction is solid."

Brew asked Stanley to step up next to him.

"Colonel Ames, please meet Mr. Stanley Bigelow. Stanley is the civilian who has designed the installation and all of the materials. Despite his youthful appearance, he is a senior civil engineer." Stanley wriggled and the colonel smiled as Brew continued. "He will lead the training here. He feels your own professional background is very important."

"Yes," Stanley said. "Most certainly. The materials are unusual. They are all here now. The concept uses completely prefabricated components."

"But I understood the installation was underground?" the colonel asked.

"It is."

"How can you fabricate the components until you match them to the foundation pilings?"

Stanley turned toward Brew with an "I told you so" look.

"Normally you couldn't. Certainly, you wouldn't, if there was any choice," Stanley said. "But we had to make an exception in this case. I drew each of the foundation stanchions and support members so that they could be aligned digitally with laser measurement equipment. They were poured in Kuwait by the army corps and aligned with the digital devices I prescribed. I have seen all of the images, and studied them the best I can from my screen."

"Those measurements are as good as the person operating the lasers," she said, not unpleasantly, but firmly. "Transmitted images can be distorted."

"True. I told the captain that I should go to inspect and verify all of them personally. But he feels I am not a soldier."

"Good thing I am," she said.

Only moments later her comment seemed prescient. Brew's phone signaled a text message. Stanley saw his face go cold. It was a directive to call CIA Director Hastings immediately on a secure line.

"You can get started with everyone in the seminar room," Brew said to Stanley and the colonel. "I'll join you as soon as I can." Then he disappeared hurriedly into the main building.

He was gone less than ten minutes. Colonel Ames had led the other reserves into the training room, arranged with crescent tables facing a large presentation screen at the front of the room. Without suggestion from Stanley, she sat in the first row of the center aisle. Stanley was attaching the clip-on microphone to his loosened tie when Brew entered with a stern bearing. He motioned Stanley over to the wall.

"You're not going to Kuwait for sure now. You're a known man."

Earlier, Stanley had concluded that it was good to be cared about. But to be *known* was a different thing.

47

A PRESIDENTIAL VACATION

★ ★ ★ Historians would not likely note it, but one of the accomplishments of Presidents Clinton, Obama, and Trump was getting the public finally used to the idea that golf was a perfectly acceptable presidential escape from the stresses of Washington. Perhaps fueled by the public's general elation at news of Del Winters's admission to the Burning Tree Golf Club, even the partisans gave up on the potshots about the president playing golf while the nation dealt with one problem or another.

She had left Washington purely for relaxation only once since her election—yes, for a week of golf in Palm Desert. Now, she needed another break. It wouldn't do her father any harm either, he reminded her. Which prompted her idea. Stanley Bigelow was ensconced in Charleston training the reserves for the installation of the Eaglets' Nest deployment base. She had told Stanley that she would like him to meet her father. She believed they would like each other. Over drinks in the White House residence she asked Henry what he thought of a golf getaway to Kiawah Island, just south of Charleston. It was a favorite of Joe Biden, going back to his vice presidential years. Biden, except for Donald Trump, the lowest handicap in any administration since Kennedy, spent most Easters there with a friend on the island. He raved about it, and the golf courses there.

239

"And we can entertain your engineer from Pittsburgh?" Henry asked. "The baseball man?"

"Just what I was thinking," she said. "We can have him over for drinks."

"It will be awfully warm, though."

"They've done the PGA tournament there as late as August," his daughter said. "It must be tolerable."

The president wanted to see Brew too while she was there, so she asked her Secret Service detail to contact him about the arrangements. The captain was not enthused about Stanley seeing the president, especially in view of the Russian tip about the North Korean surveillance. The Secret Service leader put it into perspective for him.

"Believe me, your man couldn't be safer so long as the president is in town," he told Brew. "We will be crawling all over the place. Anyone trying to take him would be crazy to come into view of so much surveillance. We bring people in to the president and take them back out all the time when she's away. Anyway, we will use an alias for him in case the press picks up on it."

Brew consented, and arrangements were detailed in the next week. Stanley would be secreted into the Sanctuary Hotel on the island the night before the president's arrival. Many from the press would be coming in then too; another early arrival wouldn't be noteworthy. He would have cocktails with the president and First Father the next evening, after they had settled in. Understandably, Stanley was delighted. Brew told him he would be registered under an alias and that identification for it would be prepared. Did he have a suggestion for the alias? A name he would not forget?

"Richard McAullife," Stanley said, immediately.

"Ohh-kay," said Brew, writing it down. "Mc or Mac?"

"Mc."

"Is there some meaning to this name?"

"Yes, but that's between Henry Winters and me."

To Stanley's surprise, the Navy SEAL did not probe further.

48

A ROOMMATE WITH BENEFITS

★ ★ ★ The intelligence about Pyongyang's interest in Stanley's work altered Brew's own personal plans. He had intended to stay at the Beaufort marine base and commute with the call-ups to the daily training at the vegetable laboratory. But in light of the new information, he decided instead to join Kitt, Stanley, and the dog in Charleston.

Hastings had followed up on the tip from Moscow. Interpol in Sweden believed the Russian contractor had been slain by two professional assailants. The CIA chief told Brew it was common for foreign assassins to stay with a matter once assigned. If the North Koreans in fact came for Stanley, it would probably be the same pair. He seconded Brew's conclusion that he should join the personal protection team for as long as Stanley remained in the low country. In the meantime, Hastings would use his influence to engage NSA resources to learn more about the North Koreans. It could be a real threat, or it could be a false alarm.

All of the rooms reserved for Stanley featured, at the big Pittsburgher's request, king-sized beds. Brew had them send up a cot for him. At first it was awkward for Stanley. He had not slept in a room with another man since college days.

"This is no longer the style to which I am accustomed," he commented on their first night in the same room.

"If it bothers you that much, I can stay with L.T.," Brew said. "But it's better to have someone in here with you and Augie."

"No, it's all right," said Stanley. "I can take one for the team."

"I suppose you'd rather have Colonel Ames in here."

"What?" Stanley sounded surprised.

"Just teasing, Stanley. She *is* impressive, though. And awfully good-looking. I think you've noticed her. You know, in that way." It seemed an odd turn of phrase from a Navy SEAL.

"Actually, I have. And that she's twelve years younger than me, and looks even younger. I'm too old for her," Stanley said. "Plus, I assume she couldn't associate with me even if she *was* interested. Aren't their rules against that?"

"Not that I can think of," said Brew. "You're a civilian."

"Oh."

"Maybe I should invite her downtown for dinner with us," Brew said.

"How would she get back to Beaufort?"

"She could bunk the night with Kitt. Or whatever."

"No whatever. She stays with Kitt," said Stanley. He was feeling nervous now.

"Fine, I'll ask her."

Stanley knew that the time for protest was at hand. Should he discourage Brew? He had felt a stirring when he first met Helen Ames. Something was new inside of him, or something old and unused. She was strong and intellectual, and attractive—very, he thought—in an unadorned sort of way, perhaps owing in part to the uniform. She had struck a chord. And she was an engineer no less, and a good one. Soon after the reserves arrival, he and Brew had agreed immediately that she was the unquestioned leader among the installers and had asked her to take responsibility, not only for the engineering aspects of the project but also for supervising the entire installation to occur soon in Kuwait. And he was almost afraid to acknowledge even to himself that she had in her own way signaled that his impressions of her were reciprocal.

"That would be kind of you, Tyler" was all he said.

49

SOUTHERN PLEASURES

★ ★ ★ It was midway into the training period, and Stanley was pleased with the effort. Each of the call-ups had some background in construction. Helpfully, one was even an ironworker with experience in underground projects. But none, except Helen Ames, had ever been asked to read and understand drawings anywhere near as detailed as Stanley's. So, he spent the first three days of the training explaining them, section by section. Wilson Bryce, the technology specialist from the defense department, had supplied an encrypted projection drive with all the drawings so that Stanley could display them on the large training room screen. He stood before the screen with a laser pointer and slowly described each component, panel, and fitting. Most of the reserves had never heard of beryllium and were amazed by its properties. On the first day, Stanley casually walked to the front of the room with his pointer in one hand and with one of the rigid ten-foot-by-twenty-seven-inch wall panels in the other. He could have been carrying an empty soda can, it was so light. Their jaws dropped.

Positioning the slotted panels and attaching them to the support stanchions would be the easiest part of the installation, Stanley and Helen knew. The edge fittings and flanges would be more tedious. The sidewall ventilation components and the hydraulically powered retracting roof would, by far, be the most difficult. But the reserves listened carefully and asked good questions. Stanley was confident the installation would go well, so long as the foundation work was in exact alignment.

In the warehouse behind the vegetable laboratory headquarters building, preparations had been made for a working classroom. A twelve-foot-deep hole the size of a small garage had been bulldozed and I-beams planted in it, simulating to scale the concrete posts at the real site. Helen worked with each of the call-ups as they practiced, making determinations as to individual skill so that she could best apportion the installation tasks among them, like a manager planning his lineup.

It was hard work for everyone. But esprit de corps was high. Brew arranged for evening relaxation and activities for the reserves when they returned each night to the Beaufort marine base. He even persuaded the major there to provide a night each week when the young reserves were welcomed at the officers' club on base. The privilege was not abused. Each was fit for duty on the mornings that followed.

Stanley found Charleston, despite the heat, as pleasant as Kitt had described it. The two of them walked early every morning with Augie, and again in the evening. Stanley worried that the heat was hard on the dog. Kitt assured him he could handle it and had been trained, at times, in worse. It helped that many of the merchants along King Street and East Bay left water bowls out as a matter of course. Stanley noticed that Augie never stopped for one of the bowls on his own initiative. He seemed oblivious to them. But whenever Stanley saw one ahead and suggested he take a drink with a motion of the leash, he did so without fail, then looked up at his master with gratitude before moving on.

The dinner invitation to Helen was readily accepted, and led to two more in the following weeks. Brew and Kitt joined for the first. Just Kitt came for the second. Stanley and Helen dined alone for the third, though Kitt and Augie took a table outside with line of site to them. Kitt could see that an attachment was forming. It pleased her, but she felt she needed to be sure that Brew was also okay with it. When she started to raise the matter to the SEAL in the hotel lobby, while Augie escorted Stanley into the men's room, Brew raised his hand to stop her, gently, in midsentence. "Know all about it," he said, smiling. "Hell, I think it's great. For both of them, probably."

The president's visit to Kiawah Island came in the final week of the scheduled training. All of Charleston was abuzz with the news that she would be vacationing at the Kiawah Island golf resort. The night before her arrival, a Secret Service Escalade pulled up to the rear entrance of the King's Inn where Stanley was lodging, his fourth venue. He waited at the appointed time, with L.T. and Augie. Only Stanley got into the car.

He was whisked south across Charleston Bay and out to the resort twenty-five miles away. Stanley noticed that the ride took them right past the United States Vegetable Laboratory where he had been driven by L.T. every morning. A few miles past the facility, the Secret Service driver turned left on to what Stanley saw was named Main Road. A sign read, Kiawah Island 15 miles.

"Main Road," Stanley heard the driver say to the other agent in the front passenger seat. "More like *Only* Road."

The driver didn't elaborate, but it was not, in fact, an idle comment. It was the only road available from the mainland to the resort island. Once crossing over the Intracoastal Waterway, the road narrowed to two lanes. The Secret Service's Presidential Protection Unit did not favor locations with a single means of paved ingress or egress. A well-staged attack on the president would likely include total prior blockage of that road, preventing evacuation of her by means of it. But there was a convenient alternate route available in this case: the Atlantic Ocean. Three coast guard vessels, two of them specially armed and equipped with high-speed engines, had moored earlier in the week just off the hotel beach. Two guarded military speedboats were docked and manned around the clock in slots just a thousand feet from the ocean-side doors to the hotel.

Large trees, "live oaks" as they were called, shrouded the two-lane passageway. In places, their broad trunks were mere inches from the road's edge. Stanley couldn't help flinching as the driver whirled through the closest ones. *Relax,* he told himself, unsuccessfully. *This guy drives the damned president.*

The resort itself was striking, to say the least. Tall palm trees blended with lush loblolly pines and the ubiquitous live oaks. There were large magnolia and striking myrtle trees too. It made for an almost jungle feel. Stanley had assumed the hotel would be near the entrance, but it was several miles inside the resort gate. The road weaved through golf holes and marsh vistas in the late day sun.

Stanley was well traveled, but he had never seen a hotel quite like the Sanctuary. It had a feel all its own. It seemed almost a museum to the South, with rich dark floors made of wide shiny planks and mammoth winding staircases at either end of a massive lobby.

The Secret Service agent stood nearby as Stanley produced the passport Brew had given him for the reception attendant.

"Oh, yes, Mr. McAuliffe. It's nice to have you. We have a very nice accommodation ready for you."

Indeed, it was. Wide plantation shutters opened to expose an ocean view observable even from the bathtub. All the furnishings were top drawer. He found a fine bourbon, Woodford Reserve, in the minibar and enjoyed it on his terrace with a cigar, before ordering his dinner from room service. The Secret Service agent stayed outside in the hall. He told Stanley that another agent would arrive soon; one of them would always be there. If he wanted to take a walk or go downstairs, just let them know; he would be accompanied. Stanley knew he could not be more secure, and he did feel relaxed in the beautiful environment.

Somehow, though, it was not same, he thought, without Augie. It was his first night apart from him since L.T. had ushered him in months ago in Pittsburgh.

Still, government service was more comfortable than people said it was, he considered. At least for Dick McAuliffe.

50

A WALK ON THE BEACH, COCKTAILS FOLLOWING

★ ★ ★ The next morning, dark-suited Secret Service agents decorated the grand premises of the Sanctuary Hotel like Christmas tree ornaments. They seemed to be everywhere. There was no mistaking the presence of the president. Stanley wondered why the spiral translucent cords of the agents' hearing pieces were worn so obviously, and why the agents telegraphed their identity by bearing US Secret Service lapel pins. He asked the agent escorting him to breakfast.

"Discourages people," the agent said.

It made sense. Better to deter confrontation if you could; better that intended trouble be aborted than attempted.

After breakfast, Stanley asked if he could take a walk. He was used to walking every day now with L.T. and the dog, and had come to look forward to it.

"Sure," said the protective agent. "The beach is packed firm. Easy to walk on. Okay to walk there?"

"Absolutely."

Normally, the long beachfront at the resort would have been dotted with morning joggers, shell hunters, and families setting up early for a day of dolphin watching under the sun, but not this morning. The resort's beach lounge chairs and umbrellas were all stored out of sight. Every boardwalk to the water was manned fore and aft by a fully suited agent, even in the temperature. Signs at each read, We Are Sorry That Beach Access Is Not Available for the Time Being. But Stanley—Richard McAuliffe—was exempt.

The Kiawah beach extended over ten miles, stretching through high, multishaded seagrasses, home to happy bobcats and less happy seabirds that wandered in to them at high tide.

They walked an hour. Stanley could have enjoyed more, but he felt awkward taking the attention of the Secret Service agent, especially when he noticed him perspiring, without complaint, in his navy-blue suit. As they approached the hotel at the end of the walk, one of the coast guard cruisers unmoored and began to circle around a perimeter that Stanley adjudged to be at least several square miles. He pointed out to the craft.

"It's sweeping," said the agent. "It'll do concentric circles with detection equipment until it can't get any closer to the shore. Then they'll deboard and do it by foot from there."

"For mines?"

"Mines and weapons that could be planted there."

"Amazing," Stanley said.

"You haven't seen the half of it, sir. She is the most powerful person on the planet, at least in government. There's a lot of hate out there."

"What do you know about me?" Stanley asked. "Do you know why I am here?"

"Not a thing, and I don't want to. All I know is that if anything goes down while you are with her and her father, you won't be evacuated with them. That's a little unusual. I guess it means it's important that no one know that Richard McAuliffe is meeting with her."

"Does someone else take me?"

"The United States Navy. Over there. See them?" The agent pointed down the beachline. Tucked beneath a hanging sea shrub, two SEALs, one eyeing them with binoculars, were crouched in a rubber speed craft. The agent gestured a thumbs-up to them, and both SEALs stood to return it. "Lucky damn guys," said the agent. "Look at those shorts they get to wear. And probably played golf yesterday before you got here."

"Well," Stanley said, "I'll bet your food tonight will be better than theirs."

"I doubt it," the agent said. "They'll send them out the same thing."

They were near where they had begun their walk an hour earlier.

"Are you with Naval Command, sir?" asked the agent.

"No."

"Retired navy?"

"No, I never served," Stanley said. "I'm not proud of it. I admire all of you people," Stanley said to him. "For your service. For the quality that you show in your work. I was a kid during Vietnam. By 9/11, I was in my forties, building my business. So, I never served. I regret it, I really do."

"Well, you must have done something pretty well. Or you are doing something important now."

"Why do you say that?" asked Stanley.

"Because you're here. And because I'm here."

At exactly six thirty, two agents greeted Stanley at the door to his room and escorted him to his appointment with Del and Henry Winters. They took the elevator down to the lobby, then walked through a ground-floor kitchen to a service elevator used for room service deliveries. Cooks and waiters looked as they passed through but seemed unimpressed, as if they had seen it many times. When the service elevator door opened, a third agent awaited inside. The agents all nodded, but said nothing until the door closed.

Then one said into his sleeve, "Mr. Guest rising."

Stanley was startled when the elevator next opened. The president was standing to greet him, flanked by other agents. She seemed taller than she appeared on television and a little slimmer, he thought. Her smile was wide. She stood straight. He was used to seeing her in the media in more formal business attire, her hair usually tied back. Now she stood before him in a light summer wrap skirt, a linen blouse, and open-toed sandals, her dark hair hanging freely to her shoulders.

"Stanley, I am so glad you are here," she said.

"I am surprised you would come out here like this," he said. He was sincere, but he wished he had not said it. He recalled his earlier comment when she had called him at his apartment, questioning if the line was secure. Now here he was again, implying a lack of caution. But her smile did not break.

"They don't like me to do it, but someone had to greet you. I thought if I sent my father out to get you, I'd never get a word in. He is eager to meet you."

For once, the presidential suite of the hotel was in fact so occupied. It warranted its name. Stanley guessed it to be nearly as large as his entire apartment residence in Pittsburgh. The president led Stanley through the open double doors into the suite. The agents remained outside in the hall and closed the doors behind them as they entered. Stanley saw the ocean beyond a wide terrace ahead, from which Henry Winters approached. Stanley noticed his step; it was quick and agile, surprising considering his large frame. He was taller even than Stanley and broad across the shoulders, enviously near normal weight. Henry carried a sheet of paper in his hand as he walked toward Stanley; it was the visitor's prep sheet. The security detail always circulated one before a guest arrived.

"I was expecting a Stanley Bigelow," called out the president's father. "But it says here we have Dick McAuliffe! Dick McAuliffe!" He was beaming. "Del said you were a baseball man, but *Dick McAuliffe*?" He extended a muscular hand.

"Well, I wanted to make sure she was leveling with me when she said you were a *Moneyball* man." Stanley looked at the president, who appeared approving but puzzled. "I wondered what your view was of Dick McAuliffe," he asked the First Father.

If you went door to door on Kiawah Island and half of Charleston, you might not find a soul who could tell you who Dick McAuliffe was, much less any who had an opinion of him. Henry Winters had one.

"One of the most underrated offensive players of his era," he said. "Played short and second for the Tigers for a dozen years. A little third base. An All Star several times in the sixties—when the players voted them in and it really meant something."

"I couldn't agree more," said Stanley.

"He hit home runs before middle infielders hit home runs."

"Also true."

"Drew plenty of walks."

"Correct."

"Probably the guy Al Kaline drove home more than anyone else. He hit two slots ahead of him."

"Impressive, General."

"Call me Henry."

"All right, I will. But what else was it about McAuliffe that was so underrated? People didn't talk about it. For my money, they still don't talk about it enough." Stanley was now standing very near the retired general.

The president wondered when the two seniors would get beyond this. Neither seemed in a hurry. She could see her father was relishing the exchange. He was pondering Stanley's last question. He turned to the side and ran a hand across his chin. His eyebrows curled in concentration.

"Double plays!" he finally exclaimed. "Double plays! Not that he turned them in the field. He wasn't too good defensively, but he didn't hit *into* them. He was uncanny! The year the Tigers won the pennant—it was 1968—he played nearly every game and didn't hit into a single double play all year. Incredible. How many runs scored later in those innings when he didn't kill a rally? No record of it. No credit for it."

"You looked that up," said Stanley.

"I didn't. Honest."

"I don't think he did, Stanley," injected the general's daughter, a little defensively. "I told you he's a baseball encyclopedia. He was only just now handed that sheet with your alias on it. But now you've got him going."

About that the president was right.

The three of them moved onto the terrace with cocktails. Henry and Stanley took turns regaling each other with statistical insights, theories, and odd facts. Henry reported something that even Stanley did not know about McAuliffe. At the end of his playing days he became a minor league manager for the Red Sox. He was not playing anymore. Near season's end, the Red Sox's regular third baseman fell ill. He had not swung a bat all year, but McAuliffe was called up and played several games in Boston's successful pennant drive.

They listened to each other intently. Henry told the story he liked to tell about Luis Tiant, the pitcher for the Yankees, Boston, and Cleveland known for an unorthodox delivery in which he swirled on the mound so severely that his back was to the batter and his face looking at second base just before whirling back and releasing the ball to home plate. Uninitiated batters were terrified and perplexed. Henry said that in a game in the Mexican league, the whirling dervish fooled a hitter facing a two–two count—and everyone else—so badly that when he threw to first base attempting to pick off a runner, instead of delivering to the plate, the batter swung anyway and was called out on strikes.

"The manager charged to home plate to protest the call," Henry recounted. "'He's not out!'"

"'He swung!' said the umpire."

"'I know,' said the manager, 'but he *ticked* it!'"

Del had heard her father tell the story before, always to amusement. But Stanley laughed uncontrollably, to the general's delight. She could not remember when she had seen her father so engaged with a nonmilitary person. She let them go on, without interruption, sitting next to them and enjoying the waves rolling in on the beach before them.

A Secret Service agent brought her a telephone. It was Vernon Lazar, calling from the Pentagon. Ben Williamson and the CIA were nearly finished with their review of the recovered data from Farah. They didn't think a briefing of the president could wait. Could it be arranged for the morning?

PART IV

PART IV

51

ONE ROOM WITH A VIEW, AND ANOTHER WITHOUT

★ ★ ★ There may be no other Holiday Inn anywhere with a view comparable to the one that rises high above Charleston Harbor and the Ashley River on the southwestern edge of the Peninsula City. To the ocean side of the ten-sided tower lie hundreds of sailboats and yachts moored in the harbor. To the inland side, tidal waters and their olive and amber grasses stretch as far as the eye can see.

The two North Korean agents rooming on the sixteenth floor were not there for the view. They had arrived four days earlier. Using forged South Korean passports, they had entered the country by way of Miami before driving north to Charleston in an Avis rental car. They chose Avis over Hertz because they had used the latter in Stockholm a month earlier, presenting the same passport to obtain it. Better not to show both trips in the same company's database, they concluded. Before checking in at the Holiday Inn, they stopped at a church parking lot nearby. No services were being held, but several cars were parked in the rear. While one of the agents stood guard, the other used the screwdriver bit from a Swiss army knife to remove the South Carolina license plate from one of them. He replaced the rental car's Pennsylvania plate, storing it in the trunk for reinstallation later.

The US president's vacation in the Charleston area was an inconvenient coincidence. Their trip to find the Pittsburgh engineer had been ordered before the president's travel plans had been announced. But the security forces surely to be surrounding her gave pause to their supervisor in Pyongyang. It was said she would be spending the week at a golf resort outside the city, but it was always the case that the travel of the head of state necessitated security measures broad in sweep. Advance teams would be sent in to prepare for contingencies, such as where the president would be taken if medical care were needed, and which routes would be used for an emergency departure. Even restaurants and entertainment venues would be scouted and diagrammed so that her security detail would be familiar with them before she visited.

The supervisor in Pyongyang directed his men to lie low until the president had left the area and things had returned more or less to normal. They could proceed with essential preparations for their mission, including surveillance of the engineer to understand his movements, but no attempt to abduct him should be made until the vacation of the US president was finished and she had returned to Washington.

They used the time efficiently. They waited each morning from different vantage points on the opposite berm of Highway 17, a safe distance from the entrance to the United States Vegetable Laboratory, studying the cars and vehicles that entered. Every day the same ones arrived with little variation. A short man wearing glasses and carrying a briefcase was usually the first to arrive. He parked his car in the first space adjacent to the walkway leading to the front doors. Reserved for him, they surmised. Perhaps the superintendent or manager. Others followed soon after, about half men, half women. Some mornings a UPS truck entered and drove to the rear. Each day a larger delivery truck came also and drove to the rear of the headquarters building. They googled its unfamiliar Latin-sounding name, Cintas; uniforms and maintenance supplies, they learned. And about nine o'clock each morning a large passenger car with dark-tinted windows pulled in. Grating of some kind was positioned in the rear of it. A large man climbed a little slowly out the passenger side, seemed to bend at the window for a moment, and then walked into the building.

On the second and third days of their observation, the North Koreans took photos of him as he exited the car. They compared them to a grainy reproduction provided by Pyongyang pulled from a newsletter published on the internet. It described a fund-raising banquet of the Pittsburgh Symphony Orchestra eleven years earlier. There were photographs of some of those who'd attended. The two North Koreans used a magnifying glass to examine the couple identified as "Mr. and Mrs. Stanley Bigelow" and held it next to the photos of the man they saw leaving the large passenger car. He was heavier now, considerably. His hair was thinner and noticeably less dark. But, they concurred, it was Bigelow; it was surely Bigelow.

The agents knew that the infiltrated email said the beryllium components had been shipped to the site on Highway 17. The emails said that the facility was an agricultural research center, which they could see it indeed was. And they now knew that Stanley Bigelow was in fact coming to that place. The contention that his work pertained to agricultural purposes, and not military ones, seemed plausible. It lined up, they thought. There was no sign of any other government presence except for the daily US Postal Service truck. They queried their authority in Pyongyang. Should they abort their mission and return?

It was nearly twenty-fours before they were answered.

"Unconvinced," the reply said. "Continue planning. Stand by to proceed."

That day they found a Target department store nearby and purchased a wooden stool and a dozen bungee cords. Then they visited a self-storage business on Highway 17 a few miles north of the vegetable laboratory toward downtown Charleston.

"Our sons are coming here for school," they said to the manager. "Can we rent a storage place for them?"

Of course they could, the manager said. Did they need climate-controlled space? Many of the students preferred it. But if they might have larger items and wanted to pull a car up to their space for loading and unloading, one of the outbuildings with overhead doors might be better. Yes, the agents said, the building with the overhead door would be best. Would one in the very rear be less expensive? No, all the units were the same price, but the rear units were somewhat shaded by the woods behind the fence; they might be cooler. Yes, yes, said the agents. We will take a cool one in the rear. Can we pay in cash for the whole school year? Why, of course they could. Do you sell packing tape, the plastic kind? Yes, regular or extra duty? The extra duty, yes, yes.

The manager gave them the card key for the unit and the North Koreans went alone to the rear of the lot to examine the space. It was ample in size for their purpose, ten feet wide and twelve feet deep. A single light bulb hung from the center of the ceiling, and there were hooks on the sidewalls. They left the wooden stool in the middle of the little room and hung half of the bungee cords on a wall hook. They returned to the Holiday Inn, awaiting further orders, with the other bungees and the extra-duty plastic tape.

52

THAT SUCKING SOUND
YOU DO NOT HEAR

★ ★ ★ Grass did not grow beneath the feet of CIA chief Hastings. The call from his Russian counterpart troubled him deeply. He was not used to believing information coming from Russians. But he believed what Marraka Yevzelsky had told him this time. Immediately after notifying Tyler Brew, he called Admiral Jennings at the NSA to ask for her help. Her teams were already monitoring all the communications between Stanley and the various suppliers. But at Hastings's request she put a new team of specialists on all data that might provide information on North Koreans entering the United States, and particularly anyone destined for Charleston. The breadth of available data was sweeping. As Richard Clarke, the cyber and national security advisor to President Bill Clinton and both Presidents Bush, had once said, the NSA operated a huge global vacuum sweeper sucking up not only telephone data but also radio transmissions, emails, social media postings, and all manner of surveillance camera data. It was stored in server farms in massive secured data warehouses around the country.

The intelligence that could be drawn from that vast sea of data was in there someplace. The trick was in synthesizing and sorting it in such a way as to isolate it for coherent examination. The billions invested in the technology to do this had paid off. Hundreds of nascent terrorist attacks and planning activities had been thwarted—entirely outside the public eye—because of this capability.

Even with all the speed and technology the government could buy at their disposal, it was still time-consuming work for the NSA specialists to filter, refilter, sort, and re-sort the immense body of possibly relevant data and reduce it to specific, actionable information. But after four days of disk-spinning scans and decryption protocols, the NSA specialists transmitted their report.

It was exactly what Hastings hoped it would not be. It stated that a week earlier two males had entered the country on a flight to Miami from Seoul. The same passports had been used to enter and leave Stockholm a month ago. An Interpol official investigating a murder there had checked the passports of all visitors to Stockholm in that time frame. Two weeks ago, he'd circulated a global report indicating that the two South Korean passports were forgeries. His report ought to have placed the Pyongyang assassins on the TSA watch lists at every United States airport. But the TSA technician to whom the report was routed at the agency's data processing center in Baltimore was off for a child's college commencement ceremony in Colorado. Fortunately for the assassins—not so much for Stanley—the report was still sitting in the technician's bulging inbox when the North Koreans entered Miami unnoticed.

But not really.

The NSA processed every digital frame of camera footage from the Miami airport, and tracked the two men through the terminal to the rental car center; from there to the Avis aisle; and from there to Interstate 95, heading north. Eerily, in view of their prey, the rental car bore a Pennsylvania license plate. Its number was clear. It would be captured by tollbooths and the NSA-installed cameras in place on nearly every highway in the country.

The NSA data specialists also ran the passports through the

other databases and learned that one of them matched that used to rent a Hertz car on the men's earlier visit to Stockholm. As a courtesy, they forwarded this information to the Swedish Interpol chief, one Lars LaToure. It became the subject of discussion over espressos the next morning in the Commercial Relations Department at the Russian Embassy.

Hastings had all the analysis dispatched directly through a secure landline to the FBI office in Charleston for immediate delivery to Brew. The Charleston field office was not large, just six agents plus Bobby Beach, the agent-in-charge. Agent L.T. Kitt made a total FBI presence of eight. Hastings asked Brew if he wanted support from the Secret Service detail in town to protect the president. An additional team could be sent from Washington and could stay on after the president's vacation to help with the protection of Stanley. Absolutely, Brew said.

"It will be a first," Hastings said. "The FBI, NSA, the CIA, Secret Service, and the goddamn navy all working on the same thing."

Someone certainly still cared about Stanley Bigelow.

53
WHAT TO MAKE OF THE IRANIANS

★ ★ ★ The First Father took a walk while his daughter sat before the video link in the presidential suite of the hotel. He knew the teleconference was scheduled, but she had not asked him to stay for it. He took no offense; she intended none. There are separations of power additional to those expressly provided in the Constitution, and each knew it. Everyone on the other side of the call sat in a special conference room in the Pentagon designed for the purpose. There had been developments since the short call to the president the evening before. A small truck carrying two uniformed men had come from Iran to visit the deserted outpost near Farah. The drone surveillance video showed one of them entering the compound with a carton and leaving with a carton minutes later. Analysts were trying to determine if the same box came and left, but results would likely be inconclusive. It could have been a delivery of additional materials, a withdrawal, or both. But analysis of the uniforms was conclusive. Magnification showed it was the garb of the Jamar Al, the Iranian elite military forces.

"This puts a new light on this," said Vernon Lazar.

"It sure does," said General Williamson.

There was a considerable pause. No one needed to be more specific. The original discovery of the data drives—and the assessment made of them since—all pointed to emerging cooperation between formerly discrete terrorist groups. But nothing, aside from the proximity of little Farah to the Iranian border, suggested the involvement of a nation-state. Last night's visit by Jamar Al soldiers changed that. But to what degree? Several scenarios were possible. The Iranian troops could have deposited additional information at the drop. That would be serious, to be sure, because it would prove outright cooperation between Jamar Al and the terrorists. But it might be that the Iranian soldiers were merely doing what the US Navy SEALs had done before them—recovering hidden data for their own assessment and benefit. A third possibility occurred to the president. It might be that the terrorist groups had agreed to share information with Iran in hopes of winning its support—a proposal of sorts.

All three possible explanations for the Iranian visit to the outpost were discussed and debated. CIA's Hastings was the most dubious of any benevolent view toward Iran's involvement. He had thought from the outset that it was no accident the terrorists' data treasure had been stashed so close to the Iranian border. And it was not realistic to believe the Iranians had done merely what the US special ops had done.

"We had to knock a door down," he said. "They must have had keys to the place to be in and out so quickly."

You could not argue with his reasoning.

But the president and Williamson were not yet ready to conclude that Iran was an antagonist in the current circumstance. For one thing, the nuclear development agreement first negotiated in Obama's second term had held up better than its critics had feared. President Trump had withdrawn the US from its terms, but other signatories had not. Even the Israelis had notched back their criticism of Iran from strident condemnation to "real concerns" about the Middle East power. Discussions looking to the deal's extension had been ongoing for six months. There were signs of progress, and Del Winters was cautiously evaluating whether she would commit the US to the agreement once again. For another, the current clerical hierarchy in Iran was measurably more moderate than earlier ones. "Death to America" rants were no longer commonplace and seemed usually attributable to fringe elements within the country, and plainly not the general populace. And, most important in the president's mind, ISIS had committed its most critical error since its early alienation from al-Qaeda by sending a team of suicide bombers into—of all places—Tehran. It was an irrational and vicious bite of a hand that could have fed it. Back-channel communications from Tehran to Washington indicated Iranian fury at the terrorist behavior and its comprehension that no one could safely ally with at least ISIS.

Against this background, the president did not rush to judgment about Iran's complicity in the terrorist planning. Williamson wondered if the State Department could quietly probe its sources in Tehran to learn more. But Hastings and the president felt that would risk disclosure to the terrorist factions and the loss of a critical asset now possessed: namely, that the Special Forces discovery of the planning data was unknown to them. So long as it remained unknown to the terrorists, it remained actionable. Once known, it spoiled almost immediately.

Also in the minds of all was the knowledge that the Eaglets' Nest deployment base in Kuwait was progressing rapidly and might be operational by mid-August. It was frightening to consider that the new capability might be called upon so quickly after its completion. But, depending on the president's assessment of the terrorist data about to be presented by Williamson and Hastings, its use could not be ruled out if she deemed the need imperative and the rewards great enough.

The general did most of the presenting. His tone was even and somber. He did not seem to emphasize any one finding over any other. All of the information was ominous. Three of the terror networks had all but formalized a cooperation agreement. Two additional networks in Africa were being solicited as well. There were two overarching themes to the terrorist planning.

First, much larger fighting forces were to be assembled and deployed to launch overwhelming surprise assaults on cities inhabited by substantial numbers of Christians. There would be no attempt to hold the cities after the eradication of the citizens and the destruction of the infrastructure. The terrorists, according to the discovered information, had concluded that trying to keep seized cities was a losing strategy. Armies, often assisted by Americans, would always be able to retake them eventually. Instead, following the destruction, the forces would disperse to multiple staging areas, then regroup to launch their next assault in a different region, again seeking to surprise.

Second, to supply the massive munitions needed for the plan, storage facilities would be stocked in unprecedented volumes and located where they could be rapidly accessed for the assaults. The hospital at Turj had been a poor choice, the data revealed, a mistake to be learned from. The Americans would always come to such a place, as they had at the Doctors without Borders hospital. Obscure compounds were to be favored instead. A dozen candidate locations were identified across Syria, Afghanistan, Iraq, and North Africa.

After the presentation, the president suggested a break. She walked to the balcony and studied the ocean silently. She did not sit down. A Secret Service agent asked if she wanted anything. She shook her head no without turning her face from the waves rolling in. She brought her advisors back in fifteen minutes.

"We will not speak to Tehran about Farah now," she announced to the group. "We will continue the surveillance." She addressed the general and the CIA chief. "Ben and Jack, see if there is any way in heaven that a team can be sent again to Farah without detection. If the Iranians are just reading drives, that's one thing. If they are leaving information to help the terrorists, it's a very different thing. It could take us to one place rather than another. Even to Eaglets' Nest."

All listening knew that Del Winters never said anything she did not mean.

54

ALL ARE HUNTERS; SOME ARE HUNTED

★ ★ ★ A good spy will always elude his hunter, or at least buy time while trying. And the two North Koreans were very good spies. The NSA's trail on the Avis rental car plate had gone cold. The last sighting was by a street camera near downtown Charleston the same day it had left the Miami airport. The foreign operatives had been wise to select a white Honda Accord. You could hardly find a more popular model. They were everywhere, it seemed, as Bobby Beach's FBI agents and the Secret Service team scoured the city. But none carried the Pennsylvania plate originally observed. Bobby Beach concluded the plates were almost certainly changed.

The North Koreans were also too smart to use their false passports for identification at the hotel. Instead they chose forged Wisconsin driver's licenses bearing long Japanese names. Only the photos were authentic. They knew the quality of the fake licenses was poor. But they also knew—correctly as it turned out—that a Holiday Inn desk clerk in South Carolina would not be familiar with the appearance of a Wisconsin license or know the difference between a Japanese person and a dairy farmer, much less a North Korean. Bobby Beach's checks of every hotel registry and parking lot failed to turn up a Korean name tied to a white Honda with or without Pennsylvania plates.

It did not help that it was high season in Charleston. Despite typical temperatures, the heart of summer drew thousands to the historical port city. The streets were flooded with tourists, many of them Asians from cruise ships and bus tours. The North Koreans felt as unremarkable on the crowded streets as in their hotel room.

Brew was concerned but calm. He knew Bobby Beach and the Secret Service were doing everything they could. The training out on Highway 17 was nearly finished. Helen Ames would lead the installation team to Kuwait within days. The president had returned to Washington. He told Stanley and Kitt that the North Koreans who had traveled from Miami may or may not still be in town. The teams would continue looking. The two of them should remain vigilant. They could continue their walks so long as they stayed together always and carried a new signaling device that he gave to each of them. It looked like an ordinary cell phone, but it had only one function. It remained in "on" mode all the time; it could not be turned off, even intentionally. The screen had no application icons, simply a photograph that never changed. To humor Stanley, Brew programmed the screen on his device to display old Wrigley Field in Chicago. Two rapid taps on the screen—any part of it— sent an instantaneous alarm message displaying the sender's GPS coordinates and graphic street location to Brew, Bobby Beach, and each of the agents on the surveillance team. Every foot of turf and pavement within Charleston County, down to the smallest alley, was programmed in.

"Don't hesitate to use it," Brew told them. "If anything doesn't look right, give it two quick taps. Don't worry if it's a false alarm."

For their part, the North Korean agents were becoming anxious. They wanted to make their move. It had been a full week since their arrival. Pyongyang was irritating. They had asked for permission to proceed now that the US president was out of the area. It might take days for the right opportunity to present itself, and they desired the option to strike if one did. Again, they waited twenty-four hours for a response. It seemed to them like another week. And then it came.

"Proceed when ready."

55

GRADUATION FOR SOLDIERS, COMMENCEMENT FOR HELEN AND STANLEY

★ ★ ★ At the United States Vegetable Laboratory on Highway 17, school was about to be let out. Brew met with Stanley and Colonel Ames, and together they walked through the instructional underground classroom in the warehouse behind the headquarters. Stanley had ordered parts for a miniature roof assembly and the colonel demonstrated its operation, all from work accomplished by the trained call-ups.

"It really is an incredible design," she said to them. "It will all work. If the support installation is right, it will go smoothly. If it is a little off, I will make it work."

Brew studied Stanley as she spoke. Did he believe her? He knew that Stanley had acquired feelings for her. Would it cloud his judgment? Would affection dilute his truest view? He had been so adamant about his desire to inspect the foundation work personally.

"Stanley, what do you think?" he asked.

"I stand by what I said before," Stanley said. "I should have gone there to measure it myself." Helen did not seem startled.

"You should have, but you couldn't," she said. "And you can't. You didn't get what you wanted. We never do all of the time."

"I've never been good at delegating," he said.

"Which is one of the reasons they wanted you," said Brew.

"*They?*" said Stanley.

"You know I was worried," answered Brew. "I was worried at first. Worried for a while. But you convinced me, Stanley. You really did."

No one spoke for a moment.

"She can do it," Stanley finally said to Brew. "She knows what she is doing." He looked at Helen. "You can do it."

"I know that I can," she said. "I know it totally."

The logistical planning was complete, and Brew explained it to them. The reserves would go back to the Beaufort marine base for a day of rest. The components, all shipped to the Highway 17 site, could not be packed into a single truck. Two would be needed. Large FedEx and UPS trucks had been arranged to move the materials, an hour apart, to the Charleston Air Force Base the next evening. Helen would go there to inspect them upon arrival and supervise their loading into an air force transport plane. The following morning the call-ups would come to the USDA facility in the usual Cintas van, like any other day, and then move to a waiting UPS truck for the drive to the air base, where Helen would be waiting for them.

"So I have one more night in Charleston?" asked Helen.

"Yes," said Brew. "I won't ask where you want to spend it."

"I don't mind your asking, Captain," said the colonel. "But I assume there will be no telling."

She knew it was not something she could properly order. But she knew she didn't have to.

It was an important night for Stanley and Helen. They had spent long days together, working through the thick blueprints and training the soldiers, and Stanley had observed her keenly as she interacted with them. "Gently authoritarian" is how he judged her manner. But attentive and surely not unkind or abrupt. And she watched Stanley too. She liked the kind glimmer in his eyes as he fielded questions from the young soldiers. He was teacher-like, and tended to end each conversation, however short, with some notion of encouragement, such as "You're doing fine" or "Atta fellow," which she found endearing. But there had been little time for them to be alone together—really none, except for the single dinner a week earlier, and then under Kitt's and Augie's nearby watchful eyes. Now, though, they could sit together, relaxed, in privacy amid the pleasant night air of Charleston.

Stanley's room that night was on the top floor of the quiet Inn at Charleston Place on Meeting Street. The inn was a lovely four-sided southern structure that rose above and wrapped around a beautifully tended garden courtyard. Broad double doors from Stanley's room gave access to an ample balcony, where the two of them sat and talked into the early hours. They drank, but not much, from the room's minibar. Stanley chose an unfamiliar southern bourbon; Helen, Jameson Irish Whisky. Stanley, a trace apprehensively, asked if she would mind if he smoked a cigar. "Of course not," she said. She enjoyed the aroma of a good cigar. "And something tells me Stanley smokes only good cigars," she said with a smile.

"On that you may be sure," he said.

The two engineers covered a lot of ground. Conversation came easily, each trusting the questions of the other as well intended. Neither dominated the discourse as they told one another much of their life histories. Helen knew that Stanley, like she, did not have children, but she did not know that he had no siblings either. She had three sisters, all younger and married, and was close to each of them, he learned. And she was an aunt to two nephews and three nieces. She saw that this pleased him; his large eyes flared with interest.

She told him she'd been motivated to join the military by her paternal grandfather, who had also served in the Army Corps of Engineers, not as an engineer but as a procurement officer. It was a mixed blessing, she told Stanley. She liked the work very much, and the travel, but relationships were difficult for her in the military. Men and women were always coming and going, and assignments were usually short term, project by project. She had worked on a half dozen bases in four countries. Her education qualified her for an immediate officer's commission, and she reenlisted for a second six-year term that took her into her midthirties and to the rank of captain. As that term neared completion, the corps tried to induce her to stay on longer, promoting her to the rank of lieutenant colonel. But it could not commit to a permanent station near any of her sisters, two of whom were raising their families in Saint Louis, where they had all been raised. She elected to leave active status and enter private engineering practice there for a medium-sized architectural engineering firm that did mostly public infrastructure work. But she happily stayed on in the reserves, attached to a small corps unit based in Missouri, about halfway to Chicago.

She had never married, though not for want of opportunity.

"You are a beautiful woman," Stanley said sincerely, quietly. "But you never married?"

"No." Her tone told him he could go further if he wished.

"You did not want to?"

"It wasn't that I didn't desire it, I don't think. I just didn't get myself there," she said.

They heard couples talking in the courtyard below. The quiet banter granted her reprieve. A minute or two passed before she resumed. Stanley looked over at her face. She was looking out over the railing, seeming to be concentrating.

"Oh, there are times I regret my choices," she finally said. "When I was younger, I think I was a perfectionist. Maybe too much. I would be with someone and everything seemed good and promising. Then a little thing would creep in. I'd get doubtful."

"What kind of little thing?" Stanley asked.

"Well, there were different ones," Helen said. "There was a navy lieutenant who really clicked with me. He wanted to make it a permanent deal. The whole thing. We were both posted in Savannah, not far from here. I was working on a fuel pipeline at the naval station there. He was a career man, which at that time was fine with me. No skeletons, no hang-ups that I could pick up on. At first. Then I could see that he didn't get along with his mother. I said, *Well, not everybody gets along with their mother. There are some lousy mothers.* But after a while, Stanley, the guy was just hard and mean about her. From what I knew about her, she was a bright woman. Successful. I met her and liked her. And liking her turned me off about *him.*"

"Maybe you thought you might become her down the road," Stanley said.

She turned to him. Her smile was seasoned with eyes showing sadness.

"I think you are right, Stanley," she said. "I think you are exactly right."

"Maybe it was *you* who was right," he said. "Even if not exactly."

And there were others whom she told Stanley about also. He could see that one, in particular, had left an imprint of lasting doubt. A friend had introduced her to a divorced veterinarian with two children, shortly after she had returned to civilian work. She fell deeply in love with him; he had seemingly all the traits she liked, and was an attentive father to his son and daughter, who were middle schoolers. In the beginning, she told herself, this was a good thing.

"*This man loves his children,* I say to myself," she recounted to Stanley. "I mean, deeply." She grew quiet.

"And maybe you could not love them the way he did," he said.

She didn't answer for a long time. She sipped her Irish whiskey. Eventually, she nodded.

"I didn't think I did. I didn't think I could. I thought he was unrealistic about them. Everything they did, everything they said, was fine, tolerable. I didn't feel that way. I wasn't proud to feel that way. I felt ashamed. I cut it off. He was very disappointed in me." There was a long pause in their conversation.

"That one I still wonder about," she said.

"How long ago?" Stanley asked.

"Ten years."

"Nothing since?"

"Nothing worth wondering about," she said. She lifted her empty glass to signal her intent, then rose and went into the room to refill her drink. Augie, lying in the middle of the hotel room, raised his head in greeting, then immediately returned to rest. The night air was cooling, the breeze waning, when Helen stepped back onto the balcony. Stanley had risen and was standing at the rail. She stood next to him.

"And you, Stanley?" she asked. "What about you?"

"*What* about me?"

"You could start by telling me about your wife." She turned and faced him.

"That isn't really about *me*," he said.

"Oh, I think it is pretty much the same thing."

Stanley let out a mild sigh, audible but not hostile. He removed his gaze from her face and looked out over the balcony rail. But she did not remove her gaze from him.

"You could start by telling me her name," she said. "You've never mentioned it."

He looked into Helen's eyes, which were glistening in the lamplight of the southern balcony lantern. At first he said nothing. His impulse was to resist, to deflect. In nearly ten years, he had uttered his wife's name to almost no one, and not at all since closing her financial accounts at the Pittsburgh bank sixty days after her death. He was keeping it, he knew unreasonably, even selfishly, in a place even safer than the bank. But safer for whom?

"Is it important to you?" he asked her. There was no rancor in his voice, no note of resentment or offense.

"It is important to you, so it is important to me," she said.

"Agnes. Her name was Agnes."

"Agnes," Helen said. "It's a beautiful name."

"Yes," he said. "I loved her name. I loved everything about her."

"Did you call her Aggie?"

"No."

"Anything else?"

"Button. I called her 'Button' sometimes. It just happened, and it lasted. I guess when you love someone, you don't call them by just one name. L.T. taught me that."

It went, Stanley later recalled, easily, so easily, from there. They talked into the early hours. As the air grew cooler and the courtyard below emptied and became silent, they retrieved light sweaters from the room. Hers was army issue. Stanley didn't have to ask about another cigar; she suggested it. He told her how he and Agnes had met as students at Carnegie Mellon. He was three years older, nearly four, studious and averse to fraternity life. His academic program in engineering was demanding. She was light and bouncy on the outside, extroverted, and one of the many theater aspirants at the school, which was renowned, unusually, for both engineering and the fine arts. To her, at least in his eyes, university life was pure joy.

"Don't misunderstand me," he said to Helen. "I don't mean to say there was no rigor in her studies. It was very hard work. So much concentration and memorization. So much experimentation. But doing it gave her such happiness! She was like a boy playing baseball. It was great to watch that in her."

"Just by watching, you were sharing," Helen observed. He nodded.

"She liked it that I wanted to go to her rehearsals," Stanley said.
"Nobody comes to rehearsals!" Agnes had told him.

"Well, I want to come to them."

The directors did not always approve, but Agnes talked them into it. Stanley said it relaxed him to sit in the rear of the practice space and watch, week to week, as the show developed. He made gentle suggestions to her on things that could be changed, which she listened to carefully but rarely pursued with the directors, except for his comments on the set design, for which he had an intuitive sense. "That side wall is not adding much," he said of one set for *A View from the Bridge*. "Dim uplighting to it would help." The next week it was there. He later teased her that he could find no stage credit in the performance program.

"Did she go on to work on the stage?" Helen asked.

"Oh, yes. I have all the playbills. I go through them sometimes. Quite a range, really. She was a regular at the Canadian Shakespeare Festival in Ontario. Not leading roles, but good parts. No interest in television. I kept urging her to try for film. She just didn't want that. I never knew why, really. Broadway she did want."

"Did she make it there?" Helen asked.

"No, she couldn't dance well enough or, I suppose, sing well enough either."

"At that level, it's almost impossible," Helen said.

"Agnes accepted it. She didn't pout about it. Not a bit."

"She knew who she was," Helen said.

"And who she wasn't."

"Sounds like a grounded woman," Helen said. Stanley turned to her, and she wondered if he'd misunderstood her. "I mean, honest. About herself."

"Oh, yes. You are right about that. She was that way to the end." It didn't seem to Helen that much should be said, at least by her, at that point, and silence arrived. After a minute or two, Stanley said, "I didn't fully appreciate that about her—her honesty about herself—until after. Along with some other things too."

He told Helen that Agnes was the granddaughter of Irish immigrants, that her grandfather Brendan Leary had come to work in the booming steel mills of Pennsylvania in the thirties, during the buildup to war. According to Agnes, he thought dropping the *O'* from "O'Leary" would disguise his brogue.

"She loved that man," Stanley said. "Really, really loved him. Always wanted to sit right next to him and talk to him, throw her arm around his shoulder. By the time I met him, he was up there. At least eighty. Still as bright-eyed as a child. Not a big man. Gentle, not a mean bone in him. Agnes said I reminded her of him. I said, 'Really? He's so much smaller.' She said, 'I mean in the important ways.'" He turned toward Helen. "It was kind of her. Agnes was very kind that way."

"And you have never stopped loving her, have you?"

"No. I don't think I ever will."

Helen took Stanley's hand and looked up to his eyes.

"You don't have to, Stanley," she said. "You never have to."

She led him from the balcony and undressed before him at the side of the bed.

The next morning, Bobby Beach sent an agent to the hotel for her. She was taken to the air base to await the trucks. On Brew's insistence, she waited alone outside to be picked up.

56
PREFERRED FOR ABDUCTION

★ ★ ★ The North Koreans were more successful at locating Stanley than the FBI and Secret Service teams had been at finding them. The spies had many advantages. They knew where Stanley went during the day—to the Department of Agriculture building south of the city—and could easily follow him at day's end to his changing hotels in Charleston. On his evening walks he was easy to spot too. He was far taller than most of the other pedestrians, and he walked a well-behaved dog on a short leash. A much younger woman seemed always to be with him. The two of them talked much as they walked. The woman knew the older man well, the foreign agents concluded. Probably a daughter, they thought. She did not appear to be armed, wearing casual walking shorts and a T-shirt, a cover-up tied around her waist in case the evening turned cool.

It was not difficult to see a pattern to the large man's walking routes. Each night the two of them walked the gallery district along Broad Street, then went north on King Street, Meeting Street, or East Bay toward the historical center of town. At Calhoun Street, they usually turned back to King Street, the principal avenue of high-end retail in the old city, and strolled south all the way back to Broad, or to their hotel in that neighborhood. Somewhere on the route they would stop for dinner, preferring venues with outdoor seating. The dog sat next to them as they ate. He didn't beg for food, the agents noticed. A very well-mannered dog, they thought. Other patrons and small children knelt to pet him. A very gentle dog too, they observed.

Normally, the agents noted, the dinner stop occurred near the middle of the walk. The dining options on East Bay Street were many, and one or another was usually selected. But on one of the earlier nights, while the agents were awaiting approval to take Stanley, they saw that he dined much later in the evening walk, off lower King Street at a small Italian restaurant on Fulton Street named for its address: Fulton Five. Fulton Street was barely an alley running west off King Street between Queen and Market in an area known more for shopping than fine food—except for Fulton Five, a small high-end eatery noted for romantic coziness. The night they tracked him there, his pattern changed. He did not dine with the short younger woman. She was there, but she stayed outside, the friendly dog sitting beside her, as the large man from Pittsburgh sat inside with a different woman. This one was taller and older than the other. She must have been waiting at the table for him to arrive, as she did not enter with him. The two diners seemed comfortable with each other, and friendly. But there was no touching as far as the watching agents could see, and their postures seemed more professional than romantic, at least the woman's. She sat straight with her shoulders back. The big engineer slumped a little forward, as he always seemed to. They did not linger long over dinner. In about ninety minutes they walked out together and greeted the younger woman with the dog. There was no kissing and no overt embrace. But the older man did gently slide one arm around the dinner companion's waist and seemed to press against it very slightly. The woman stepped into a taxi and left.

The North Koreans considered this night of surveillance particularly valuable. Little Fulton Street offered something that precious few other locations did in old Charleston: a place to park a car. Directly across the narrow street from the entrance to Fulton Five lay a stretch of pavement three hundred feet in length owned by a large cosmetics and perfume store around the corner on King Street. It was a parking strip reserved for the perfumery's patrons' free use during daytime business hours. But after five o'clock, the perfumery looked the other way at its use by the restaurant customers. At that hour each day there was room for a dozen or so lucky drivers to leave—for free—a vehicle within steps of busy King Street. The next closest reliable option was the multilevel public parking garage on Queen Street. For shoppers or diners, those garages were quite serviceable. But for abductors, they were not preferred. Yes, thought the North Koreans, this is the place to move on him once Pyongyang sends authority. He eventually will walk to the corner of King Street and tiny Fulton. He has crossed it every evening. They could leave the white Honda Accord parked in a free place just three hundred feet from the corner and wait for him. With the getaway car so nearby, they could leave it unattended. Both would conduct the assault; one would grab the big man from behind and start him to the car, then be assisted by the second as soon as he had disposed of the younger woman, who would surely be along as she always was, with the gentle dog.

57

WALKING OFF DINNER

★ ★ ★ Stanley wanted to see off Helen and the call-ups when they departed the air force base for the Middle East on Saturday, but Brew would have none of it. It was known that the Russians had detected his work and apparently accepted the cover story. But it also was known that the North Koreans had learned of him over the shoulder of the Russians, and there was strong evidence they had *not* bought into the cover—and might even be in Charleston watching Stanley now. Any behaviors inconsistent with the work at the United States Vegetable Laboratory on Savannah Highway were out of the question. Stanley was not getting near the Charleston Air Force Base.

Brew considered sending Stanley and L.T. home to Pittsburgh immediately. But Bobby Beach had arranged for a secure video link to his office that Helen could use from Kuwait after her initial inspection the next day of the foundation work performed earlier by the army corps to Stanley's blueprints. It would extend Stanley's stay in Charleston by only a couple of days and would give the two engineers the chance to work through any early problems that Helen observed upon arrival. Brew decided the Pittsburghers would wait in Charleston for Colonel Ames's report from Kuwait.

It was a beautiful July Saturday in the historical city, cooler than

291

average. A pleasing breeze rolled in over the Atlantic waves. Stanley and Kitt thought a horse-and-buggy tour of the old town in the afternoon would be interesting but feared Augie's company would prevent it. They were wrong. The stable manager said smaller dogs went all the time. It was up to the carriage driver. The first two who were asked declined, not unreasonably, it seemed to Stanley, though the dog looked up with an expression of unaggressive disbelief. The third driver said it was just fine. Augie hopped up agreeably and sat on the outer edge of the carriage floor next to Stanley. Stanley tried to make him sit in the middle of the floor between Kitt and himself, but the dog refused, insisting on his outside position.

"Forget it, Stanley," Kitt said, as he continued to tug vainly on the dog's collar, hoping to move him to the center. "He's not going to do it. He won't sit between us. He always has to be looking to the outside—next to you, looking to the outside—in case someone comes from there."

"Oh," said Stanley. "I guess I forgot. He's still on duty."

"He always is."

The ride through the narrow streets was relaxing and educational. The driver was well versed in the history and lore of each building and scene, and had a pleasing southern delivery seasoned with humor. "Is anyone getting lightheaded?" he asked, turning toward them, at an address on King Street not far from the corner of little Fulton Lane where Stanley had dined so pleasurably with Helen the week before. The driver wondered, he said, because they were at that moment at the highest elevation in Charleston: *twelve feet* above sea level. "Don't come here when it floods; it's too crowded," he said. He talked about the French Huguenots who had been welcomed by the South Carolina settlers as early as 1680, fleeing from religious persecution in their homeland. Stanley marveled at the design of their place of worship on Church Street.

Over Stanley's half-hearted protest, Brew had moved their place of lodging again. Their final night would be stayed at the John

Rutledge House Inn on Broad Street just off King Street. Kitt said Stanley had nothing to complain about, and when Bobby Beach checked them in after the carriage tour, he saw why. The inn was stunning.

It looked impressive also to the two North Korean operatives. They had waited that morning for Stanley and his young woman companion and the gentle dog to leave their prior hotel, and had been following them all day. The foreigners were pleased that it was the weekend. Their target did not go on Saturdays to the government building outside of town. It was boring to move back and forth all day on the highway out there, watching to see if the large man left it—which he never did—before the end of the day. They preferred this day, when they could walk the streets of the city and even separate, so long as one of them kept the man in view. One of the agents even took interest in the descriptions of the carriage driver and tried to walk close enough to hear, drawing a rebuke from the other, who thought it imprudent.

It was nearly four in the afternoon when Stanley entered the room he was to share with Brew at the John Rutledge. Brew was already there, with the luggage he had brought over. He reviewed the protocol for the evening ahead. As usual, Brew would stay back at the hotel to ensure there was no entry. He would be out for an hour or so, though, he told Stanley. He was meeting with Bobby Beach and the Secret Service detail at the federal court center, very near the hotel, to compare notes on the continuing sweep for the foreign agents. Stanley, L.T., and Augie could go out together for dinner. Kitt wanted to try the Peninsula Grill on Meeting Street, up near the public market, Brew told him. There was plenty of outdoor seating for Augie. He reminded him to bring his messaging device.

The Pirates were playing the Cardinals that afternoon in Saint Louis. The one-hour time difference meant the game was still going, and Stanley found the audio broadcast on his laptop. He texted Kitt to say he would be ready to walk to dinner at six. She replied, simply, "Fine." *Such an easy person to deal with,* thought Stanley.

When Kitt, Stanley, and the dog emerged from the hotel minutes after six o'clock, one of the North Koreans stood watching at the edge of Courthouse Square, only a few hundred yards ahead of them. If his prey turned northward on King Street toward Fulton, he would follow close behind. The other agent was already waiting at the corner of Fulton, where he had parked the Honda Accord down the lane in one of the perfumery spaces. They would seize the opportunity to take the large man right then. They considered the timing optimal; many of the shops were closing and the streets were not too full. There would be many more people in the dinner hours, but not this early.

But, to the agents' momentary disappointment, Kitt and Stanley did not turn on King Street. Instead, they led Augie straight up Broad and across King, passing directly in front of the North Korean scout who held a cigarette in one hand and a street map in the other, this time not of Stockholm. He watched as Kitt and Stanley made their way to Meeting Street and turned left, heading, as he would soon learn, to the Peninsula Grill at Meeting and Market Streets, three blocks up. He consulted his map and texted the other agent.

"Taking deferred for now. Stay put. Will trail."

Shortly into their meal at the Peninsula Grill, Stanley regretted they had not dined there earlier in their Charleston stay. The outside tables were nestled in a lush garden. The menu was extensive; the service, impeccable. He ordered a bone-in strip steak, and every fifth or sixth slice he carved found its way to Augie, who lay beside him facing the garden entryway. Kitt noticed but didn't comment. She was relaxed and talkative, more so than usual, Stanley thought. It had been a long duty for her. Her protection assignments rarely lasted more than a few weeks. She told Stanley that her longest prior duty had been the safekeeping of an organized crime informant during a trial in Philadelphia three years ago. But Stanley's protection was twice that. She said she felt the way a long-distance runner must feel near the end of a race. The hardest part was over. A second wind had arrived. A feeling of comfort, approaching exhilaration, was setting in. For the first time, she discussed her personal life in some depth. Stanley listened quietly. She had been married once, to a fellow agent early in her career. It was a poor decision. Their work seemed all-encompassing, and the unpredictable hours were too long. Her position in witness protection was especially difficult because it often meant around-the-clock duty away from home. It all left little room for real togetherness. In fact, it suffocated it. The breakup was not hostile—more professional than emotional, she said. She touched Stanley by saying that she had never come to know or understand "an assignment," as she called him, as well as she felt she knew him.

"And you showed me something about living downtown," she said. "I really like it down there."

"Then maybe you can stay right where you are," he said. "It would be nice to have you and Augie next door." He meant it.

"*Way* above my pay grade, Stanley," she said. "But there are some lofts going in across the river on the North Shore. Some one-bedrooms. By the ballpark. Maybe there."

Stanley had started with a bourbon on the rocks, and when Kitt ordered coffee after the meal, he asked if he might have another. Normally, Kitt limited him to a single drink on their dinner walks. She knew she probably should not consent this night, but it was, after all, probably their last one in Charleston. Brew had told her to be ready to drive back to Pittsburgh after the video briefing from Colonel Ames, expected tomorrow.

"Go ahead," she said. "But take your time with it."

Stanley complied, ordering it neat so that he could sip it slowly without too much dilution from ice. *If you want to stretch out a bourbon, have it neat,* he thought. A half hour later, just past eight, she paid the bill and they left the garden. While Stanley and Kitt dined, the hungry North Korean operative trailing them had fetched his own meal in the open-air vendors' market bordering the Peninsula Grill. He had returned to his observation post by the time they appeared on the Meeting Street sidewalk outside the restaurant. Stanley and Kitt could have returned the same way they came. It was the most direct route back to the hotel. If they had, they would have avoided the little corner of Fulton Street and King. It would have made the walk back a mere five minutes. Stanley hoped for more.

"Care to walk off this dinner a bit?" he asked Kitt.

"Sure," she said. "And Augie needs some exercise too." She didn't mean the kind he would soon get.

They headed north on Meeting Street toward Calhoun and the large open square in the center of the city where slaves had been traded for 150 years, across from the old Francis Marion hotel. The operative immediately texted his mate.

"Be ready. Looks like usual way. Coming to join."

Once Stanley, Kitt, and the dog walked left on Calhoun and then went left again on King Street in the direction of their hotel, the die was cast. To reach the John Rutledge House Hotel on Broad, they would have to cross little Fulton Street and the waiting abductors.

The unseasonably cool day was turning even cooler as the sun fell. Kitt thought about putting on the windbreaker wrapped around her waist but decided it best not to expose her firearm. The hotel was just twenty minutes away and their pace was brisk; she would stay warm enough. The two North Koreans were now stationed a few blocks ahead of them as they walked south on King Street, which narrowed and became one-way in the direction they walked. Tiny Fulton Street ran off to the right ahead. The white Honda was backed into a space down the lane one hundred yards. Its driver's-side front and rear doors were ajar for rapid entry.

One of the operatives hid out of view, a few feet down from the corner, standing straight and rigid, his back to the side wall of the shop that fronted the street. In that position, he would not be seen as the walkers entered the small intersection; he could then attack the large man from behind. The other operative stood in plain view ahead on the other side of the crossing, looking casually into a store window, with a cigarette in one hand and a street map in the other.

It could have been her training. It could have been instinct. Maybe it was Providence. Whichever it was, it likely saved her life. Kitt's glimpse of the cigarette and street map in the hands of the Asian man ahead, just as she and Stanley were halfway across the skinny lane, fired an alarm to her brain as instantly as a rifle shot. Even before the North Korean began his lunge toward her, she threw her right hand into the pocket of her slacks and tapped twice on her emergency messaging screen. She needed the same hand to reach across her waist to retrieve her gun from her left hip. She could not get it there in time. The athletic attacker dropped the map and cigarette and rushed at her like a lineman attempting a high hit on a quarterback. There was no opportunity for her, or for Augie, to look behind them to see the other abductor springing toward Stanley. Augie set his fury on the first agent, leaping between him and Kitt, thrashing wildly and knocking the assailant off balance. The North Korean by then had drawn a gleaming knife, brandishing it waist-high and charging again at Kitt. The other attacker grabbed Stanley from behind, spinning him forcefully around by the shoulder and, knife in hand, forcing him down Fulton Lane toward the waiting car.

Augie raged in fury, relentlessly launching himself at Kitt's aggressor. His first two leaps drove the man back, a step and a half each. Kitt went to the ground and rolled to her left, drawing her gun. She wanted to find a line between the assailant and the dog, but Augie was leaping high, higher than the face of the attacker. As he descended from his second leap, she fired from the ground, trying for a head shot. She missed. She saw a dozen onlookers frozen in fright, some diving to the ground, but she knew the trajectory of her shot was upward enough to sail above them.

Augie's third launch was laser-like, to the man's right wrist, inches above the knife blade. Stanley tried to turn so that he could see Kitt and Augie, but the stout North Korean, a thick hand now to the back of Stanley's neck, was too strong for him. But perhaps, he later considered, it was better he could not see it. The hearing was enough. It was sound he had never heard or imagined before. The dog made a full-jawed clamp on the aggressor's wrist and tore the man to the earth, refusing to release his grip, shaking his strong head back and forth, dragging his teeth through flesh and tendon. The attacker let out a piercing prolonged scream, a rush of alternating long and short vowels—"eeaaheeaheeah"—pounding like white water over downstream boulders.

Stanley did not know what he should do. But he knew what he did *not want* to do. He did not want to stay on his feet and let his attacker lead him away. He didn't think about it; he just did it. He slumped to his knees, taking his 260 pounds to the ground. The North Korean screamed at him to get up and shook his knife near his face. He tried to drag him. But Stanley lowered his shoulders as far as he could and slackened his long, heavy legs. *Augie will come for me,* he told himself. *Augie will come for me.*

And Augie did come. Kitt had subdued the other abductor, who was badly wounded by Augie's final leap. The dog instantly bounded down the lane to the other assailant, who was trying to force Stanley to his feet. When the attacker saw the dog racing at full speed and Kitt standing over his groaning cohort behind him, he let go of Stanley and started running to the white Honda. Stanley was certain Augie would pursue the man, but he didn't. Instead, he leapt to a halt at Stanley's side, ran his snout within inches of his face, and then stepped over him as he lay on the ground, placing himself on all fours between Stanley and the fleeing abductor. The dog stood there in a crouch next to Stanley, glaring at the retreating attacker, every one of his teeth showing, it seemed to Stanley, and an unstopping baritone growl vibrating deep in his throat.

Stanley lay there, seemingly frozen. Later he would recall feeling oddly safe. He looked toward the corner to see Kitt. He saw Brew racing around the corner, Bobby Beach behind him. Seeing that Kitt had secured the first assailant, Brew did not pause—not in the slightest.

Even a very good spy will not make much of a living trying to outrun a Navy SEAL in open field. Brew flashed by Stanley and Augie, running fully upright, his open-palmed hands pumping up and down like an Olympian's. Bobby Beach followed, doing his best to keep up, quite admirably, Kitt thought, for a sixty-year-old agent-in-charge. The North Korean was a few feet from his car when Brew reached him. Stanley, Kitt, and Bobby Beach were never able to satisfactorily describe the takedown that ensued. The best they could say was that there was a dive, the rapid chopping of wrists and arms, the thrust of a hand beneath a chin, and the loud crack of two large bones.

Within minutes three Secret Service agents and two others from Bobby Beach's local FBI team flooded into little Fulton Lane, all responding to Kitt's emergency message. Brew and Bobby Beach were together in the federal court building when the alarm was sounded, so nearby that they came on foot. The Charleston County Sheriff's Department was called to the scene. An SUV was needed to take away the North Koreans. Five minutes later three deputies arrived from the sheriff's department. The deputies all knew Bobby Beach, but he showed them his credentials anyway.

"Will y'all transport these two over to the federal detention center?" he asked the ranking deputy. "Be much obliged." He told them to take their cell phones and any other devices, such as wristwatches, that might contain GPS tracking sensors.

"Sure, Bobby," the deputy replied.

As the two would-be abductors were loaded, Brew and Bobby Beach conferred near the white Honda. They looked in the trunk and found the Pennsylvania license plate, the plastic tape, and the bungee cords. Both knew there was no time for delay. Stanley was safe—for now. But for how long? And was his cover about to be

blown in a barrage of media coverage? Brew had not shared with
Bobby the true nature of Stanley's work, only that it was a matter
of national security involving the military. The FBI veteran knew
better than to press for details. But he looked around at the crowd
that had gathered. You didn't have a shot fired on King Street
in downtown Charleston on Saturday night and two abductors
apprehended without questions—lots of them.

"You have to get out in front of this, Brew," he said. "Somehow
you've got to keep this from blowing up."

"Any ideas?" Brew asked him.

"There is a way," said Bobby Beach. "There is someone who can
do it." He looked at his watch; it was nearly eight thirty. "And I know
where to find him right now."

58

THERE'S RIGHT, THERE'S WRONG, AND THERE'S THE SHERIFF

★ ★ ★ The "way" that Bobby Beach meant was a public version of the night's events that would protect Stanley Bigelow's cover story. The man to do it, Bobby Beach knew, was Weldon Bechant, the long-serving sheriff of Charleston County. And the place he could be found was the place he always was at eight thirty in the evening, nearly seven nights a week: the bar of Halls Chophouse on the other end of King Street.

The local FBI leader asked a Secret Service man from the Presidential Protection Unit to drive him and Brew down to Halls and to come in with them to see the sheriff.

"Nothing impresses like a presidential bodyguard," he told Brew.

When the three of them walked in to the crowded restaurant, Bobby Beach spotted the sheriff immediately. He was at his usual seat at a large high top near the back of the bar area, holding forth in full uniform with the amiable owner of the establishment and his other high-profile regulars. The sheriff rose instinctively when he saw his colleague approaching. He said nothing, just made a slight motion to the owner and started to the rear door, walking down a hallway and past the restrooms, knowing Bobby Beach and his guests would follow. The sheriff knew official business when he saw it. He waited for them at the rear door. When they were all there, he opened it and stepped out first. A line cook and a dishwasher, smoking on their break, were huddled near a screen door to the kitchen in the small rear area large enough only for the food supply trucks and the owner's parked Cadillac. They did not require asking; they scurried into the kitchen when the sheriff emerged.

Weldon Bechant breathed rarified air in greater Charleston, and most people believed he had earned it. And he'd earned it against the usual odds in elected service. In many ways he was unlikely for the role. At seventy-one years of age, he was not a strapping, muscular man who stretched the shoulder stitching of a police uniform the way most southern—or for that matter, northern—sheriffs did. If he were to stand on the Charleston phone book, he might be five feet seven inches tall. But he was trim, handsome in his own way, and signature in his appearance. He liked to wear his trousers cinched high, a preference that seemed accented by the wide-brimmed trooper's hat he wore above a perfectly knotted black tie, no matter the weather. He had a taste for the finer things and an unsurpassed knowledge of wines, spirits, and things culinary. Out of uniform, he was an impeccable dresser, standing out at charity benefits in crisp suits and two-hundred dollar neckties from Grady Ervin, one of Charleston's upscale clothiers. "A man of the law ought to look the part," he liked to say. "It's a civic duty," he said, which often as not meant the haberdasher on King Street ought to look elsewhere when it came to expecting payment.

And Weldon Bechant was as bright as bright could be. They said he could tell a lie before it was uttered, and could remember the smallest details of witness statements in every murder investigation in forty years.

But the secret to the stature of the sheriff of Charleston County was not in his dress or style, or even his erudition. It was the credibility he had built over more than four decades among the people of his sprawling county. He had that most rare of qualities in an elected official. He understood the people he served and knew what they needed—at times, it seemed, better than they themselves understood it. No one mistook him for an angel. His drinking antics were well-known. He could carry his power with a heavy hand. And no one ever accused him of modesty. But he was, above all else, a man who could be trusted to do the right thing when it was important. That made his words as good as the gospels, and probably why they were consulted by his devoted public more often than they were. But doing the right thing in Charleston County and keeping the law at the same time was not always an obvious correlation. Part of what endeared the sheriff to the people was his unvarnished acknowledgment of that reality.

"The law is the truth and the truth is the law," the old sheriff was fond of saying. "And sometimes you have to bend one of them to keep it that way."

Brew and Bobby Beach hoped he would apply that principle this night.

"I don't suppose this is about that dustup down the street just now?" the sheriff asked when they were all outside. "Just got a text about it. A *shot* was fired? Who the hell did that? A *shot* on goddamned King Street?"

"It all happened pretty fast, Weldon," said Bobby Beach. "But, yes, that's why we're here." He introduced Brew and the Secret Service agent and told the sheriff they had come for a favor.

"So I've got a shot fired on King Street, a Navy SEAL, and the goddamned presidential guard here. This is some kind of Saturday night," he said. The back door to the restaurant opened and a waiter in a white tuxedo shirt emerged with a tray holding four whiskeys in rocks glasses.

"From the boss for the sheriff and his friends," the waiter said. Weldon smiled approvingly but not broadly. He took one and gestured to the others to do the same. The Secret Service agent complied, but held the glass at his chest, not partaking, it being against the rules. Brew and Bobby Beach were not so particular.

"What kind of favor?" asked the sheriff.

Bobby Beach looked to Brew to see if the SEAL wanted to explain. But Brew deferred to the local officer.

"I don't even know why, Weldon, but the two men arrested down there were North Korean spies trying to kidnap an old civilian engineer from Pittsburgh who's working with Captain Brew here," Bobby Beach explained. "The shot was fired by a bureau agent from Pittsburgh who's been guarding him, with a trained dog. She's a good officer. She was on the ground, under attack."

The sheriff listened closely, standing inches from the FBI man. His hearing was poor, but he made it a practice never to miss a pertinent word. Bobby Beach went on, saying that a cover story had been prepared to keep the engineer's work secret. He outlined the cover. The government knew some foreign intelligence forces had believed it. But not the North Koreans. They had been stalking the engineer during the president's visit, and tried to take him tonight to learn what he was doing.

"They must think it's really military," said the local agent-in-charge.

"Which it probably is," said the sheriff.

"As I said, Weldon, I don't even know myself. But I know it's important to the captain here, and even to the president. That's why the Secret Service is helping too. They need the right spin on this to protect the man. Protect his work. I told the captain and the president's man here I hoped you might do them a favor."

The sheriff removed his glasses and held them with his drink hand. He ran his other hand over his nose and across his temple, then over his nose again. The wheels were turning.

"I don't suppose you mind if I take a little credit for the department?" the sheriff asked.

"That would be just fine, Weldon," said Bobby Beach. "Probably even better that way."

Bechant raised his glass to Bobby Beach's.

"I've been doing favors like this my whole life, Bobby," said the sheriff of Charleston County, smiling. "Almost my damned specialty. I'll get the reporters over to my office in an hour to take care of this," he said, stepping toward the door. "You fellas finish your drinks. I won't need ya."

59

THE MORNING AFTER

★ ★ ★ Kitt went to the lobby early the next morning and picked up the early edition of *The Charleston Post & Courier*. She and Stanley read the front-page story together.

VISITOR ATTACKED ON KING STREET

SHOT FIRED

SHERIFF ASSURES PUBLIC

A Pittsburgh man was assaulted last night on busy King Street, but Sheriff Weldon Bechant said citizens have no reason for alarm. The sheriff said two assailants were arrested at the scene and placed in federal custody after an apparent kidnapping attempt.

Speaking to reporters at his office late last evening, Bechant said the intended victim was an engineer working at the United States Vegetable Laboratory on Savannah Highway. The sheriff said the incident was unrelated to two recent robberies in the Queen

Street parking garage, for which separate arrests have already been made.

"The streets of our city remain safe for all," assured Bechant. "The Sheriff's Department responded immediately, professionally, and successfully. There are no perpetrators at large."

Witnesses described a frightening scene at the corner of King and Fulton Street about 8:15 Saturday night. Sheriff Bechant confirmed that two men wielding knives attempted to overtake the seventy-year-old Pittsburgh man as he walked after dinner but were thwarted by a canine unit of the Charleston County Sheriff's Department. Bechant said that a member of the sheriff's canine force, a German shepherd named Nelson, disabled one of the assailants and protected the intended victim from the other until his officers took both into custody.

The name of the Pittsburgh visitor was not released, in keeping with the department's privacy policy. The sheriff said the man was in town to supervise the installation of a special storage container at the Department of Agriculture facility on Highway 17. The assailants are being held in federal custody because the assault of a United States contractor is a federal offense, the sheriff said.

The sheriff confirmed witness reports that a gunshot was fired in the incident. He said it was fired by an FBI agent who came to the assistance of his deputies at the scene.

"Agent-in-Charge Bobby Beach of the Charleston FBI happened to be working the area with a team of his people on another investigation," Sheriff Bechant said. "They came to the assistance of my deputies and our dog, and one of them fired a warning shot into the sky. The discharge was entirely appropriate in the circumstances," he said. The sheriff said he had filed a report, required by FBI procedures, certifying that public safety was not endangered by the agent's action.

The sheriff would not comment on reports that the two assailants appeared to be of Asian descent, saying only that they were not from the Charleston area.

Kitt and Stanley howled at the newspaper's description of events. "*Nelson!*" exclaimed Kitt. "A German shepherd named Nelson! He even took credit for Augie!"

But each knew, as did Tyler Brew in helping orchestrate the relation of the incident the night before, that Sheriff Bechant and Bobby Beach were solidifying the cover story intended from the beginning to protect Stanley and the secrecy of the Eaglets' Nest project. The sheriff and his friends at the *Post and Courier* made certain that the news story was picked up and repeated by the Associated Press. The involvement of a police dog broadened interest in the story. It was widely reported, with a photo of the department's canine Nelson, sitting resolutely next to the sheriff, that Bechant had released to the press. An abbreviated version even appeared internationally in the *News Herald* in its Europe and Asia editions. The local television outlets featured the sheriff's conference prominently, and one of them provided taped footage to CNN. There could be no question but that Pyongyang and Moscow would learn what happened or—more accurately—what was said to have happened. The latter might derive some satisfaction from the course of events; the former—quite likely, Brew believed—might conclude that it had misconstrued its stolen intelligence all along.

Brew had breakfast with Bobby Beach to thank him, and then he went to the hotel to recount the night's events together with Stanley and Kitt. He was pleased and grateful to both Bobby Beach and Sheriff Bechant. Kitt asked if the sheriff really had made the report about the discharge of her firearm. Brew said he had, and without needing to be asked. She was relieved and said it was not always the case that local law enforcement worked so cooperatively with the FBI. Rivalry was more the norm, she said. Agent Beach had clearly cultivated the respectful relationship he enjoyed with the slow-drawling southern sheriff with the high-cinched pants. And it had surely inured to everyone's benefit last evening.

Brew reported that Helen Ames and the call-ups had arrived safely at Bagram Air Base and were secretly transported to Kuwait in oil field uniforms. Helen had already made an initial inspection of the foundation work and would be leading a video uplink to discuss it with Stanley in an hour in Bobby Beach's conference room at the FBI office. If the videoconference went well, Stanley and Kitt could return to Pittsburgh that afternoon. And he said the president had been briefed on everything, including the abduction attempt.

"She was very concerned about you, Stanley," Brew said. "She really was."

"Well, that's kind of her," said Stanley.

"I told her we believed the threat was likely over and that it would not be repeated. But she told me to offer you Augie permanently. To look after you. Just as a precaution. If you would like to have the dog, that is. She would like you to accept, but it's up to you."

"That's even more kind of her," Stanley said, looking down at the dog resting on the floor near the door of the hotel room, wearing his customary long-tongued smile. "Kitt?" he asked. "Is that okay with you?"

"I think it's wonderful," she said convincingly. But at least Brew thought he saw the briefest sweep of sadness cross her eyes.

"Please tell the president that I accept, with gratitude," said Stanley. "So long as August does."

60

THE PRESIDENT'S SPECIAL ORDER

★ ★ ★ General Williamson had three separate Special Forces teams study the prospects for a return visit to the compound at Farah. He did not tip his hand to any of them when he gave them their assignments. But in his heart, he was deeply skeptical about another mission, and thought the president probably was too. He was not surprised by the independent conclusions of the planning teams. It could not be done with any assurance of success, and with less of nondetection. In the face of undeniable knowledge that the Iranian military knew of the compound and its contents, any attempt would certainly be "contested," a bland if not misleading term for, at best, a diplomatic mess or, worse, an all-out firefight.

One of the teams did devise an ingenious scheme, with somewhat better chances, in which diversionary events would be staged north and south of the compound in hopes that Iranian forces would pursue those provocations en masse while a small Special Forces team was inserted quickly at Farah. Williamson commended the team for its creative thinking but knew that such provocative action, requiring the dropping of substantial ordnance into Afghan territory near the Iranian border, carried too much risk in and of itself. Even if the Farah visit could be conducted during the distractions, civilian casualties were probable. The Iranians and

Afghans would—with justification—decry the military actions as inflammatory, or worse.

As is so often the case with military planning, the assessments were mooted before the general could even report them. The French ambassador to the United States made an unscheduled visit to the State Department in Washington. France's embassy in Tehran had been asked to pass an urgent message to the United States. It was said to come from the highest levels in Iran, with authorization from both the civil leadership and the religious clergy. The assistant secretary of state who received the written communiqué had the good sense to know when he was out of his league. But he also had the good sense to ask one critical question before calling Defense Secretary Lazar.

"Do you have clear assurance that the Iranian *military* is also aware of this message?" he asked the French official. It was statecraft protocol. A diplomat acting as an intermediary should always ask for confirmation of the full scope of the source's authority. The Frenchman in Tehran had done so.

"Yes. Unequivocal" was his response.

Lazar called Williamson at his base in Florida and suggested he take an air force command jet to Washington immediately. Next he called Jack Hastings at the CIA and asked him to stay in the Eisenhower Executive Office Building adjoining the White House for the rest of the day. A meeting with the president was likely. Then he called the White House and asked the president's chief of staff to arrange a meeting with her as soon as possible.

"What do I tell her?" asked the White House official.

"Farah and Eaglets' Nest," Lazar said. "She'll know."

Three hours later they convened in the Oval Office. Lazar produced the writing that had been funneled by Iran through the French. If genuine, it was a breakthrough. But the ramifications—and risks—were enormous. The message was not long, barely more than a page. Its content was direct. The Iranians wanted the United

States to know that ISIS, al-Qaeda, and Hasikan Jahideen had solicited Iran's involvement in a series of broad-scale offensives across several nations. The Iranians had asked for proof of the planning and claimed resources. The terrorist groups had made such proof available, Iran said. Iran's military and intelligence leaders believed it credible. The plans called for the consolidation of terrorist forces exponentially larger than any heretofore seen, equipped with massive armaments. Wholesale slaughter of civilians was contemplated.

Williamson confirmed that the details recited by the Iranians matched the information revealed in the data drives discovered by the SEALs at the Farah compound. That much was certain. Iran was disclosing what was found by its two soldiers filmed by the US drone entering and leaving the otherwise deserted outpost.

Some of the message was difficult to accept on its face. It said Iran would not support the plan or participate in its execution. It also would not disclose to the terror groups its transmission of this information to the United States. Accepting these claims as true required a leap of faith for everyone reading the communiqué in the Oval Office. But at least the president was open to the possibility that the claims were true. The message stated that Iran did not approve of the expansionist goals of the terrorist groups. It also did not believe that the terrorists would target only Christian civilians, as they had already killed scores of Muslims—in fact more Muslims than anyone else. It singled out ISIS and the newer entrant to the terrorist web, Hasikan Jahideen, calling the latter's seizure of the Doctors without Borders hospital in Turj and the execution of the doctor and patient there "raw barbarity."

But while Iran said it would not support the terrorist groups, its message was less clear as to whether it might join in any countermeasures against them. And the message contained one sentence that piqued the president's interest in particular. It read as follows:

The United States should know that any military
actions undertaken by it to obstruct the offensive
planning of the terrorists will be unnoticed by the
Islamic Republic of Iran.

Unnoticed? It seemed an odd word. *Any* military actions? Even if
the Iranians could be trusted—and she had not yet concluded they
should be—she did not for a minute believe that this expression
could be taken literally. The Iranian promise was made without
Iran's knowledge of Eaglets' Nest. Surely Iran would not encourage
the use of *nuclear* force in its own region—and never would do so
against Muslims, however extreme. Whatever the bona fides of the
Iranian outreach, *any* did not truly mean "any."

There was not much time to deliberate options. The message
from Tehran did not say it, but the intelligence digested by
Williamson and the CIA indicated that the first—and largest—
consolidated terrorist assault on an urban center was planned to
occur in only eight days, in the third week of August. The general
and his Special Forces command had already developed military
options for the president's decision. According to the Farah data, the
terrorist groups intended to infiltrate numerous small villages and
compounds north of the Afghan city of Qalat, a city on the Ring
Road that circles much of Afghanistan, located in Zabul Province
in the southeast section of the country near the Pakistan border.
Bands of fifty to two hundred fighters would move to their stations
near Qalat over the next week. Thirty thousand were expected to be
in place and ready to attack together on a coordinated command.
Williamson's preferred counterapproach called for waiting until the
terrorists had consolidated and advanced to an agonizing extent—
when the large force was nearly at the steps of the city. At that time,
and not until then, a devastating US air campaign would descend
upon them. Just hours before, while the terrorists were streaming
toward their target, an initial force of ten thousand US paratroopers

and support vehicles would be dropped on the other side of the city. A second force of half that size would be airborne and ready if the initial force proved too small. Most of the paratroopers would move around the city's eastern side and engage any terrorists who survived the air attack. The rest would enter Qalat and safeguard the civilians inside.

The message from Iran presented new possibilities but also new risks and, at least to the president, almost a need to involve the temperamental power, if such a thing could be arranged.

"Why do you want them in this?" asked Lazar. It was a fair question.

"Because we've been dancing around the edges with this government since its revolution in the seventies," she said. "Hot and cold, hot and cold. Never any sustained cooperation. It is the largest population in the Middle East. Its technology is the most advanced. We forget it was a bitter enemy of Saddam Hussein. Despite all that's gone before, we have *some* things in common."

"This communiqué could be a setup," said Lazar. "Can we really trust them that they have not told the terror groups? What if there is a whole other plan altogether? We could be dropping troops into an ambush."

Williamson said he thought there was a way to test the honesty of the Iranians and use the Farah intelligence at the same time. He outlined his thinking generally in the Oval Office meeting. The president asked him to refine it with operational details to be presented in another meeting the day after next.

The same group met with the president two days later near the dinner hour. General Williamson's plan was intricate, ambitious, and it seemed to all, doable. The plan called for asking the Iranians for human intelligence assistance on the ground—and only that— as the terrorist offensive took shape. Communication lines directly to the American commanders in the theater would be provided to the Iranians. Iranian operatives, to be planted in a broad semicircle north of Qalat, would be asked to call in details and coordinates of the terrorists' consolidation as the groups began to move. All of these arrangements would be made through the French Embassy in Tehran working with one of Williamson's direct commanders. The French had been contacted; they were pleased to act as the intermediary and knew how to reach the correct authorities. If the Iranians in fact agreed to do this and then did *not* come through during the operation, the president would have her answer as to whether they could be trusted. But if they did perform, she could have even more positive news to announce at the completion of the mission than the destruction of an unprecedented number of terrorists. She could tell the world that meaningful cooperation in the fight against terror had been provided by a major Middle East power, and a troublesome one at that.

But the general's plan had one more element. Once the paratroopers jumped south of the Afghan city and formed into units, the American soldiers would be vulnerable to rocket fire or encirclement by an Iranian ambush. The concentration of ten thousand men and women in an open area was every commander's worst fear—and every enemy's dream.

Eaglets' Nest was complete—barely—and four Eaglets were in their hidden base, armed with two Talon missiles each, enough to obliterate the Iranian capital. Stanley's design had achieved its essential purpose of undetectability. The NSA and the air force had conducted numerous reconnaissance and satellite sweeps employing every detection technology available at every conceivable vector and altitude. The area adjoining the Kuwaiti oil field appeared merely a piece of sandy earth.

The general and the president had never contemplated such early use of the new weapons. But a double cross by the Iranians would constitute a game-changing blow to the United States. Williamson asked for authority to deploy two Eaglet drones two hours before the paratroopers were dropped. They would stay within Afghan airspace and return to the underground base in Kuwait if the mission went as planned and Iran fulfilled its promise. But if the American troops were ambushed, they would fly to Tehran and await the president's instruction.

The commanders and advisors in the meeting said later they could not recall a session in which President Winters was so quiet. It was not that she was unengaged. She sat forward in her chair the whole time, and did not touch her coffee, unusual for her. She listened intently to every word. She stared at Williamson with serious eyes as he detailed every aspect of the operation. She never once smiled. She did not even formally close the meeting. She simply stood up and asked the general if he was finished. He said he was. She gave no instruction or any indication of one. She just walked out of the Oval Office and over to the East Wing residence.

Staff in the residence recounted later that the president asked that her dinner be deferred until later and that her father be located and brought to the study. They remembered there was no drinking by either of them as they talked behind closed doors in the study for an hour and a half. Then the president called for a folio and presidential stationery. In her own hand, she wrote the following order and sent it by courier to the Secretary of Defense:

> The military operation of the United States Armed Forces, detailed by SOCOM commander Williamson for execution on or about August 17 of this year, is hereby authorized, approved, and directed to be executed, with the following exception: the SOCOM commander's plan specified the dispatch of two Eaglet drones, equipped with two Talon warheads each, for potential use on my order during or after the mission. The SOCOM

commander is instead ordered to dispatch *four* Eaglet drones, similarly equipped, for use on my order during or after the mission.

DJW, President

The First Father looked at what she had written.

"Never send a boy to do a woman's work," he said.

61

FOUR HOURS

★ ★ ★ On the night of the operation, the president waited once again in her study in the upstairs residence of the White House. Henry Winters did not come to the study on his own. He waited until she asked, at about seven o'clock. General Williamson led his team, joined by Captain Brew, and watched live feed from a dozen drones in the central SOCOM command room at MacDill. The general asked the president if she wanted him to divert the video feed to her at the White House. She declined. She knew that President Obama had been criticized, even by his former defense secretary Gates in his memoirs, for micromanaging military operations. She passed no judgment on the earlier president, and would not have even if he had not been the one most responsible, on account of his recommendation years earlier, for her sitting that night in the White House in the first place. But it was her style, nerve-racking as it was for her, to let the military leaders implement on their own once the largest tactical orders had been made. As hard as it was to sit and wait for word, she knew their job was even harder. Nothing ever went exactly as planned or hoped; snap judgments were always necessary at the line of scrimmage. They didn't need an overseer watching from 1600 Pennsylvania Avenue, and especially not one with a general for a father.

Brew and Williamson watched in real time as the four Eaglet drones rose, one after another, from Stanley Bigelow's subterranean deployment locker next to the Kuwaiti oil field. Stanley's box top-roof lifted perfectly and, when the drones carrying their Talon missiles were safely away, closed on command with a gentle thud. Once down, the canvas-covered beryllium roof sections looked like just another piece of desert. Williamson called the president to say the Eaglets were airborne.

The French had reported that the Iranians agreed on all aspects of their assignment. The Iranians said they had infiltrated the region over the past thirty hours and had positioned intelligence personnel along an eighty-mile radius of Afghan territory at the precise coordinates supplied by the US command. They were to initiate the first contact at 20:45 EDT. It did not come. It did not come at 20:46. It did not come at 20:47. Henry Winters saw the gravity on his daughter's face as she paced in the upstairs study. He reached for her hand.

"Conclude nothing," he said. "You cannot tell anything from this yet."

But at MacDill, on screens covering an entire wall, disconcerting images appeared. The screens showed feeds filming the Iranian border near Farah. A mobilization was taking place. An Iranian armored tank division was forming up. Williamson called the president immediately in the White House study. His voice was calm but very serious.

"We have Iranian troops gathering on their side of the border. They have nothing in the Afghan airspace, though," he said to her. "The Airborne has already started sending our people out of the planes."

"And still no contact from the Iranian agents in the field?" she asked. It was 20:49.

"Nothing," he said. "I don't like it. Maybe they are not even out there. We picked up small movements around the coordinates yesterday, but it could have been anybody. Locals, farmers." He paused. "Wait." Another pause. "The first contact just came in. He reports a group of ISIS fighters gathering on the Ring Road sixty miles out of Qalat. He said he was late because he had to take cover; they passed right in front of him."

The strain fell from the president's face as if gravity had removed it.

"Thank you, General," she said. "Get back to it."

The next four hours unfolded so rapidly that it seemed to President Del Winters like twenty minutes. The Iranian troops continued to build on the border, but her father urged that she not make too much of that. They didn't trust us any more than we trusted them, he reminded her. "If you had some other power landing ten thousand soldiers in Mexico, what would you do?" he asked. "You'd get people ready in Texas and Arizona. It's the intelligence reports from the coordinates that are important." And those reports continued to come, nearly all of them at the specified intervals.

Williamson had maintained that it was necessary to wait as long as possible before commencing the air attack on the marching terrorists, to allow for as many as possible to become exposed and limit the number that could retreat. The Farah data seemed to be dead-on. The aggregate terrorist head count reported by the Iranian field network ultimately reached nearly thirty-one thousand. The armed mob was only a mile from the border of Qalat when the first of dozens of waves of US fighter jets descended upon it. For sixty minutes, they pilloried the terrorists with alternating waves of laser-guided missiles and strafing gunfire. All the while, the paratroopers raced into and around the city. Three special units did nothing but find older adult citizens—mothers, fathers, and elders—to tell them what was happening, helping them to gather their families, and telling them to stay in the city where, the soldiers assured them, they would be safe. The terrorists had consolidated and had tried to take their city, but the Americans were destroying them before they could reach it. It was not a hard sell to civilians living in fear and disgust for years under constant threat from Taliban bands and terrorist assaults.

It was past midnight. Nearly all the attackers had been killed. Few surrendered. The president did not wait to be asked; she called Williamson and directed him to send the Eaglets back to Kuwait. Then she asked for Tyler Brew.

"Captain," she said, "I didn't want a feed of what happened tonight. I didn't want to meddle. But now the Eaglets are flying back to their base. They will be landing in a little while. That, I would like to see. I would like to see what Stanley built."

"Done," Brew said.

She watched the Eaglets descend, one by one in two-minute intervals, Stanley's roof panels reaching up to them like welcoming arms until the last was safely home. Henry Winters watched with her; only he with bourbon.

62

TWO FAVORS FOR ONE

★ ★ ★ The president addressed the nation the next morning to inform the people what had happened. *Most* of what happened, of course. There was no gloating, and she maintained her customary tone of understatement. But she did say that for the first time the United States had sought and received intelligence assistance from the Islamic Republic of Iran and was grateful—very much so—for its support in dealing this blow to terrorism. No one was calling Iran an ally of the United States, she said, or the United States an ally of Iran. But the ability to work together on matters of common security and human decency was a good sign, she said, for both countries and for the world.

The Eaglets' Nest had been deployed, but went unmentioned. It had functioned flawlessly. It remained a secret. All that remained was the issue of what to do with the North Korean assassins sent to abduct Stanley Bigelow and learn the nature of his assignment. They could have been charged with espionage, assault, and kidnapping and made to face US justice. But no one was much interested in the public display, much less the intelligence disclosure, that could accompany prosecution in the homeland.

President Winters had an idea. It may have been her best idea since thinking of a dog for the overweight engineer from Pittsburgh.

The Russian president came on the line to answer her call. She had placed the call, intentionally, at a time convenient for him, eight in the morning, Moscow time. It was less convenient for her, sitting alone in the White House residence late in the evening.

"Madam President," he greeted her. "I am surprised to have your call. I have nothing before me concerning any matters between us. I think all is quiet. Are you calling about your victory over the terrorists in Afghanistan?"

"No, Mr. President," she said. "I am not calling about that. And happily, there are no problems between us, other than the ones that always seem to be there."

"You really can address me as Dmitri," he said. "We get along well enough. It is a good thing, no? To be on a first name basis?"

"Thank you, Mr. President." Deliberately, she did not accept his first-name overture. She thought it would be interesting to see if he assumed it anyway and adopted the practice himself.

"I am calling about something new. It is nothing disturbing," she said. "In the past, your country has normally had standing requests on file through our diplomatic channels that should persons whom we know have harmed you in some way come into the custody of the United States, they be transferred to your custody, confidentially."

"Of course. We have a protocol for that. It has been a long-standing arrangement. And reciprocal," he said.

"Well, I cannot agree it has always been reciprocal," she answered.

"Really?"

"There was a certain Mr. Snowden, I recall."

"Oh, that. Yes, except for that. I hope you are not calling about that old episode."

"I am not," the president said. "I am calling because we have in custody two foreign agents we have reason to believe you are interested in."

"Oh, really?" he said.

"Yes, we are quite sure they are of interest to you. But when I checked with our ambassador, she advised me you presently have no formal request on file for operatives of North Korea."

"That must be an oversight, Madam President. There should always be an open request for citizens of each country listed in the protocol. Both Koreas are on that list. Someone has erred on our end."

"I thought so too. Perhaps you could see to it that one is formally filed for North Koreans. Today yet, even."

"Most assuredly, Madam President."

"Goodbye then, Mr. President. Perhaps you and your wife will plan a visit to Washington soon. It's been too long."

"Thank you for your graciousness. My regards to your father." He hung up.

Six hours later a black armored FBI Suburban drove onto a tarmac at the far end of Dulles International Airport. It pulled up to a Boeing 727 with diplomatic markings of the Russian Federation. Four hefty federal agents emerged from the vehicle and led out the two North Korean operatives. They were dressed in black pants and black short-sleeved shirts. They were handcuffed behind their backs, and an ankle chain connected the leg of one to the leg of the other. One was in a shoulder sling with an arm heavily bandaged from the top of the hand to the elbow. The other wore plaster casts on both arms. Taking each side of the handrail of the stairs lowered from the fuselage, they ascended one step at a time, unhurried. They were being returned as a favor.

Just not to their own country.

63

THE ACCIDENTAL PATRIOT

★ ★ ★ Stanley couldn't sleep. In truth, he didn't want to. Helen was already asleep next to him, exhausted, as he should have been, from the day's events. But Stanley's mind was running. It was running with a sense of quiet excitement and contemplation. He was looking back at all that had happened and trying to put it together, sum it up. He rose from the bed gently. Helen did not stir. Augie, sleeping between the foot of the bed and the door, sprung up instantly, soundlessly, and followed him out of the room. Stanley went to his liquor cabinet and poured a double of Jefferson's Reserve. He remembered it was the same bourbon he had ordered at the JW Marriott from the oddly silent bartender the day that all of this began.

Augie watched him closely as he poured his drink. When Stanley opened the double doors to the balcony, the dog moved a few steps, as if measuring a line between Stanley and the apartment foyer. Then he lay down, snout on paws. He always rested between Stanley and the door. He did it even when Stanley asked him to do otherwise. Stanley had worried that Augie might be showing signs of disobedience; maybe he was not happy. He had called Kitt to ask her about it. Augie would not sit by the fireplace with him and would not come up onto the bed or sofa, no matter how Stanley coaxed him, he told her.

"He will always take a position between you and the door, Stanley," she told him. "When you are inside, that's what he will do. He may never stop it." There were some things you could never take out of a protection dog, she said. "Don't worry. He's crazy about you. How is he otherwise? Not chewing your slide rules, I hope." Stanley could tell that she missed the creature.

It was two weeks past Labor Day, but the late-night air in Pittsburgh was warm as he sat on the balcony. The weather people on television always called it "unseasonably warm." He didn't understand why. It happened every year, it seemed. And it was lovely to have on this evening, he thought. It suited his mood.

His journey had finished that day as it had begun six months before, with an unexpected trip to Washington. Two weeks earlier, the president had invited Stanley and Helen to the White House for lunch with her and Tyler Brew. She wanted to thank Colonel Ames in person for her supervision of the installation in Kuwait, and Stanley and Brew too, for all they had been through since their meeting on Kiawah Island. Before extending the invitation, she checked with Admiral Jennings at the NSA, who was relaxed about the idea of the visit, even if it should attract public notice. There was nothing remotely unusual about a senior military officer visiting the White House, and Stanley could be welcomed under an assumed name. She reminded the president that Stanley and Helen were seeing each other and that the relationship might be romantic. She said she knew.

Del chose to have the meal upstairs in the residential quarters. It was mainly because her father, taken greatly by Stanley at Kiawah, wanted to see him again. The president said that was fine, but urged him not to talk baseball all of the time; she didn't know if Colonel Ames was a fan or not.

"Are they a couple?" asked her father. His tone reflected surprise, mixed with a little concern.

"So what if they are?" she said.

"I'm just surprised, that's all."

"Well, if they are, I am very pleased," the president said.

She did not explain why, but her father thought he knew. There had always been an element of discomfort for her in all of this, involving an ordinary citizen—a senior citizen at that—in a matter of secret and hazardous national security, and after the murder of the first engineer recruited. But if there might be some unexpected reward for him that came of it, maybe the discomfort could be discounted. Maybe he had not been taken too much advantage of after all.

Helen, upon receiving the invitation and knowing that Stanley had been asked too, suggested she could come to Pittsburgh for a visit a day or two in advance. They could travel to Washington together. What did he think about that? "Why, that would be nice," he said. Even better if she would plan on returning to Pittsburgh after the lunch and staying a few days then too. The new symphony season was beginning. If there was a pause before she agreed, it was negligible.

They took a morning flight to Reagan National and emerged at the same arrival door where the small blue Toyota had awaited Stanley when his odyssey began. But this time, a black Secret Service Escalade awaited, out of which Tyler Brew stepped with a brilliant smile. "Stanley! Stanley! Stanley!" he exclaimed, and they embraced beside the car. He was wearing his dress blues, cutting an impressive figure. His left breast was a sea of bright ribbons, emblems, and shining pins. Stanley had never seen him so dressed, so formal. Even so, he seemed to Stanley more relaxed than he had ever seen him, save perhaps in his kitchen apron. Remembering their greeting that morning from his balcony chair in the Pittsburgh air, Stanley smiled in the silent evening. How far he and Brew had come since the day he met the intense, skeptical, unsmiling Navy SEAL.

The president greeted them warmly at the front entrance of the White House. She separately saluted the colonel and the captain, and shook Stanley's hand firmly.

"Stanley, you are looking fitter than ever," she said. He did look good; a few more pounds had departed. "Augie must be doing his job even in retirement," she said. "How is he doing?"

"He is a fixture in the neighborhood. Well respected. He goes to the office with me now."

"Outstanding."

"I have not seen any of his pension checks in the mailbox, though."

"An oversight, I assure you."

The good humor continued upstairs, where Henry Winters waited. He hurried to Stanley like one player rushing to congratulate another after a triumph on the field. They embraced and stepped a small distance to the side. Immediately, they seemed to be in energetic conversation. The president and the colonel overhead something about pitches per plate appearance in relation to on-base percentage and reaching on error. They appeared to agree on the point. As far as the president was concerned, though, her father's promise to keep baseball talk in tow was being honored, as the bard had said, more in the breach than in the observance. She walked over and steered them into the dining room. Cleverly, she led Stanley to one end of the long table and Henry to the other. If the two of them intended to keep this up, they would have to do it over the bow of a colonel, a Navy SEAL, and the president of the United States. It worked.

Over lunch the president asked Stanley and Helen to talk about highlights of the project. Stanley described the conniption of the Pentagon officials over wilted salad vegetables during his vetting, and Brew's cuisine in his apartment. He recounted the newspaper story from *The Charleston Post and Courier*, mentioning how he and Kitt had roared at its reading. Helen disclosed, slightly to Stanley's discomfort, the way in which she had expressed interest in him personally. After the second day of training in Charleston, Brew and Stanley had decided that she would lead the installation team in Kuwait. Stanley handed her a thick set of his blueprints and suggested she study them that evening. The next morning, she brought the prints back to Stanley. He was confounded by an entry she had made, in standardized engineering calligraphy, in the margin of an interior page.

"What is the meaning of these ten digits?" he asked, pointing to her marking.

"It's my phone number" was all she said.

After the meal, the president suggested they see the Oval Office on their way out. Of course, it was formidable to all the visitors, though Brew had been there before. As they departed the office, the president asked Stanley to stay behind with her.

"Stanley, what you did, everything you did, was above and beyond," she said. "You are truly a patriot."

"I am just a citizen," he said. She seemed to disapprove of his reaction.

"I have learned in this office that there are all manner of citizens and all manner of patriots. And just once in a great while they are the same thing, when citizenship *is* patriotism. I believe that happened to you, Stanley." She moved closer to him. "You know that I hope that your work will never be used. After all you did, I hope it will come to nothing. Because the *having of it* will hopefully mean it will not be needed. But there would be no having it without what you did." Then she looked to see that the others were well away. "I wonder, Stanley, if there should be another need, would you serve again?"

"I still don't know how or why I was asked for this one," Stanley said to her. "Or why I agreed to do it, other than I had the wherewithal to do it. And I suppose I understood that gave me a duty of some kind."

"Trust me, you are a patriot," she said.

"If I am a patriot, I am an accidental one," he replied. "I am just glad that I could serve. And, yes, I will do it again, if I am capable."

Now as he sat waxing contemplative on his balcony above the river, he knew that what he had said to Delores Winters was only partly honest. It was true that he had not sought to make any great contribution and did not seek recognition for any. And it was certainly true that he did not consider himself a hero or a patriot. Augie, Brew, Kitt, and Bobby Beach—they were heroes. He had simply done what he was asked to do, and that was to make something that—should the president be wrong—could change the face of the world in horrible ways.

But he also had told the president that after all that had happened he was merely glad to have been of service, as if the experience had not deeply affected him, as if it were just another day at the office. And that, he knew, was not true. He was glad about much more, and knew that he was deeply marked by everything that had happened. He had been just an ordinary, overweight lonely man—he could admit now—who happened to have attributes and skills in need of being needed. Completely without aforethought, he had climbed into a strange car simply because he was asked to do so, and from there he had gone on to live five months that changed, in nearly every way imaginable, the sum of the seventy years lived before them. He still had all that he had learned in those many years, all the love he had given and received, all the memories of his life with Agnes. But now there was Helen, for whom his feelings deepened every day. And Kitt, the daughter he never had, whom he enjoyed so much. All the walks they could have together, the advice he might offer, for her taking or her leaving. He had a loyal companion to care for in August, and a new friend to call who was no less than the First Father. And who knew? Maybe Tyler Brew or the president would call on him again. Nothing had been taken from him, while so much had been added, even now, in the last chapter of his life.

He stepped in from the balcony to retrieve a cigar from the humidor atop the liquor cabinet. Augie lay at his post halfway to the foyer. He was sleeping, breathing evenly. Stanley could hear a soft snore from the creature. He was pleased that he had not awakened him. He returned to the balcony and leaned against the rail. The lights of PNC Park still blazed many hours after the final out.

He remembered that Yogi Berra was said to have remarked that you could observe a lot by just watching. Stanley, in that moment, sensed he could learn also by just looking back, taking stock of it all, summing it all up in his soul. He had selected a good cigar, full-bodied but mellow. He knew a rich cigar this late might make sleep even more elusive. He didn't care.

He was going to look back on everything once more. Slowly.

He could sleep anytime.

AFTERWORD

When fiction weaves real persons, places, and events with purely invented ones, the author seems obliged to acknowledge which is which. Here is a scorecard of sorts for the reader of this work.

All descriptions of Pittsburgh, Pennsylvania, and Charleston, South Carolina, including street names, restaurants, hotels, and public places, are intended to be materially accurate. There actually *is* the unusual United States Vegetable Laboratory on Highway 17 south of Charleston, but it was not originally built as part of Reconstruction after the American Civil War, and the current modern facility was not funded with federal stimulus money following the 2008 financial crisis. There is no RiverBridge Place apartment building on Fort Duquesne Boulevard in Pittsburgh, but there are other such luxury residences there. Kista, Sweden, is indeed a large northern suburb of Stockholm comprised of a commercial sector and a residential one, as described. Little Schliist Street, however, is imaginary. There is no city of Turj in Afghanistan; but Farah, the Farah River, and Qalat are real places located as described. I worked from a declassified military map of the region, used by US military officers in the field, provided me by an active duty general at a public speaking event.

The Accidental Patriot is not meant to teach US presidential history in any meaningful way. But the references to United States presidents and advisors, and anecdotes about them, are intended to be accurate and inspired by the scholarly (unlike mine) work of others, including Walter Isaacson in his definitive biography *Kissinger*, and the reportorial history *The President's Club*, by Nancy Gibbs and Michael Duffy. Of course, the action ascribed to President Obama in confidentially recommending Delores Winters to a successor is fiction, as are the advisory comments attributed to President Trump.

I also wish to note the influence on several of the book's themes of the PBS documentary *Top Secret America*, Frontline Series, aired April 30, 2013. Among other things, the fictionalized statement attributed to Richard A. Clarke about the data collection capabilities of the NSA was inspired by that program.

Though I wish I could, I cannot take credit for the account of baseball pitcher Luis Tiant's delivery acrobatics recited by Henry Winters near the end of *The Accidental Patriot*. I first heard that story while listening to a Detroit Tigers radio broadcast many years ago, as told by the team's legendary Hall of Fame announcer, Ernie Harwell.

Many persons assisted me as I wrote *The Accidental Patriot*. Lon Nordeen, an accomplished author of a series of books on military aircraft and their deployments in Middle East conflicts, read the original manuscript as it progressed and offered excellent suggestions. My close friend Neal Bechant, whose surname I used in inventing the Charleston County sheriff, was the first to review my early drafts. His comments meaningfully informed the numerous changes reflected in subsequent drafts and the final work. And by the way, except for his intelligence, he bears no resemblance to the fictional Weldon Bechant.

Jim Donald, retired CEO of Starbucks, whom I chanced to meet on a golf course, read my manuscript and could not have been more gracious with his insights and support. And the observations of Robert Burden, a retired Westinghouse executive living in Georgia, were also very helpful.

Boston friends Carmen and Kathy D'Angelo, and Michigan neighbors Dr. T. J. Spencer and Brooke Spencer, read my work and supported me from the beginning. So did Ohio readers Polly Herman, Carla A. Moore, and Susie Beach.

South Carolinians including Todd Lynch, Denise Kotva, John Reock, Ken Kavanaugh, Elison Atkinson, Deena Ralph, Jack Wilson, Don Romano, Caren Breen, Dr. Walt Leonard, Deborah Leonard, David Cruse, Bruce Stemerman, Bid Sikes, Pam Paroli, Ed Leary, J.T. Carpenter, Paul DePalma, Michael Jones, Bob Simpson, Dr. Ed Rigtrup, Lynne Davis, Deana Hubbard, Patricia Huff, Glenn Cocciola, Barbara Blasch, Larry Blasch, Warren McCulloch, Gary Huckaby and Jeanne Huckaby were manuscript readers who encouraged me in the journey. And John Wilson made important technical points on military protocol that I heeded.

When I thought the manuscript was finally finished, Cleveland lawyer David J. Hooker showed me that his true calling may have been professional editing. His suggestions made the book materially better.

My brother, the Rev. Daniel J. Bauer SVD, was a particularly generous and insightful advisor. Dan is a writer, priest, and college professor (including of English literature) and was a weekly columnist for *The China Post* in Taipei, Taiwan, for twenty years, publishing more words than I can ever hope to bring to print. His thorough and honest appraisals were invaluable, and his tenderness in the delivery of them was much appreciated too.

Lastly, many authors have said that writing is harder work for the author's spouse than for the author. It's true. Thank you, Gloria.

JB

ABOUT THE AUTHOR

Joseph Bauer writes novels from his homes in Charleston, SC and Cleveland, OH. *The Accidental Patriot* is the first in a three-book series. The others will be published in coming months.